## SPOCK WAS IN THE GRIP OF SOME TERRIBLE CONVULSION . . .

He looked flushed—feverish—his eyes wide. And he was breathing much too quickly, as evidenced by the rapid rise and fall of his chest. The captain had expected some fractured ribs, maybe internal bleeding. But not *this.*

"Bones," Kirk breathed. "What's *happening* to him?"

McCoy scowled. "Something's gotten into his bloodstream—some kind of poison I can't identify. It's accelerating Spock's vital processes."

Abruptly, the captain flashed back to the sight of the creature's tentacle brushing Spock's shoulder. He cursed, drawing McCoy's attention. "Bones, I saw the thing touch him with one of its tentacles . . . *there* . . . " He pointed to the juncture of Spock's neck and his shoulder.

Pulling the material of the first officer's tunic aside, McCoy exposed three tiny puncture marks, still green with clotting blood. "Damn," he said. "Jim, I've got to get him up to sickbay . . ."

# Look for STAR TREK Fiction from Pocket Books

## Star Trek: The Original Series

*Final Frontier*
*Strangers from the Sky*
*Enterprise*
*Star Trek IV:*
  *The Voyage Home*
*Star Trek V:*
  *The Final Frontier*
*Spock's World*
*The Lost Years*
#1 *Star Trek:*
  *The Motion Picture*
#2 *The Entropy Effect*
#3 *The Klingon Gambit*
#4 *The Covenant of the Crown*
#5 *The Prometheus Design*
#6 *The Abode of Life*
#7 *Star Trek II:*
  *The Wrath of Khan*
#8 *Black Fire*
#9 *Triangle*
#10 *Web of the Romulans*
#11 *Yesterday's Son*
#12 *Mutiny on the Enterprise*
#13 *The Wounded Sky*
#14 *The Trellisane Confrontation*
#15 *Corona*
#16 *The Final Reflection*
#17 *Star Trek III:*
  *The Search for Spock*
#18 *My Enemy, My Ally*
#19 *The Tears of the Singers*
#20 *The Vulcan Academy Murders*
#21 *Uhura's Song*
#22 *Shadow Lord*

#23 *Ishmael*
#24 *Killing Time*
#25 *Dwellers in the Crucible*
#26 *Pawns and Symbols*
#27 *Mindshadow*
#28 *Crisis on Centaurus*
#29 *Dreadnought!*
#30 *Demons*
#31 *Battlestations!*
#32 *Chain of Attack*
#33 *Deep Domain*
#34 *Dreams of the Raven*
#35 *The Romulan Way*
#36 *How Much for Just the Planet?*
#37 *Bloodthirst*
#38 *The IDIC Epidemic*
#39 *Time for Yesterday*
#40 *Timetrap*
#41 *The Three-Minute Universe*
#42 *Memory Prime*
#43 *The Final Nexus*
#44 *Vulcan's Glory*
#45 *Double, Double*
#46 *The Cry of the Onlies*
#47 *The Kobayashi Maru*
#48 *Rules of Engagement*
#49 *The Pandora Principle*
#50 *Doctor's Orders*
#51 *Enemy Unseen*
#52 *Home Is the Hunter*
#53 *Ghost Walker*
#54 *A Flag Full of Stars*
#55 *Renegade*
#56 *Legacy*

## Star Trek: The Next Generation

*Metamorphosis*
*Vendetta*
*Encounter at Farpoint*
#1 *Ghost Ship*
#2 *The Peacekeepers*
#3 *The Children of Hamlin*
#4 *Survivors*
#5 *Strike Zone*
#6 *Power Hungry*
#7 *Masks*

#8 *The Captains' Honor*
#9 *A Call to Darkness*
#10 *A Rock and a Hard Place*
#11 *Gulliver's Fugitives*
#12 *Doomsday World*
#13 *The Eyes of the Beholders*
#14 *Exiles*
#15 *Fortune's Light*
#16 *Contamination*
#17 *Boogeymen*

# STAR TREK®

# LEGACY

## MICHAEL JAN FRIEDMAN

**POCKET BOOKS**

New York   London   Toronto   Sydney   Tokyo   Singapore

An *Original* Publication of POCKET BOOKS

POCKET BOOKS, a division of Simon & Schuster Inc.
1230 Avenue of the Americas, New York, NY 10020

Copyright © 1991 Paramount Pictures. All Rights Reserved.

STAR TREK is a Registered Trademark of
Paramount Pictures.

This book is published by Pocket Books, a division of
Simon & Schuster Inc., under exclusive license from
Paramount Pictures.

ISBN: 0-671-74468-2

First Pocket Books printing August 1991

10  9  8  7  6  5  4  3  2  1

POCKET and colophon are registered trademarks of
Simon & Schuster Inc.

Printed in the U.S.A.

*For Lorraine, alias Susan:*

Trekkie without peer and the best
mother-in-law a guy could have

## Historian's Note

This story begins on Stardate 5258.7, which would place it approximately four-fifths of the way through the starship *Enterprise*'s original five-year mission.

# Prologue

ON THE MERKAAN interstellar ship *Clodiaan*, Acquisitor Hamesaad Dreen considered his reflection in the gilt-edged, freeform mirror that hung on his anteroom wall. Try as he might, he could not make himself believe that the image before him was that of the young stalwart who had commanded the *Clodiaan* ten years before.

*Ten years.*

His eyes, once dark and unflinching, had sunk into the striated flesh around them like large, vicious insects taking shelter in their nests. His cheekbones, at one time his best feature, had lost their definition; the skin around them sagged, flowing into the beginning of jowls at his jawline. And his mane of black hair, in which he used to take such pride, had thinned and lost its luster.

*Ten years.*

Dreen cursed and lifted his goblet to his lips. The tawny Maratekkan brandy—actually better than the overrated Saurian variety—was every bit as chilled as he liked it. But it didn't begin to wash away the bitter taste in his mouth—or cool the heat that climbed into

1

his cheeks as he thought about the time that had been stolen from him.

If all had gone well, he might have *owned* the *Clodiaan* by now—and a few more like her. He might have been a frequent visitor to the potentate's court, like Gareed Welt and that fat fool Luarkh. He might have been a state *hero*.

Instead, he'd spent a decade redeeming himself, proving he was worthy of leading an expedition again. Ferrying booty from one manor moon to another—or if not booty, then some lord's snotnosed broodlings off to see their aunt on the homeworld. Finally cajoling his way back onto a privateer, where he had to play the subordinate to one pompous, self-important fop after another until the owner conceded he was capable of his own command. And even then, he'd been allowed to pursue few real opportunities— mostly half-empty Dardathian cargo ships and creaking Confaari freighters.

And all through that agonizing time, the memory of his undoing had irritated him as a grain of sand might irritate a Tellarite bloodworm and churned up his digestive juices until they literally ate away at his insides. The result? A couple of years ago, the doctors had been forced to replace his stomach cavity with a prosthesis.

Since the operation, the physical pain had gone away, even to the point where he could indulge his taste in liquor again. But the mental anguish hadn't diminished a single iota.

*Ten years.*

Dreen looked at the mirror again over the rim of his goblet. He considered the scowling, somewhat less-than-dashing figure he saw there. Another man in the same circumstances might have counted himself lucky. After all, he had salvaged his career. He had regained what was rightfully his—command of an acquisition triad, and one of the very finest triads at that. He had beaten the odds.

But it wasn't enough. It didn't make up for his humiliation, his suffering. It didn't come close to what might have been.

There was only one balm that would soothe his pain: revenge on those who had disgraced him. Not only their deaths, but their complete and utter mortification. Of course, he harbored no illusions about his chances of finding them, much less exacting his retribution.

The Federation was immense. And starships seldom stayed in the same sector for very long.

The acquisitor wondered what had become of the hated ones. Had their lives been happy? Had they prospered from his defeat? The very thought made his heart beat faster with rage.

And then a worse possibility occurred to him—that they might not even remember. That if he stood eye to eye with them, they might not even know who he was.

*Hamesaad who? It's been so long, it's hard to recall.*

His fury boiling to the surface, Dreen rose and hurled his goblet at the mirror. Instantly, his reflected image exploded, littering the carpeting with a swarm of prismatic shards.

The brandy spattered over the wall. The goblet bounced once and came to rest among the shards.

A moment later, his *mesirii*—a matched white pair, rare even on the homeworld—slunk into the anteroom from their place in his sleeping quarters, their tiny earflaps erect. Naturally, they'd heard the sound; the acuteness of *mesirii* senses was legendary. There was both caution and curiosity in the way they held their lean, powerful bodies—muscles bunched at the shoulders and the haunches, as if ready to spring—in the way their long black tongues snapped in and out past ridges of sharp fangs and in the cast of their protuberant golden eyes. Without question, they knew something was amiss.

Dreen stared at them and at the ruin he'd created,

shocked by the intensity of his own emotions. Then he swore under his breath.

The mirror would have fetched a tidy sum from some manor lord. Now it was junk. Nor did the symbolism elude him.

He snorted. At least he wouldn't have to be reminded of his age anymore—and his loss. Falling back into his chair, he reached out and pressed the communications plate.

A moment later, his personal servant poked his head into the room. His eyes were drawn to the gleam of broken mirror-glass on the floor—to the goblet, and to the dark spot which was slowly spreading down the wall. Looking past the beasts, he considered the master they had in common.

"Is everything all right, Acquisitor?"

"Obviously not. My mirror has fallen and broken. See to it that the damned thing's cleaned up."

The servant bowed as he withdrew. "Yes, Acquisitor."

The sun was hot on his naked back. Raising his head to see over the forearm that was cradling it, he peered at the woman lying next to him on the beach blanket.

Her eyes, the color of the ocean, were open. She was looking at him—and had been for some time, probably. She was smiling.

But then, that was nothing new. She smiled a lot.

So, come to think of it, did he.

"Don't tell me," she said, speaking over the rush of surf against the distant shoreline. "Your back hurts."

He nodded. "Do you think you could douse me again with that lotion?"

Getting to her knees with uncommon grace, Vina reached for the brown plastic container of sunscreen. The late afternoon light caressed her hair, touching off sparks of pale gold as she tossed it back over one firm brown shoulder.

"You know," she said, pouring some of the lotion into a cupped hand, "you don't have to burn."

"Don't I?" he asked. "I thought our friends wanted to experience the whole picture." There was a sprinkling of sand on the blanket, having been deposited by the wind. He brushed it off.

"They do," she replied. "But not if it causes us discomfort." Popping the container top back into place with her thumb, she let the lotion slide out of her other hand, onto his back.

It felt like ice-water, which was to say it felt great. He sighed.

"Anyway," Vina told him, "I'm onto you, Christopher Pike. You invite these sunburns—just to get me to rub this stuff into your back."

He chuckled. "Interesting theory."

As Vina worked the sunscreen into his skin with slender, supple fingers, Pike considered the beach house she'd conjured up—a wooden affair, rising against the azure sky on a set of rather ungainly-looking poles. The poles, Vina had informed him, were a protection against storm-driven tides—or so her aunt had told her when she'd visited this place as a little girl.

It was funny how he'd stopped trying to find flaws in the Keeper's illusions—stopped questioning the benign turn of events that had landed him on Talos IV, the one place in the universe where he could find happiness.

Somewhere, in some other reality, he was a scarred hulk of an ex–starship captain, dependent on a machine to do the work of his crippled organs. And Vina, the survivor of a crash landing, wasn't in much better shape herself. But in *this* reality, in this world of their own choosing, they were young, whole—alive. They had all two people could ask for.

"Honestly," his companion said, "it's not as if you need to *trick* me into massaging you." Suddenly, her face was pressed against his. She smelled like the beach blossoms they'd found earlier up by the dunes —sweet and fresh and vigorously alive. "All you have to do," Vina whispered, "is *ask*."

Rolling over, the heat in his back forgotten, Pike drew her to him. Running his fingers through her hair, he kissed her.

Maybe it wasn't a real kiss, but it certainly felt like the genuine article. And that was good enough.

Hell, it was more than good enough.

# Chapter One

McCoy FROWNED, giving new emphasis to the worry lines in his face. He looked up at the captain, his blue eyes full of pathos. "It's dead, Jim."

Kirk's first inclination was to laugh. But when he saw the look on the doctor's face, he decided against it. "Bones," he said, keeping his voice down so not everyone in the rec room would hear him, "it's just a marrae-marrae plant. It's not supposed to live forever."

No question about it: the Balphasian houseplant McCoy called *Lulu* had seen better days. Its leaves, normally a lusty scarlet in color, had faded, shriveled, and gone brittle.

McCoy held the sorry-looking specimen up to the light. He shook his head in that doctorly way he had. "*I* know that. It's just that I've had it for so long, I sort of expected it to be around until Doomsday." He sighed. "Besides, it's practically a family heirloom. It's been a McCoy now for—"

"Two and a half years?" the captain estimated. "Including the time your daughter had it?"

The doctor snorted. "Longer. Nearly three."

Ruefully, Kirk glanced at the game of Chinese checkers he'd set up. The original idea had been for him and his chief medical officer to engage in a quick contest—at least, until Spock completed his preparations for their survey of the planet below. And since Chinese checkers were more McCoy's speed than three-dimensional chess, that's the diversion Kirk had agreed to.

But when Bones had entered the rec room with his marrae-marrae cradled in his arms, the captain sensed their game was in jeopardy. It appeared now that his instincts were on the money.

McCoy must have noticed Kirk's glance, because he suddenly looked contrite. "Sorry. We came here to play a game, didn't we?" He looked at Lulu. "Just excuse me for a second, will you?"

Getting up from his seat, the doctor crossed the rec room and deposited the deceased plant in the waste disposal unit. When he returned to the table, his mood had lifted a little—but *just* a little.

"All right," McCoy said, "let's play."

"You sure?"

"Of course I'm sure. Why? Don't I *look* sure?"

"To be honest," Kirk observed, "you look like a pallbearer."

The doctor grunted and sat back in his seat. "It's not so much that the damned thing died on me," he explained, unable to keep an ironic quirk out of his voice, "it's that I never got a chance to say goodbye."

"You know," Kirk said, "I have a feeling you'll get over it. Maybe even get a new plant someday."

"No." McCoy looked the captain in the eye, maintaining a perfect deadpan. "There'll never be another marrae-marrae like Lulu."

"Captain Kirk?"

Recognizing Spock's voice, Jim looked up at the intercom grid. "Yes, Commander?"

"The survey team has been assembled. We are ready to beam down to Octavius Four."

McCoy raised an eyebrow. "That was quick."

"I saw no reason to delay, Doctor," the Vulcan answered, never breaking conversational stride.

Bones snorted. "I guess respect for the dead isn't a reason."

"I beg your pardon?" the science officer said.

"Nothing," Kirk assured him. "We'll meet you in the transporter room in five minutes, Spock."

"Acknowledged." The Vulcan wasn't inclined to mince words today, Kirk noted. But then, wasn't that always the case when a planet survey beckoned?

"Come on," the captain told McCoy. "If we're late, Spock'll never let us forget it."

The doctor got up, though not with any great alacrity. "I don't know what all the fuss is. You've seen *one* Class M world, you've seen them all."

As Kirk and McCoy entered the transporter room, they found Spock, Sulu, and a couple of young science officers waiting for them on the platform, while the rest of the survey team stood off to one side. Turning his tall, slender form ever so slightly, the Vulcan trained his dark eyes on them. Though the Vulcan's features were characteristically devoid of emotion, his posture fairly reeked of impatience.

"All right, Spock," the doctor commented, "don't get your knickers in a twist. You'll be sniffing the undersides of those rocks before you know it."

The first officer shot McCoy a wilting glance. "Doctor, I fail to see the relevance of—"

*"Gentlemen,"* the captain said, cutting them short before they really got started. "I want this to be a peaceful survey. Not like the last one."

Out of the corner of his eye, Kirk couldn't help but notice a rather attractive blonde among the other members of the survey team. Purposely, he ignored the distraction, focusing on the task ahead of them.

Stepping up onto the raised platform, Kirk watched

Bones do the same, then turned to Lieutenant Kyle. "Energize."

"Aye, sir," the transporter chief replied.

A fraction of a second later, Kirk found himself standing in six inches of diamond-bright, gently swirling water—part of a stream which bisected the clearing in which they had materialized. In fact, they were all standing in the stream—a necessary inconvenience, considering it was the only parcel in the area that was both level and completely free of foliage. Outside of the clearing, there was a great, aromatic tangle of green and growing things rippling in a warm, tropical wind. Your basic jungle, Kirk mused, except for the absence of whistles and squawks that one normally expected in a place such as this.

Not that he'd been expecting any of that here. Starfleet's long-range sensor readings of Octavius Four had declared this world devoid of complex life forms. Of course, there had been some holes in the scans, attributed to sensor-foiling minerals in the planet's crust, which was why the *Enterprise* had been dispatched for a closer analysis. A "hands-on analysis," as Admiral Kowalski liked to put it.

"Of all the damned—"

Turning, the captain saw McCoy pick up one of his feet and consider it sourly. There was something slender and brown and slimy encircling the doctor's boot at the ankle. As if it knew it were being watched, it lifted its head and returned McCoy's scrutiny with what looked like tiny black eyes.

"It appears you've made a friend, Bones," Kirk observed.

The chief medical officer grunted and aimed his tricorder at the creature. "Well," he said, consulting the device's monitor, "at least it's not poisonous." Reaching down, he pulled the thing off his boot and dropped it into the water downstream.

"I didn't notice any snakes in the survey," Sulu remarked.

Spock trained his tricorder on the creature as it wriggled away. "Actually," he said, "this life form is considerably less evolved than either the Serpentes or Ophidia suborders. It only *looks* like a snake."

That was when the second half of the team arrived, including the woman that Kirk had tried to not notice *too* much up in the transporter room. What was her name—Karras? That's right, he thought. Selena Karras.

Slowly but surely, he recalled the details from her personnel file. Karras had signed on less than a month ago, straight out of the Academy, after completing both the Science and Command curriculums. A bright woman, but one who seemed a little out of place at times—not all that unusual, perhaps, for dual-curriculum graduates, who often seemed torn between the captain's chair and the lab.

"If something slithers up your leg," McCoy warned the newcomers, "it's nothing to worry about. I have it on good authority."

If that was meant to be another jibe, Spock didn't even seem to hear it. He had turned his attention from the snakelike thing to a small marshy pool that fed off the stream. As Kirk watched, he knelt and used his tricorder again. When the captain came closer to get a better look, he saw some greenish-brown spots in the water.

Obviously aware of Kirk's approach, the Vulcan turned to him. "Free-swimming invertebrates," he said. "Not unlike those we have encountered elsewhere, except this species seems not to have any active defense structures."

The captain knelt too. For a moment, he watched the small, round opacities make their way around the pool. Then he looked up at Spock.

His first officer would never show it, but he was having a good time. Spock was really in his element when it came to exploring virgin territory.

"Sir?"

Kirk shielded his eyes from the direct sunlight and found himself looking up at Sulu. "Yes, Lieutenant?"

"I'd like to take a group over that rise," the helmsman told him. He pointed to a long, green ridge that hunkered up out of the jungle a few hundred yards distant. Turning back to Kirk, he said: "According to the survey, the vegetation's a little different there. We may get a different set of fauna samples." A grin. "Besides, there's no point in *all* of us getting wet."

The captain smiled back. "You've convinced me, Lieutenant. Take three of the others and see what you can see."

"Aye, sir." And Sulu was off, not wasting a moment. But then, that was no surprise. Spock wasn't the only one who looked forward to survey duty.

The wind moved, blowing about large, spade-shaped leaves and long, fuzzy tendrils. It made an almost musical sound, like those that came from a Sonsfilian feather-lyre.

Kirk recalled something he'd heard at the Academy: *Watch out for the places that lull you to sleep. More often than not, you don't wake up.*

He laughed softly. By now, he'd seen enough planets to know that every cautionary maxim had an application somewhere.

So, you watched your step. But you didn't have to go around with your heart in your mouth.

Spock looked up and cocked an eyebrow. "Something . . . amusing?" he asked.

The captain shrugged. "You had to be there, I think."

The Vulcan nodded and returned to his study of the invertebrates without giving the matter another thought.

*I guess he's getting used to his captain's whimsical behavior,* Kirk thought. He took a moment to check in with Scotty and to inform him that there were now two parties for Lieutenant Kyle to keep track of. The engineer already knew about it, however—Kyle had noted the change in the configuration of communicator signals and informed him before Kirk could. The captain smiled at his transporter chief's efficiency.

In the meantime, the landing party—or what was left of it after Sulu had finished his recruiting efforts—had fanned out from the stream and was taking samples of the plant life. McCoy was among them, perhaps looking for a replacement for Lulu, despite his earlier protestations.

Suddenly, one of the younger science officers—a lanky black man named Owens—came thrashing through the undergrowth, in Kirk's direction. Out of reflex, the captain stood.

"What is it?" he called.

Owens jerked a thumb over his shoulder. "Sir, there are some caves back there. Big ones."

By then, Spock was standing as well. He and Kirk regarded one another. "Sounds intriguing," the captain said.

"Indeed," Spock agreed, starting off in the direction Owens had indicated. "We will see what, if anything, grows without benefit of sunlight on this world."

The caves became visible after they'd gone about thirty meters into the jungle. There were two of them, about four feet high and twice as wide, set into the base of a grassy slope and overgrown with flowering vines.

"Actually," Owens told the captain, "it was the flowers that caught my eye. If not for them, I might never have seen the caves at all."

Spock was the first one to reach the openings. Running his tricorder past the vines, he made certain that they weren't harmful. Then he bent over, held a yellow blossom to his nose, and inhaled.

Kirk couldn't help but stiffen a little at the sight, recalling their experiences on Omicron Ceti III. But the vine blossoms emitted no spores—just a pleasing fragrance, judging by his first officer's reaction.

As the captain caught up with Spock, he felt a

breath of cool air from the caves—cool enough, in fact, to dry the perspiration on his face and hands. It felt good, providing a break from the humid warmth of the jungle.

Unfortunately, it didn't smell very good. Kirk's nose wrinkled at the odor.

"What the hell is that?" McCoy asked as he joined them. He waved a hand in front of his face, as if to dispel the scent. "It's like the time a raccoon died in the chimney."

"You're exaggerating," the captain told him.

The doctor inhaled another sampling. "Not by much," he insisted.

Spock looked back over his shoulder at Kirk. "There does appear to be something rotting in there," he concluded. "However, I cannot obtain a tricorder reading. The sensor signal is blocked, probably by a mineral deposit of the variety that thwarted the long-range survey."

The captain nodded. By then, everyone in the party had clustered around the caves—not only Kirk, Spock, Owens, and McCoy, but also Karras and a squarish, stolid-looking security officer named Autry.

The Vulcan stuck his head into the larger of the two openings, ignoring the rude smell coming out of it. "It may be possible," he reported, "to crawl inside and circumvent the mineral deposit."

"Not while I'm in command," Kirk told him. "I don't know what's down there, Spock, but it's not worth risking your hide for."

The Vulcan lingered, as if reluctant to leave even this small mystery unsolved. But after a moment or two, he withdrew and got to his feet.

"Now, then," the captain said, "we've still got a lot of ground to—" He stopped as a vibration climbed through the soles of his boots and up his legs. He looked around.

Karras had a strange expression on her face. "I

think I just felt a tremor," she said, sounding not at all certain.

"You did," Spock advised her. He consulted his tricorder. "Albeit a small one."

McCoy cursed under his breath. "Terrific. I thought the long-range survey showed no indication of seismic activity."

"That's what I thought too," Kirk said. "Of course, vibrations as small as that one might not have been noticed."

"True," the Vulcan confirmed. "And in any case, long-range surveys are not flawless."

Autry looked to the captain. "We *are* going to continue, aren't we, sir?"

Kirk considered the alternative, but for only a second. "Yes," he assured the security officer. "We're going to continue. It'd take a lot more than that to scare us out of—"

As if on cue, the earth shook again. And this time, it was more than just slightly noticeable. It was a full-fledged earthquake, one that made the captain's teeth grind together.

Before it was over, Spock was announcing his readings: "Twelve-point-four times the strength of the last tremor. And three times the duration."

McCoy glanced at Kirk. He looked a bit pale—not exactly the picture of confidence. But he had too much respect for his friend to sound a retreat without his say-so.

Frowning, the captain flipped open his communicator. "Mister Sulu?"

The helmsman's voice came through loud and clear. "Aye, sir?"

"Everyone all right over there?"

There was a moment of hesitation, which the captain translated into surprise on Sulu's part. "Of course, Captain. Why shouldn't we be?"

Was it possible that Sulu's party hadn't felt the

tremor? Kirk posed the question via his communicator.

"We haven't felt a thing," the helmsman reported.

Spock raised an eyebrow. "Apparently, a localized phenomenon."

"Apparently," Kirk echoed. He addressed Sulu again. "Carry on, Lieutenant—for now. But be prepared to beam up on short notice."

The response was crisp and immediate. "Acknowledged, Captain."

Closing his communicator and replacing it on his belt, Kirk listened to the wind sighing through the dense foliage. There were no fallen trees, he noticed, which probably meant that the quakes didn't get any worse than that second one.

Unless, of course, the tremors were unusual occurrences—which just happened to coincide with the survey team's arrival.

Somehow, he couldn't buy that. The first possibility was far more likely—that the quakes were just a periodic fact of life here.

He looked at Autry. This time, the man didn't have to ask.

"We're staying," Kirk told him. "Still."

Autry smiled. "Glad to hear it, sir."

Bones looked as if he would have liked to have protested. But, scowling, he kept his thoughts to himself and headed back toward the stream.

"Acquisitor?"

Dreen had been studying the specs of Vandren Luarkh's new triad. When he heard his attendant's voice, however, he swung aside his library monitor and got to his feet.

"You may come in," he said.

Obediently, the servant pushed aside the heavy metal door and stepped gingerly across the threshold, making way for a larger figure who stood behind him, a figure dressed in field attire, complete with disruptor and the ritual pair of ancient daggers. This was Kinter Balac, Dreen's second-in-command.

Balac smiled that thin-lipped smile of his. "It is time, Acquisitor."

Dreen had never much liked Balac. The man was too crude, too eager. There was no subtlety in his manner. But he did his job thoroughly and efficiently, and that was infinitely more important than any of the acquisitor's personal predilections.

"We have locked into orbit?" Dreen asked.

"We have indeed."

"And the acquisition force?"

"Assembled and awaiting your pleasure," Balac reported.

Thorough and efficient, all right. Dreen nodded approvingly.

"The optimum time for transport is in sixteen minutes," the man went on. "Will the acquisitor be leading this expedition personally?"

Dreen searched his second's eyes. Was there a little too much ambition glinting there? A bit too much desire for advancement?

He would have to keep a watch on his friend Balac. "Of course I will," Dreen replied. And then, more pointedly: "Don't I always?"

Balac inclined his head. "As you wish, Acquisitor."

*As I wish indeed,* Dreen thought as he gestured casually to his attendant. Without a moment's hesitation, the man scurried across the room and opened the acquisitor's cleverly tooled chest. Selecting the more ornate of Dreen's two field tunics, a blue one, he draped it gently across his forearm and carried it to his master, who had already begun stripping off his silken cabin jacket.

Dropping the cabin garment on the floor, Dreen pulled on the brocaded tunic. It felt coarse against his skin—irritating. *But that is as it should be,* he mused. *One should not be too comfortable in the course of an expedition; it leads to laxity, and laxity leads to failure.*

No, he thought, it was much better to be *un*comfortable and on one's guard.

Dreen was still pondering this philosophy as his servant finished fastening the last of the clasps on the front of the tunic. Making sure the garment fit correctly, the man then bent to retrieve the cabin jacket and returned to the chest to lay it inside. It was bad luck to clean a cabin jacket before its owner returned from an expedition; Dreen had heard tales of acquisitors' attendants who'd lost their lives for such a transgression.

Turning to his arms cabinet, Dreen pulled out the drawer that held his disruptors. Taking one out, he checked to make sure it was fully charged. Satisfied, he tucked it into the holster pocket provided in his tunic. Then he closed the drawer and opened a set of glass doors, behind which his daggers were displayed on a background of red velvet.

Being a full-fledged acquisitor, he naturally had a selection of them. Perusing that selection for an appropriate amount of time, disinclined to rush any part of an expedition—no matter how trivial—he decided at last on the pair given to him as a token of his current commission. Esthetically speaking, they were not his favorites; that distinction went to the oldest set in the cabinet, the daggers he had worn on that fateful foray ten years earlier.

But he would never wear those again, despite their beauty. The last thing he needed was another reminder of failures past.

Removing the newer set from its place on the red velvet, Dreen slipped the daggers into the leather belts sewn into his tunic for just that purpose. Considering them critically, he decided he liked the way they looked. He had made the correct choice.

Fully prepared now, he shut the arms cabinet, turned, and called to his *mesirii.* "Memsac. Sarif." A second later, the beasts came padding out of the next room.

Dreen knelt, lowering his face to the level of their long, tapered muzzles, and they came to him. They licked his hands, their black tongues hot and wet on his skin.

How he loved these beasts—and not only for their comeliness, for their grace and intelligence, but also for what they signified. Who owned *mesirii* these days? Especially a pair of matched whites? Only manor lords. Manor lords and Hamesaad Dreen.

Memsac and Sarif had cost a good deal more than he could afford. And he'd had to train them himself, shivering in the mountains with them for weeks on end—lacking the wealth to pay someone else to do it. But it had all been worth it. They were a symbol to him—a symbol of how far he had come, and how far he would ultimately go. A taste of the rewards that had been denied him, but would soon be his in full.

The *mesirii* looked up at him with their large golden eyes. They were alight with hunger—not for food, but for a challenge commensurate with their abilities. They seemed to glow with a confidence that bordered on arrogance.

Hunter's eyes, Dreen mused. The kind that couldn't imagine failure.

Which was just as well. Homeworld law called for the destruction of *mesirii* who fell short of their masters' expectations. It was a measure to maintain the integrity of the breed, and in Dreen's view a good one. After all, it was their unerring talent for success that made the beasts so sought after.

"I will see you soon enough," he told them. "Go now."

Absolutely compliant, they did as they were told. He watched them move, his heart swelling with pride.

Then he remembered where he was. Getting up, he strode out of the cabin. Without looking, he knew that Balac had fallen in behind him and that his servant—whose name he could never seem to remember—had closed the door on his way out.

The *Clodiaan* had been designed more with storage capacity in mind than efficiency. The way from the acquisitor's quarters to the transporter hall was a long and circuitous one, leading as it did past the computer core and the starboard weapons center. And it was bare of decorations, like all the ship's corridors, which made the journey seem even longer.

Finally, however, Dreen entered the high-ceilinged facility, with Balac the requisite two strides behind him. Every one of the cabin's five platforms was full to capacity with expeditors, each a veteran of one or more of the *Clodiaan*'s previous ventures. They raised their fists in salute.

With calculated detachment, he returned the gesture. Turning to the transport technician, he barked an order: "Proceed on my command."

"It will be done, Acquisitor," the technician responded. At the same time, he sent a signal to his counterparts on the triad's other two ships, where similar masses of expeditors were ready to aid in the expedition. All in all, nearly a hundred men.

Dreen glanced surreptitiously at the chronometer on the transporter console. He was right on time. They were directly over their target. Smiling to himself, he ascended to one of the two empty spots on the central transporter pad. A moment later, Balac assumed his place on the other.

Eyeing the transport technician, the acquisitor snapped off a second command: "Dispatch."

Immediately, they were caught in the crackling scarlet clouds of energy that indicated imminent transport. For a full second, the energy mounted. Then the transport facility was gone, and they stood, instead, in the crowded main plaza of a wintry Federation mining colony, surrounded by square and guileless buildings of indeterminate color and substance.

The plaza was full of people, all of them moving briskly—each, no doubt, intent on an assignment related to the colony's mining and processing functions. They wore heavy primary-colored coats against the chill.

As the invaders took on form and substance, the colonists started. Some cried out. All withdrew.

Dreen's eyes narrowed with amusement as he saw the looks on their faces. Without exception, the colonists just stood there, mouths open, waiting to see what would happen next. They clearly had no idea what was going on, or what to do about it, and could sense only that the Merkaans, with their weapons in their hands, meant danger.

To Dreen, they looked for all the world like ripe fruit, waiting to be picked. Ripe, juicy fruit.

He would not give them a chance to recover from their surprise. Drawing his disruptor, he aimed it into a crowd at the edge of a stone fountain. There were screams, but he ignored them and activated the weapon.

An intense burst of pale green force speared one of the colonists, creating a gaping hole in his middle that spread to his extremities in less than a second. By the time the acquisitor removed his thumb from the trigger, there was nothing left of the man.

On the other side of the square, a woman was sharing the same fate, the victim of Balac's disruptor. At least Dreen *thought* it was a woman—he had so little time in which to decide before she vanished.

Horrified, paralyzed with fear for their own lives, the colonists put up no resistance as Dreen's expeditors moved among them. A couple of people picked up children and held them protectively, but that was hardly an act of defiance.

So far, so good. Picking out a likely subject—a middle-aged man who looked more fearful than the rest—the acquisitor approached him. As the man retreated, an expeditor thrust him forward again. Dreen stopped only after he'd come close enough to smell the human's anxiety.

Towering over his chosen informant, the acquisitor asked: "Where is your seat of government?"

The man's brows came together. There was perspiration on his forehead, despite the cold. He glanced to the side and pointed.

"There. That's the colony administrator's office. But—"

Dreen's nostrils flared at the man's impudence. "But *what?*"

Quickly, the human shook his head. "Nothing. Nothing at all."

The acquisitor nodded. "I thought not." Looking past the colonist, he established eye contact with the expeditor who had pushed him forward. He didn't have to say anything; his look was enough.

Turning his back on the human, he headed for the building identified as the administrator's office, his expeditors spreading out on either side of him to protect his flanks from the possibility of foolhardy resistors.

It was never a good idea to let acts of rebellion— even tiny ones—go unpunished. Especially at the beginning. First impressions were so important.

Dreen never heard the disruptor—he hadn't expected to. The weapon barely made a sound even when one held it to one's ear. But the humans' loud and high-pitched reaction told him that the informant had been dispatched—and the lesson completed.

When he heard it, he smiled and quickened his pace. This was going to be easier than he'd thought.

"My god," said Bradford Wayne, administrator of the Beta Cabrini mining colony. And then again: "My god."

Outside his window, the main square—which had been such a picture of tranquillity moments earlier— was a scene of terror. Armed aliens—a variety he couldn't immediately place—were jamming the colonists up against buildings in tight groups of ten to twenty.

"You see?" Santelli hissed from behind him.

Wayne nodded, loosening a lock of unruly red hair. "I see," he replied grimly. He was fighting for balance, trying to think of what to do.

"Who are they?" his assistant asked. "Where did they come from?"

The administrator shook his head. He didn't know the answers.

As Wayne watched, a protest was met with an abrupt blast of green energy, and then the protestor was gone. It hit the administrator like a physical blow. "Those *bas*tards," he rasped.

He still didn't know what was going on. But he was sure of one thing: he couldn't allow it to continue. These were his people, his charges. He had to keep the invaders from killing any more of them. Setting his jaw, he headed for the front door.

But before he could hit the panel that would open it, the door slid aside, revealing a bunch of the same aliens who were terrorizing the colonists outside. And with a chill, Wayne realized that he knew who they were after all.

Particularly the one who stood before the others, a cruel grin festering on his sunken, cadaveric face. Of course, the last time he'd seen it was on a starship viewscreen, a number of years ago, but he recognized it all the same.

The insight wasn't shared, however. At least, it didn't appear to be. Dreen gave no sign that he had ever seen Wayne before.

As the Merkaans entered the administrator's office, one of them pushed him back against his desk. Wayne found himself looking into the business end of a disruptor.

Santelli was manhandled in a similar fashion. Stumbling backward, he was pinned against a wall.

"Greetings," the acquisitor spat, as guttural as ever. He eyed Wayne. "You are the administrator of this colony?"

"I am," the human responded.

Dreen's mouth pulled up at the corners. "Good. I will require your help."

Wayne returned the scrutiny. "And what makes you think I'll give it to you?"

The acquisitor's brow wrinkled. "Perhaps you did not see the object lessons I administered in the plaza. Perhaps I should make a lesson of you as well."

The administrator kept his mouth shut. He didn't want to die. He desperately didn't want to die. But he wasn't going to just roll over for this murderer either.

"On the other hand," Dreen went on, "you will make my job here much easier. So perhaps my next lesson should be—" He turned to Santelli. *"Him."*

The Merkaan pinning Wayne's assistant raised his disruptor to the man's face and moved his finger to press the firing mechanism.

Santelli's eyes grew wide with fear as he turned to his superior. *Please,* they said. *Don't let them kill me.*

The Merkaan's finger reached the firing stud. "No!" the administrator bellowed.

Dreen gestured casually. "Spare him," he instructed.

The Merkaan stopped and lowered his weapon. He looked disappointed.

"I think we have struck a bargain," the acquisitor told Wayne. "At least, in symbolic terms. Cooperate and your people live. Fail to cooperate and . . ." He left the rest to the human's imagination.

Wayne sucked in his pride. He had no choice but to give in, to go along with Dreen's demands.

"All right," he said slowly, hating the words. "What is it you want?"

# Chapter Two

KIRK WATCHED as his survey group began to spread out again. Spock, of course, remained by the cave openings. The captain wasn't sure how much could be learned there, but he knew better than to argue with his first officer's instincts in such matters.

If anyone knew how to unearth something interesting, it was Spock.

Kirk scanned the jungle. Speaking of something interesting . . .

Taking out the tricorder he'd borrowed from the science section, he approached a likely enough–looking specimen—a tree with a bubbly, almost animal-like membrane running in zigzag patterns through its bark—and recorded its cellular structure for posterity. Then he went on to its neighbor—a different variety entirely, one whose branches ended in large tufts of reddish . . . well, hair is what it looked like as it tossed in the breeze.

Early in his career, Kirk had thought survey work boring. Over the years, however, he'd developed an appreciation for the minutiae of the galaxy. Nothing as deep and multi-faceted as Spock's, perhaps, but an appreciation nonetheless.

Besides, he hated to lose touch with the skills he'd learned en route to becoming a captain. So every now and then, when he beamed down to a planet different enough to interest him personally, he took part in its survey—just to stay in practice.

On this occasion, however, he found it difficult to keep his mind on the task at hand. His thoughts kept returning to the tremors.

What if his earlier supposition was wrong? What if the quakes did have something to do with their arrival here?

Had they inadvertently disturbed something? Upset some sort of balance? He took another look at the tree he was scanning with his tricorder. It was difficult to tell what kind of roots it might have, or how much movement they might be capable of. He scrutinized some of the other trees around him.

If their roots could move—and enough of them had done so at the same time—it could have caused a shift in the subterranean structures that held the surface in place. *The next thing you know,* Kirk mused, *you've got an earthquake—a little one, at least.*

Of course, it was just a theory. But it was one he intended to test before they departed. Maybe by digging around the root system of a sapling, so as to minimize the damage to—

Suddenly, a cry split the jungle silence. Unprepared for it, Kirk froze for a moment.

Then he was sprinting in the direction from which the cry had come. As he hurtled past one leafy frond after another, he realized he'd recognized the voice.

It was *Owen's.* And the man wouldn't have bellowed like that unless there was something seriously wrong.

By the time the captain reached the vicinity of the caves, his tricorder was secured and his phaser was in his hand. Ducking under a thick, twisting branch, he came in sight of Owens.

"What is it?" he yelled.

The crewmember turned, showing Kirk a mask of pure terror. He didn't answer—he just pointed with the phaser.

Following the gesture, the captain saw one of the others through the branches of the trees. He couldn't tell who it was, not right away, but the figure seemed to be struggling.

And then, to Kirk's surprise, it lifted into the air. As it cleared the intervening treetops, the captain saw it was *Spock*—writhing and clutching at his midsection, though it wasn't readily apparent why.

Then Kirk saw the pale, slender tentacle wrapped around Spock's waist. Tracing the thing's source to one of the caves, he set his weapon on Heavy Stun and fired away.

A red lance of phaserlight hit the tentacle halfway between Spock and the cave opening. The impact made the thing recoil as if in pain, but it didn't let go. On the contrary, it seemed to squeeze harder, eliciting a grunt of agony from its captive.

From off to Kirk's left, two more phaser beams sliced through the air. One missed; the other hit the tentacle at its lowest visible point. Like the captain's shot, it failed to set Spock free.

Torn by the anguish on his first officer's face, Kirk adjusted his phaser to its highest setting. He hated to seriously damage something that might not have the brains to mean them any harm, but he wasn't going to give Spock up without a fight.

Unfortunately, just as the captain depressed the firing pad, the ground shuddered beneath his feet, causing him to miss his target. But this was not just another earthquake—that became apparent rather quickly. Before Kirk's startled eyes, the terrain behind him *erupted*—as if some natural subterranean force had suddenly come to life.

The jungle floor hunkered up, trees teetered and fell, and something white—so white it was almost luminous—surged out of the mess of rocks and earth and severed roots. Rearing, it rose to its full height—a good ten times the size of a man.

It reminded Kirk of a grub—the kind they used to dig out of the earth back in Iowa. But this one was huge, and as he watched, momentarily spellbound, it unfolded a series of tentacles, some long, some short. Tentacles—like the one that held Spock!

No sooner had the captain made the connection than the ground between the creature and the cave openings began to rip open in a straight line. What emerged from the debris was a good ten meters' worth of thick, powerful limb—the rest of the tentacle that had encircled Spock's middle. Finally, it collapsed the cave opening in its effort to shrug free.

"Get back!" cried McCoy, on the far side of the creature. He was doing his best to shield Ensign Karras from it, though she seemed calmer than he was.

Meanwhile, the thing was raising Spock into the air, bringing him closer to its topmost portion, where a small pink maw was beginning to open. Deciding to make that his target, Kirk sent a beam directly into the orifice.

The creature shuddered and recoiled, and there was a sickening stench of seared flesh. But even a high-intensity beam couldn't make it loosen its hold on Spock. Reeling him in, the thing brought him not to its ruined mouth, but to one of its smaller tentacles.

Something happened then, though the captain wasn't sure exactly what. The smaller tentacle seemed to touch the Vulcan on the shoulder, nothing more. And a moment later, the larger limb—the one that had held him all along—dropped him to the torn-up turf below.

Maybe the phaser beam had had an effect after all. Maybe it had just taken some time for the pain of its wound to reach the creature's primitive nerve center.

Or maybe, with its mouth no longer functioning, it didn't know quite what to do with Spock.

In any case, the thing didn't wait around to provide an explanation. As Owens and Autry sprang forward to claim the first officer, the creature withdrew into the pit from which it had emerged.

Kirk came forward to the edge of the gaping hole to make sure the creature was really going, not just regrouping. On the other side of the gap, he saw Karras do the same—phaser in hand, as in control as one could hope to be under the circumstances. After a few seconds had gone by, the captain decided that the creature had really departed; he put his phaser away and signed for Karras to do the same.

By that time, McCoy had reached Spock's prone form and was assessing the damage with his tricorder. Kirk skirted the hole and joined them.

As he got closer, he realized that the Vulcan was shuddering, as if in the grip of some terrible convulsion. He looked flushed and feverish, his eyes wide. And he was breathing much too quickly, as evidenced by the rapid rise and fall of his chest.

The captain had expected some fractured ribs, maybe internal bleeding. But not *this*.

"Bones," Kirk breathed, hunkering down beside the doctor. "What's happening to him?"

McCoy only scowled. As the captain watched, helpless, Bones removed a hypo from his kit, set it to the proper mix, and pressed it against Spock's upper arm. A moment later, there was a hissing sound, and Spock's shuddering stopped, though he still showed no sign of awareness.

Using his tricorder again, McCoy scanned the Vulcan. When he saw the readouts, he relaxed a little. Turning at last to Kirk, he said: "Something's gotten into his bloodstream—some kind of poison I can't identify. It's accelerating Spock's vital processes." He turned back to Spock and took yet another tricorder reading—apparently, one he wasn't too displeased with. "Before I gave him that sedative," he went on, "his metabolism was approaching twice its normal pace. If I'd let him alone, his heart would eventually have burst."

Abruptly, the captain flashed back to the sight of the creature's tentacle brushing Spock's shoulder. He cursed, drawing McCoy's attention. "Bones, I saw the thing touch him with one of its tentacles . . . *here* . . ." He pointed to the juncture of Spock's neck and shoulder.

Pulling the material of the first officer's tunic aside, McCoy exposed three tiny puncture marks, still green with clotting blood. "Damn," he said. "That's it, all right. That's how it happened." He shook his head, still glaring at the puncture wounds. "Jim, I've got to get him up to sickbay. I need to analyze the substance, figure out why it's affecting him this way . . ."

Kirk got the message. Taking out his communicator, he flipped it open again.

"Mister Scott?"

The answer was only a moment in coming. "Aye, sir."

"Spock's been hurt. He'll be beaming up immediately with Doctor McCoy. Have a gurney ready for him when they arrive."

Scotty's voice was heavy with concern as he answered. "No sooner said than done, Captain."

McCoy shot him a glance, as if to say "only *two?*"

"And Scotty," Kirk added, "let Kyle know the rest of us will be returning as well, as soon as I can contact Sulu's group." He looked at the doctor; after all, this last part was for *his* benefit. "I want to make sure they're all right before I pull up stakes completely."

"Understood, sir," the chief engineer replied. "Scott out."

The captain waited for the blink that signified the end of the communications link, then addressed the device again. "Sulu—report."

"Everything's fine, Captain. In fact, I was just going to call you. Ensign Ellis came across—"

"Not now, Lieutenant. We found out what was causing those tremors—a subterranean creature, and it's not exactly docile. Mister Spock's already been hurt; I'm not going to risk that happening to anyone else. We're beaming up."

"I see," Sulu responded. He sounded disappointed, Kirk noted. But whatever it was Ellis had found, it could wait.

It was at that moment that Spock and McCoy were enveloped in the telltale glow of the transporter effect. As they began to dematerialize, the captain took one last look at the Vulcan—sedate now, but still dark and feverish looking. With any luck, the doctor would be able to find an antidote for the poison before there was any permanent damage.

Then they were gone, leaving only a series of depressions in the soft soil the creature had brought up with it.

*With any luck.* Kirk sighed. "Stand by," he told Sulu.

"Will do, Captain."

Kirk was waiting for the light on his communicator to blink again, when he felt the ground give way beneath him. He fell, but only a few feet, landing awkwardly on all fours. As he looked around, he saw that the same thing had happened to his companions. They were raising their heads cautiously, wondering what had happened—and what to do next.

For a good ten meters in every direction, including the spot where the creature had emerged, the terrain had become confused, chaotic. Trees tilted at crazy angles; stones large and small were rolling toward them, slowly converging on them. At the fringe of the turmoil, there was a short barricade of earth and shredded roots.

"It's all right," the captain announced. He pointed

to the perimeter of the area and the barricade. "Make your way out of here—slowly. Try not to—"

Suddenly, there was another shift, and the unstable plot seemed to tilt down at one end, as if they were pieces of food on some impossibly huge plate, and they were being emptied off into a disposal unit. At the end that was tilted down, Kirk got a glimpse of darkness—a yawning hole, waiting to devour them. Scrabbling in the opposite direction, he tried to escape it. The others followed his lead.

But there was nothing to latch onto. It was all loose earth and debris that gave way as the captain grasped for it, and a moment later he felt himself sliding helter-skelter in the direction of the hole. On the periphery of his awareness, he heard someone shouting for help.

Then he plunged headlong into blackness. He had a vague impression of something slamming down on top of him—just before the earth swallowed him whole.

Geologist Ron Gross lay belly down on the roof of the Beta Cabrini colony's administration building, watching the square where the marauders had first materialized through a chink in the low retaining wall. The entire population of the colony was being herded like cattle into the open area, around a makeshift platform that had gone up over the last few hours.

The entire population, that is, except for Gross himself and, of course, the man laying prone beside him. "What's happening?" asked Rumiel Green, Gross's assistant, who had no chink to peer through.

The older man shrugged. "They're gathering everyone together. Wayne is stepping up to the stage."

Gross saw Administrator Wayne file through the armed Merkaans surrounding the wooden platform. The man held his head high—not an easy thing to do, under the circumstances. Nor could it have been easy to resist looking in the direction of his offices, where he knew Gross and Green would be on the roof, waiting for their chance.

In just a few short hours of occupation, the invaders had killed seven colonists, not including the three that were slaughtered right off the bat. Wayne had told the Merkaans he could not permit this to go on. What's more, he had said, bloodshed was not in the invaders' interests; it would only stiffen the colonists' resistance. But if he had an opportunity to address his people, he might be able to persuade them to cooperate, thereby benefiting both the humans and the Merkaans.

Of course, stemming the violence was only part of Wayne's real agenda. He knew that if the marauders' attention were focused on him, it might leave others free to act. He also knew that the colony's scientists were watched less closely than anyone else and that of all their scientists, Gross had the most experience with subspace communications.

It hadn't been easy getting word to the geologist. The message had had to go through three or four intermediaries before it finally reached him, and all under the watchful eyes of the disruptor-happy Merkaans.

The younger man frowned. "How much longer are we going to wait?"

Gross saw Wayne assume a position at the front of the platform. What crowd noises there had been—and they were few, thanks to the ubiquitous presence of the Merkaans—settled into near-silence. The administrator began to speak.

"No longer," the geologist said. "Let's go."

Making their way on elbows and knees to the rear end of the building, they came to another chink in the barrier. This time, Green peeked through it.

"All clear?"

"So far," the younger man whispered.

But that didn't mean there wasn't someone directly below them, guarding the back door. With great care, Green poked his head out past the wall. A moment later, he drew it back in.

"All clear," he reported.

Now came the hardest part—getting down from the roof and into the building without being seen. Gross had never been trained in clandestine activities. Hell, he wasn't even much of a climber. And neither was his accomplice.

But they'd both known people whom the Merkaans had killed for little or no reason over the past several hours. One of them had been Green's closest friend, and there was no telling who would be next. Training or no training, they had no choice but to try.

Slithering over the wall, the older man hung for a second by his fingertips. Then he let go and dropped. The ground rushed up more quickly than he expected, but he landed on his feet. Looking around quickly, he saw that the street was deserted and let go of a breath he didn't know he'd been holding. It puffed out, cold and white, and evaporated a second later.

Green came down beside him, his footwear scraping the hard, dry ground as he landed awkwardly and fought for balance. But the sound wasn't loud enough to attract attention.

So far, so good. Reaching into his pocket, Gross removed the key to the administration building that had been passed on to him along with Wayne's message. Normally, the building was unlocked, but the Merkaan leader, the one named Dreen, had decided that all potentially "troublesome" facilities should be kept under lock and key and had posted guards around such facilities as well.

At the moment, however, all the Merkaans were out in the square, listening to Wayne and studying the crowd. Slipping his magnetic key into the slot intended for it, Gross watched the door slide open.

Exchanging glances with his assistant, he led the way inside. Fortunately, the only window showed the side of the building across the way. There were no views of the square or, for that matter, of any of the other rooms in the building. There was only a door. And it was closed.

Once Green had cleared the threshold, the door whooshed shut behind them. The stillness seemed deep and impenetrable—a comforting perception, if not an entirely dependable one.

"Over there," Gross said. He pointed to the back-up communications unit.

It was a good deal more advanced than the ones he was used to. But then, his communications experience was fifteen or twenty years old, a product of the days when most planet surveys were carried out by small expeditions, and the only way for a young geologist to be considered for an assignment was to be a jack of all trades. Since he couldn't cook worth a damn, communications had seemed like a good way to go.

As they approached the unit, keeping low to avoid being seen from the window, Gross hoped he could figure the damned thing out before Wayne was done with his speech. There was too much riding on this roll for him to come up snake eyes.

"What can I do?" Green asked.

"Just keep an eye out." Gross turned his attention to the control panel, wishing he'd paid more attention to it *before* the crisis. Nothing was labeled; it had been designed for experts. And in a colony this size, there were plenty of those; too bad they were out there in the square now, under heavy scrutiny and unable to assist.

The geologist rubbed his hands together to warm them. They'd gotten cold and stiff up on the roof.

*All right,* he told himself. *This doesn't look all that difficult. A hell of a lot different, but not necessarily difficult. All I've got to do is activate it . . .*

He turned the machine on. It hummed a little.

*. . . set it for the nearest target, so there's a decent chance of someone picking it up in time to react . . .*

Gross instructed the unit to direct its transmission to Starbase 22. Instantly, the monitor confirmed that the system's orbiting satellite dish had been repositioned as required.

*. . . program a message . . .*

Request immediate assistance. Colony has been occupied by Merkaans under one Hamesaad Dreen. This matter is of utmost—

Gross never got a chance to finish the sentence. Before he knew it, Green was grabbing his arm, tugging him back the way they'd come in.

*"Merkaans,"* he hissed, his eyes wide with apprehension.

Listening, the older man heard guttural voices—distant but loud, it seemed to him—carrying in the frigid air. Were they coming this way?

It didn't matter. He couldn't leave—not yet. First, he had to input the command to transmit. Even if the message was incomplete, it would alert Starfleet to their danger. Pulling his arm back, Gross tapped what looked like the "execute" pad.

The system responded: READY TO RECEIVE.

It was the wrong pad. He pressed it again, negating the command and clearing it.

Damn Starfleet! Why'd they have to go and move the "execute" pad on him? Probably trying to simplify things again, and they'd only made them that much harder. And without any labels—

"We've got to go," Green insisted. His face was taut with fear.

Gross shook his head, trying to clear his mind of its mounting apprehension. "Not yet. I just need a few seconds."

He turned back to the control panel, feeling stupid. Up until now, he'd been fine. To get stuck trying to find the "execute" pad was the height of absurdity.

It had to be *somewhere.* If not where he'd thought it was, then *here*—or *here.* Or *here.*

Another guttural exchange, closer now. The Merkaans were definitely heading this way. Had they been discovered? Was the door going to slide aside soon, revealing a half-dozen gray devils with disruptor pistols?

Abruptly, Green made for the exit. Anger rising, Gross rasped at him: "Where do you think you're going?"

The younger man swallowed. "Out there. I'm going to give them something to think about."

The geologist understood. His accomplice meant to let the Merkaans see him—to draw them off, so Gross could complete his task. "You're crazy," he said. "It's suicide."

Green looked scared to death, but he shook his head. "No time to argue. Got to go."

And then the door whooshed open and he was gone, and Gross was all alone. Resolutely, the geologist turned back to the problem at hand.

Which pad? Which one? The wrong choice might dump this message, and he'd have to start all over again.

He pressed the one on the left. The monitor read: MESSAGE LOGGED.

No, he didn't want that. If the Merkaans were to find the device, it would enable them to know that a message had been sent. Pressing the button again, he countermanded the instruction.

That left two pads. One of them had to be what he was looking for.

Somewhere outside the door, there were deep-throated shouts, urgent ones. Had Green been discovered? Or were they coming after *him?*

Two pads left. He had to choose, and quickly.

Abruptly, without thinking, he pressed the larger one. Fortunately, it had the desired effect: MESSAGE SENT.

Gross breathed a sigh of relief. Finally giving way to his terror, he bolted for the back door. And froze.

More shouting, almost frantic. The sound of boots hitting the frozen ground. And they were coming from the street just outside.

For a moment, he thought they were onto him. He could almost feel them grabbing him by his coat, tossing him aside as they realized what he was up to. He could almost see them training their disruptors on him . . .

Then the pounding sounds went past him. They faded.

He whispered his gratitude to the empty room. At the same time, however, he couldn't help but think about his assistant. Couldn't help but picture him sprinting headlong from alley to alley, with a clot of Merkaan thugs in close pursuit—getting closer, closer . . .

Putting the image aside, he got hold of himself. After all, his task wasn't over. If he were found here, the Merkaans would wonder what he'd been up to. They'd find the communications device and realize he'd sent a call for help. And they'd be prepared for the rescue attempt when it came.

Gross steeled himself and touched the panel beside the exit. It engaged the mechanism, causing the door to retract into the wall.

Poking his head out into the alley, the geologist saw that it was free of Merkaans. He slipped out, waiting only long enough to see the door close behind him. Then he hurried away from the administration building, seeking shelter in one of the outlying facilities, as far from the communication device as possible. That had been the plan all along, except he'd expected to have Green beside him.

No sooner had the man's name crossed his mind than Gross heard a cry of pain. And not from far off. It had come from one, maybe two streets away.

By rights, he should have fled in the opposite

direction. If his assistant had been caught, there was nothing he could do for him.

Nonetheless, he headed in the direction of the cry. *If there's even a chance,* he told himself, *even a wisp of a chance of helping Green to get away . . .*

At the intersection, he heard another cry, from the next street over to his right. As much as it tore at him, Gross knew that a cry was good; a cry meant they hadn't killed him yet. It meant Green was still alive.

Looking around, making sure he himself wasn't spotted, the geologist negotiated the length of the street and approached the corner. And taking a deep breath, he peered around it.

He caught a glimpse of his assistant being held by a pair of husky Merkaans. Then they thrust him toward a third Merkaan—one who was holding a disruptor pistol.

*Balac.* Gross recognized the pistol-wielder as Dreen's second-in-command.

Balac brought his face close to Green's. "What were you doing here, human? What kind of treachery were you up to?"

Gross knew the younger man wouldn't last under interrogation. He didn't have that kind of willpower. In time, he'd incriminate Gross and Wayne and everybody who had been involved.

Green must have known it too. Because instead of pleading for mercy, he struck Balac across the face as hard as he could. Startled as much as anything else, the Merkaan staggered back a step, cursing at the top of his lungs.

For a moment, Gross had the satisfaction of seeing the blood trickling from Balac's nose. Then Balac drew his disruptor and unleashed its energy on Green.

The man looked as if he wanted to scream but couldn't, as the nothingness at the heart of the light spread and enveloped him. Half a heartbeat later, there was no sign of him.

Gross began to tremble. He'd heard about what the

disruptor did to people, but he'd never actually seen it. Stumbling in his haste to escape, he nonetheless got back down the street before anyone could notice him.

The strength was ebbing from his legs, however. His knees were turning to jelly. Sprawling, he made it to the nearest doorway before collapsing altogether. Sensing his presence, the door opened.

He pulled himself inside, and put his head down on the floor. And for what seemed like an eternity, he listened to his heart hammering in the darkness.

# Chapter Three

THIS TIME, Sulu felt the tremor. So did the three science officers with him.

Instantly, he opened his communicator and tried to contact the captain. He waited one second, two, three.

No response.

"Captain Kirk," he said. "Please acknowledge."

Still no response.

"Damn," the helmsman muttered. He looked back at the ridge which separated them from the beam-down site. The blue skies above that high ground yielded no clues, but something had happened to Kirk and the others.

Sulu's first impulse was to go see for himself. But it wasn't just his welfare he'd have been risking. He had three other lives to think about.

Bridling his instincts, he called up to the ship. The reply was tinged with concern.

"Mister Scott here," said the engineering chief. "What's going on down there, Lieutenant? Mister Kyle says he's lost the captain's signal!"

Sulu felt his throat tighten. "There's been an earth

41

tremor in the vicinity," he told Scotty. "I've tried to contact Captain Kirk, but he's not answering."

The Scotsman swore softly, though not so softly that it didn't come over the communications link. *"Another* tremor?"

"Affirmative." Sulu licked his lips. "You've heard about them, then?"

"Aye," Scotty said. "I heard, all right. Doctor McCoy told me about them, if only briefly. He also told me about the creature that caused them—the one that poisoned Mister Spock." He swore again—this time, a good deal less softly. "If that creature could do what it did to a *Vulcan* . . ."

The helmsman finished the thought in his head: *Imagine what kind of damage it could inflict on a human.*

"Well," Scotty said, "we cannae just write them off. We've got to find out what happened to them."

"Permission to do that," the helmsman volunteered.

"Permission granted. But keep us posted. I dinnae want any more surprises, Lieutenant—ye understand?"

"Perfectly," Sulu assured him. He closed his communicator and motioned to his entourage. "You heard the man. Let's go."

Of all of them, only Ellis hesitated. After all, this place was *her* find. She glanced at it longingly, but only for a moment.

Then she joined the rest of them as they started off in the direction of the ridge.

Lieutenant Commander Montgomery Scott sat in the captain's chair and drummed his fingers on the armrest. He hated this. If he'd wanted to be in charge of four hundred some-odd lives, he'd never have gone into engineering.

Out of the corner of his eye, he noticed Uhura looking at him. He turned and saw her expression. It was a mixture of anxiety and uncertainty, but also one of compassion—her way of telling him he wasn't alone in this. And to an extent, it worked. He felt as if he'd been relieved of a small portion of the weight on his shoulders.

But by no means could he relax altogether. Not with the captain and his party missing, and Spock in sickbay and a mammoth creature running around that might take down Sulu's group, too, before it was all over.

Rising from the command seat, Scotty took a couple of steps toward the forward viewscreen, where Octavius Four was a sweep of blue and green softened by white cloud formations. He locked his hands behind his back and glared at it.

The place had looked so damned inviting when they'd established orbit around it. Not at all like the deadly trap it turned out to be.

Pavel Chekov looked up at him from his customary place at the navigation console. Nor did Scotty have any trouble divining what was in Chekov's mind.

He would have preferred to be planetside, like Sulu, *doing* something, not sitting on his rump and waiting.

The engineering chief didn't blame him. Hell, he felt that way himself. There was nothing harder than—

"Mister Scott?"

He turned at the sound of Uhura's voice. "Aye, Lieutenant?"

Her expression had changed, but not for the better. "Sir, I have Admiral Kowalski on subspace. He wants to speak with Captain Kirk."

*Great,* Scotty thought. *Just what I needed—to get involved with Starfleet brass when I should be concentratin' on getting our people back.*

"Put him on screen," he instructed, with obvious reluctance.

The admiral was a tall, elegant-looking man with a touch of gray in his hair. One of those people, Scotty observed, that wouldn't look flustered if there were fire ants crawling up their pant legs.

However, Kowalski did evidence a little surprise at seeing Scott on the bridge instead of the captain. "I asked to speak with Captain Kirk," he said, somehow managing not to sound as if he were complaining.

Scotty took a deep breath. "I'm Lieutenant Commander Scott, sir. Captain Kirk and three crewpeople are missing, lost on the planet's surface. We're doing our best to locate them, even as we speak."

Kowalski's brow creased ever so slightly. "Missing," he echoed, digesting the information.

"That's right, Admiral. Now if ye've got something to tell me, I ask that ye do it quickly. I need to devote my full attention to the search."

The man on the screen seemed to hesitate just a bit, as if weighing something before he spoke. "Your search will have to wait, Commander Scott. Your orders are to proceed immediately to the Beta Cabrini mining colony. A member of my staff is issuing briefing data and coordinates now."

For a moment, Scotty just stood there, openmouthed. Then it sank in, and he exploded.

"Do ye know what ye're sayin'?" he asked the admiral. The chief engineer shook his head vehemently. "I'm *nae* leavin' the captain down there!"

Kowalski seemed unperturbed by the outburst. "I know exactly what I'm saying. Do you?"

Scotty's teeth ground together as he restrained himself. *You're nae doing anybody any good by blowing up,* he thought—*least of all the captain.* "Admiral, I've got a duty to the captain and crew of this vessel. I cannae just abandon them at the drop of a hat."

The admiral's eyes became hard, but his voice remained under control. "Commander," he said, "the Beta Cabrini colonists are in immediate and deadly danger—all two hundred and eighty four of them. Yours is the only ship anywhere near enough to provide help."

*Immediate and deadly indeed,* Scotty thought. It was a chilling phrase. But how many times had they pushed the engines to perdition when answering a distress call—only to find out some supposed danger wasn't as great or immediate as they'd been given to believe? On the other hand, what if Kowalski was right? What if the colony *was* in some terrible danger?

"Now," Kowalski continued, "I appreciate your concern for your crewmates, but it cannot supersede Starfleet's obligation to these colonists. Especially when there are so many of them, and only—how many did you say were missing from your crew? *Four?*"

The old numbers game. Unfortunately, it made sense. Could he let four take precedence over two hundred and eighty-four—especially when the captain and the others might already be beyond help? Scott bit his lip. "Sir," he began in a carefully measured tone, "I'm nae sayin' the colonists dinnae need help. But if ye just give me a little more time, I can—"

"There is no time," the admiral insisted, leaning forward. "For all we know, some of the colonists have died already. Now, I've already told you I understand your situation. Believe me, I've been there myself. But it is absolutely essential that you leave Octavius Four at once and proceed to Beta Cabrini with all the speed you can muster."

Scotty scowled. "Admiral, at least let me—"

"Maybe you didn't hear me, Mister Scott. The matter is not open for debate. Either you lay in a course for Beta Cabrini—immediately—or I'll see you face a court martial. Do I make myself clear?"

Scott's nostrils flared. The very idea of leaving Captain Kirk behind was an abomination. Nor was he particularly frightened of a court martial; it wasn't the first time he'd been threatened with one.

But it was obvious he wasn't going to get anywhere jabbering with Admiral Kowalski. "Aye, sir," he responded at last. "*Crystal* clear."

Inwardly, though, he made a vow to himself. He would go over the information in the subspace briefing packet. And if he wasn't convinced Beta Cabrini was in serious trouble, he was going to remain in orbit around Octavius Four; the admiral be *damned.*

"My god," Ellis said, still breathing hard from their hasty return to the beam-down site. "Could they be down there?"

Sulu and the others stood around a massive pit into which the land seemed to have collapsed, taking trees and soil and vegetation with it. It was as if someone had pulled out a plug and the jungle had just drained into it.

As Ferriter played his tricorder over the mess in the pit, the helmsman's mind raced. According to his communicator, this was the exact spot from which the captain had sent his most recent message. It was possible that Kirk and his team had moved off from here afterward, but they couldn't have gone very far. And if they *had* moved off a bit, where were they?

No, it was too much of a coincidence that they'd disappeared just as this hole opened up. One way or the other, they were down there.

But alive? They would know soon enough.

Ferriter finished his inspection and read the results. He frowned deeply, but he stopped short of saying why.

Steeling himself, Sulu said it instead. "No signs of life."

Ferriter nodded. "True, in the areas I can scan. But I'm getting holes in my readings, just like the ones in the long-range sensor studies."

The helmsman clutched at the straw. "Then they might still be alive down there," he concluded.

Ferriter nodded. "It's possible, sir."

"The creature might be alive down there too," Margolis—the last member of their party—reminded them. He looked warily at the pit, as if something might leap up from it at any moment.

"We'll take our chances with the creature," Sulu decided. Securing his tricorder, he took out his phaser instead. "Until we find their bodies, we're going to assume the captain and the others are alive." Then, aiming his weapon at the center of the pit, he began to burn a hole in the debris. A plume of white smoke arose from the point where his beam struck a tree trunk, vaporizing it. "Let's go," he told the others, not even looking up from his target. "Even with all of us working on this, it's going to take a long time. And if they *are* still alive, they may not have much air."

Ellis, Ferriter, and Margolis were in various stages of joining in the effort, when Sulu's communicator beeped. His heart leaping, hoping against hope that it might be Kirk, he flipped it open.

"Sulu?"

It was Scotty. The helmsman bit back his disappointment. "We found the last spot where the captain communicated," he reported. "The ground here has just caved in, and we think his party was caught in the collapse. We're—"

The engineering chief cursed, cutting him short. "Never mind that," he said. "We're goin' to beam ye back up."

Sulu couldn't believe what he'd heard. "Mister Scott, they may still be alive. If there's even a chance—"

"It's out of my hands, lad," Scotty barked. "Prepare for transport."

And before Sulu could decipher what "out of my hands" meant, he was enveloped in the transporter effect.

"Mister Scott?" Kyle's British accent was unmistakable, even over the intercom.

The engineering chief had sat down again, but he

was beginning to regret it. Was it his imagination, or was the damned chair tightening around him?

"Aye," he said, responding to Kyle. "Ye've got Sulu's party, I hope?"

"Affirmative, sir."

"Thank goodness for that," Scotty declared. "Have Mister Sulu report to the bridge. The others can log their findings in the science section." He turned to Chekov, who had already swiveled around in his seat.

"Course laid in for Beta Cabrini," the ensign reported, without Scott having to prod him. Chekov didn't look happy about leaving the captain behind either, but he wasn't letting it prevent him from doing his job.

"Thank you, Ensign." Scotty looked to Pierce, the helmsman on duty. "Warp Factor Six," he said.

"Warp Factor Six," the man confirmed.

As the *Enterprise* came about, Octavius Four slipped out of the forward view, giving way to a sea of stars, but Scotty did not ask to have the rear view posted on the screen, as Kirk sometimes did.

He didn't want to think about what he was leaving behind.

Not more than a few moments later, the turbolift doors opened and Sulu strode out onto the bridge. Still red-faced and sweaty from his exertions on the planet, he headed straight for the helmsman's station, glancing only once at the viewscreen—and studiously avoiding a confrontation with Scotty.

But the Scotsman had other ideas. "Mister Sulu," he said.

The lieutenant stopped abruptly and looked at him. "Aye, sir?"

"Dinnae bother to sit down. Ye've got the conn."

And without another word, Scotty rose, tugged down on his tunic, and made his way to the lift from which Sulu had just emerged.

\* \* \*

Leonard McCoy leaned back against a counter ledge in critical care, his arms crossed over his chest, and scrutinized the life-signs display above Spock's biobed. Then he looked at Spock.

Only the greenish flush in the Vulcan's cheeks gave away the intensity of the struggle within him. On one hand, the alien serum—injected by the creature—was encouraging his metabolism to run wild. On the other hand, the doctor's sedative, which he'd had to boost after Spock arrived in sickbay, was depressing that same metabolism.

A stalemate, but one that couldn't last forever. Though Spock's condition was stable for the moment, the tug of war for control of his life processes was taking its toll, slowly but surely. In time, the strain would damage him permanently, maybe even kill him.

Frowning, the doctor shook his head. He couldn't let that happen.

As much as Spock annoyed him sometimes, as much as the very mention of Vulcan logic made his hackles rise, McCoy had a grudging respect for the ship's first officer. *Maybe more than respect,* he admitted, if only to himself.

His frown deepening, he made his way back across sickbay to the lab. As he entered, Doctor M'Benga and Nurse Chapel turned to look at him.

"How's it going?" McCoy asked.

Even before they had pumped more tranquilizer into Spock, M'Benga—their specialist in Vulcan medicine—had extracted samples of the patient's blood for analysis. He was engaged in that analysis now.

M'Benga shrugged. "Well enough. We've isolated the poison, but I've never seen anything like it. It'll take a while before—" The man stopped himself and smiled. "I guess I don't have to tell *you* that, do I?"

"It's all right," McCoy assured him. "You're talking

to the man who once told the captain how to steer the ship."

Before the doctor had quite finished his sentence, he heard the muffled sound of someone approaching. Turning, he saw an unexpected visitor.

"Scotty," he said. "What brings you down to sickbay?"

The engineering chief had a strange look on his face, almost apologetic. "Well," he began, "first off, I wanted to see how Mister Spock was comin' along."

McCoy grunted. "He's not in any immediate danger, though we're a long way from a cure." He paused. "Why, did the captain ask about him?"

The strange look got even stranger. "No," Scotty replied, "though Captain Kirk is the other reason I came to see ye."

Something cold and clammy slithered up the doctor's spine. A premonition?

"Scotty," he said slowly, "if you're going to tell me something's happened to Jim, you'd better not beat around the bush."

Scott sighed. "All right," he agreed, "I won't."

He was true to his word.

# Chapter Four

As HE RAISED HIS HEAD from beneath the cover of his arms, Kirk could feel a load of moist dirt spill off his neck and shoulders. Coughing at the stench in the air—as of something rotting—he looked around.

And felt his heart sink. It was as if he'd gone blind. All around him was darkness—pure, unrelieved darkness.

In space, there were at least some stars to navigate by. Here, there was no illumination at all, no point of reference.

Reminding himself that his phaser could provide some light, the captain reached for it—and found that it was gone. What's more, his communicator was gone, though now that he thought about it, he'd probably dropped it in the early stages of the ground collapse.

Again, he peered into the darkness, willing his eyes to adjust to it, as if will alone could make a difference. If there wasn't any light, there was nothing to adjust to.

*Buried alive.* It was a chilling thought. Like something out of a ghost story his brother might have told around a campfire when they were kids. But this was real. And he was no kid—he was a starship captain with a crew to worry about.

What had happened to the others? He remembered seeing them caught in the collapse, but . . .

"Owens?" he called. The stench made his eyes water. "Karras? Autry?"

Nothing. No one answered. Kirk's heart sank a little more. Could it be that he was the only one who'd survived the cave-in?

He started to get up and immediately banged his head on something, the impact driving him back to his knees. Cursing, he reached up and examined the area above him with his fingertips. It only took a couple of seconds to determine that there was a rocky ceiling of sorts there—one which seemed uniform and fairly solid, though its solidity might be a dangerous illusion.

"Captain? Is that you?"

It was Karras. He could tell by her voice, muffled as it was.

"I hear you," he answered. "Are you all right, Ensign?"

"I'm fine."

"Have you still got your phaser?"

A pause. "No, it must've come off."

*There,* the captain told himself. *Her voice is coming from over* there.

"How about your communicator?" he asked, starting to crawl in what he thought was the right direction. Pulling himself over the uneven terrain, he could feel the cuts and bruises he'd suffered in his fall. Nothing terrible, though—he was lucky.

Another pause. "That I've got."

"Try calling the ship."

He heard her follow his order. Not once, but twice.

"No response," she reported. "I don't think I'm getting through."

Damn. He'd had a feeling that might happen.

"You may not be," he told her, continuing to creep forward. "Whatever blocked our long-range sensors could be blocking communications as well."

Kirk thought he could make out the click of her communicator snapping shut. It was a sign he was proceeding in the right direction.

"What happened?" asked the ensign.

"Don't know," he responded. But he could guess. If the creature traveled underground, the bedrock was probably full of weak spots. And the creature's emergence had to have weakened this area even further.

Of course, this wasn't the time to discuss the matter at length. They could do that after they were safely out of here.

Suddenly, the captain came up against a hard surface, something jutting from the ground at an odd angle. Feeling with his fingers, he tried to get an idea of its limits so he could go around it. Or over it. Or even under it, if that's what it took.

The thing was big, but it couldn't go on forever. Kirk kept crawling to his right. Farther. Farther. Finally, he found an edge and negotiated a path around it. "Keep talking," he told Karras. "I'm following the sound of your voice."

"Sir," she said, "I heard something. I think I'm right near one of the others."

A moaning. The captain spoke into the darkness. "Owens? Autry?"

"Here," came the response, barely more than a whisper. "Owens, sir."

The voice was coming from somewhere off to the right of Karras, if Kirk had reckoned correctly. "Are you hurt?" he asked Owens.

Another moan, another whispered reply: "My leg, sir. I think it's broken."

It could have been worse. The captain started to worry about Autry, and then put it from his mind.

You'll find him, he told himself. One step at a time, just the way they taught you at the Academy.

Well, maybe not a step, exactly. More of a slither.

Pulling himself forward, he felt something else in his path—a big rock, judging by the size and shape and hardness of it. Just like all those boulders he'd seen on the surface.

If one of these had fallen on Autry . . .

No. A second time, he had to focus himself on the task ahead. A moment later, he was past the boulder and making good progress.

"Karras? How am I doing?"

"You're getting closer, sir, I think. I don't have a very good sense of direction."

*Maybe not,* Kirk noted inwardly, *but you've got a lot of guts.* There wasn't the least quiver of fear or complaint in her voice.

Somewhere above, there was a crunch, followed by the hiss of falling dirt. Instinctively, the captain stopped wriggling and held his breath.

But that was it. The sounds stopped and nothing happened.

Of course, the initial ground collapse had given them even less warning than that. There were no guarantees that this cavern they found themselves in was stable, or that the rocky structure overhead wouldn't give way and finish them off.

They had to find a way out. And they had to do it as quickly as possible.

Kirk worked his way forward again, and his hand brushed against something soft. *And dry,* he thought —*strangely dry.*

Backing up a bit, he groped around in the darkness. After a moment or two, he found it again.

It was soft, all right. As soft as the material of a Starfleet uniform.

He'd found Autry—or more specifically, his arm. Quickly, he followed the contour of it to the man's neck and felt for a pulse.

He was alive. But clearly injured—how seriously . . .

Lowering his ear to the spot where he thought Autry's mouth would be, Kirk listened. A wave of relief washed over him; his crewman was respiring without any problem.

He'd just been knocked out, though there was no way of knowing how badly, or of determining what other injuries he might have suffered. The captain stopped to think. Moving Autry would involve some risk. But if he left the injured man here, he might have a devil of a time finding him again, and his instincts told him they'd have a better chance if they were all together.

As if to underline the wisdom of his decision, there was another crunch like the one he'd heard before. And this time, the hiss that followed was a prolonged one.

"Captain?" It was Karras.

"I'm here, Ensign. And I've found Autry."

Her tone was tentative as she asked, "How is he?"

"He's alive, but unconscious. I—"

Kirk was interrupted by a grunt, and then a weakly mumbled curse.

"Autry?" the captain ventured, wishing he could see his crewman's face.

A pause. "Is that you, sir?" The voice was parched and reedy.

Kirk couldn't help but smile. "Yes, it's me."

"Where are we?" Autry asked. He sounded dazed, though that was no surprise. "What happened—"

"Not now." The captain gripped his shoulder reassuringly. "Can you move?"

Another pause. "Aye, sir. I'm just a little sore, is all."

"Good. Follow me."

Kirk crawled ahead a bit, then listened to make sure Autry was with him. When he heard the man scraping along after him, he started forward again.

"You're definitely getting closer now," Karras advised him. "It sounds as if I could reach out and touch you."

It sounded that way to the captain too. "Hold out your hand," he told her. "Wave it in front of you."

As he crept on, he did the same. And made contact.

At first, their hands only brushed one another. On the second pass, though, they caught and locked.

Karras' hand seemed cold and small in his. Maybe it was his instinctive need to protect; maybe it was some other impulse entirely, but he held onto it a little longer than he had to.

"I've got you," he said.

"Yes," she replied, releasing him finally.

Kirk looked back over his shoulder, as if he could actually see something. "Still with me, Mister Autry?"

"Still with you, sir."

The captain peered into the unbroken darkness. "What about you, Mister Owens?"

"I haven't gone anywhere," the crewman answered, somehow masking his pain for a moment. It was good to see he still had a sense of humor, despite everything.

Kirk wasn't going to miss an opportunity to lift his people's morale. "I hate to disturb you, but it's time to join the group."

They all laughed, even Owens. "I wish I could," the crewman said, injecting a more sober note.

"Here," Kirk responded, heading for Owens—or at least, where he perceived Owens to be. "Let me give you a hand."

Above, there was a heavy grating sound—stones shifting their positions in a slow, deadly dance. *Hssst* —the trickle of dirt again, a reminder that time was running out. And not just one trickle, but a few. It took what seemed like a long time for the last of them to dry up.

Owens was farther away than the captain had

thought. In time, however, he reached the man. Karras and Autry were right behind him.

At last, they were together. But it wouldn't do them any good if they didn't find a way out.

*A tool—something to dig with—would sure come in handy,* Kirk mused.

"Owens—Autry—you wouldn't by any chance still have your phasers, would you?"

"No, sir," Autry replied. "Mine's gone."

Owens took longer to react to the question. But when he did, his answer was a good deal more favorable: "I've got mine, sir. Here it is."

A moment later, Kirk felt Owens' fingers close lightly on his wrist, and then the familiar shape of a phaser was pressed into his palm. He grasped it.

"Captain?" Karras again.

"Yes?"

"I'm not so sure that's a good idea, sir. The smell in here, it might be some sort of natural gas."

Kirk frowned. He hadn't thought of that, but the woman was right.

Of course, it might get to the point where he'd have to take that risk. But not now. The situation wasn't that desperate yet.

Funny, he'd actually forgotten about the stench. It was amazing what one could get used to.

Even now that he was concentrating on it, he could barely detect anything unpleasant in the air. Which was kind of strange. He couldn't have become *that* accustomed to it.

Unless . . . it was fainter here. And why would that be the case, unless there was fresh air coming in to dispel the odor?

"Excuse me," he said, making his way past Owens on his knees and elbows, still holding the phaser in his right hand, "I may be onto something." He had no idea if he was headed in the right direction or not, but he had to start somewhere, didn't he?

If luck was with him, he'd find the limits of the cavern before too long. Then it would just be a matter of searching for the source of the air.

*If* he was right about there being an opening to the outside.

*If* it was large enough for him to detect.

*If* the cavern didn't collapse on them first.

*Too damned many ifs,* the captain told himself as he snaked forward. His shoulder grazed an obstruction, but when he examined it, it turned out to be nothing more than a rock. He hadn't reached the cavern wall yet.

Crunch. Grate. *Hsst.*

He tried to ignore the warning sounds. *Lord knows,* he mused, *I don't need any more reminders. What I need is to concentrate on the task at hand.*

Then he reached out and came up against the wall of the cavern. Feeling around, he made sure of it.

"Captain?"

Kirk jumped. He hadn't known there was anyone behind him.

"Autry," he said.

"Aye, sir. I thought you might be able to use some help."

The captain nodded, even though he knew he couldn't be seen. "You thought right, crewman. Here —you go left and I'll go right. We're looking for a hole through which air is entering the cave."

Autry didn't ask any questions. He didn't cast any doubts. He just did as he was told.

Kirk, meanwhile, put away his phaser. He'd need both hands if he was to—

The thought died stillborn. There was a draft on the back of his hand. An honest-to-goodness draft!

Moving his hand from one side to the other, then up and down, the captain pinpointed its location. Finally, he lowered his face to the spot, pressed his cheek against the rock, and tried to find the opening.

No light. Not even a glimmer.

But there was a channel to the outside. There had to be. Digging his fingers into the crust of rock and hard earth, Kirk tugged. Nothing, again. This time, a small piece of rock came away in his hand.

"Autry," he called. "I need your help."

Before the crewman found him, he wrested another piece of rock from the barrier, making the opening as big as a man's fist. The draft was a little stronger now.

"Sir?"

"Give me your hand."

The captain found it in the dark and guided it to the hole he'd made. The crewman grunted as he realized the import of it.

"See if you can make this any bigger," he told Autry. "In the meantime, I'm going back for Karras and Owens."

"I hear you, sir."

Judging from the sounds of his exertions, Autry wasted no time in applying himself to his task, as Kirk held up his part of the bargain. His little injuries were getting worse now, aggravated by all the crawling he was doing, but this was no time to start counting his aches and pains.

"Karras?" he called. "Owens?"

Homing in on their voices as he had before, he reached them more quickly than he'd expected. Distances were tricky here in the dark.

"Sir, what is it?" Karras asked.

"We found a way out," the captain told her. "At least, it might be—there's a draft coming from it." He found Owens' shoulder, then hooked his hand under the injured man's armpit. "The only problem is, it's not very big—but Autry is working on that right now. Ready to travel?"

There was no hesitation in Owens' voice. "You bet, sir."

"Good. Then let's—"

Suddenly, there was an enormous grinding sound, as of huge teeth gnashing together. And somewhere in the cavern, maybe not too far away, a thunderous crash. Kirk just hoped the cave-in hadn't put any obstacles in their path. If they'd been cut off from Autry and the opening . . .

Not wanting to think about that, the captain forged ahead and pulled Owens after him. The crewman cried out in pain as his bad leg dragged over the uneven terrain, but he did his best to help propel himself with his other leg.

A moment later, Kirk heard Karras' voice, less than a meter away and on the other side of Owens: "I've got his other arm, sir."

"Glad to hear it," he told her.

Together, they made good progress. They didn't hear another peep out of Owens; if it hurt, he was keeping it to himself. Nor did they find any new obstacles in their way. Before long, they could hear Autry's labored breathing as he worked to enlarge the gap in the wall.

Unfortunately, there was still no light in sight. Not a good omen, the captain mused. Not a good omen at all.

"Captain?" Autry asked.

"All three of us," Kirk amended.

"Sir, that sound . . ."

"Pay no attention," the captain instructed him. "How're we doing?"

"Pretty well," Autry replied, though despite Kirk's advice, it seemed part of his mind was on the cave-in. "I've made some headway. Here, see for yourself."

Kirk took him up on the invitation. With Autry's help, he found the opening. It was quite a bit larger than when he'd left it—large enough for him to stick his hand through and reach in up to his shoulder. He couldn't feel anything on the other side. Even if it wasn't the way out they were hoping for, it would at least give them an alternative to the crumbling environs of the cavern.

"You do excellent work," he told Autry as he withdrew his arm.

"Thank you, sir."

"But there's still more to do. Here, you take one side and I'll take the other."

"Sir," Owens ventured, "I can lend a hand."

"I'm afraid not," Kirk responded. "There's only so much room here, and you've got that bad leg."

Scrabbling for a promising rock to tug on, the captain heard it again: grating protests from the cavern's structural supports. He found a likely protrusion, pulled, and felt it give a little. Pushing it forward, he felt it give a little more. The next pull did it: with a gravelly sound, the rock came free in Kirk's fingers. And a hefty specimen it was too.

Autry grunted and another gravelly sound followed. There was a distinct thud as he dropped his prize on the ground.

Encouraged, the captain got a grip on another protrusion and yanked. Unfortunately, this one wasn't coming loose so easily. Before he could try again, there was a terrible screeching noise and a crash so ponderous that the whole cavern seemed to shake with the impact.

"Damn," Owens shouted over the racket of settling debris, his voice full of apprehension. "That one was close."

*Too close*, Kirk recognized. At any moment, the rocky ceiling might come crashing down around their heads.

Kirk was sorely tempted to use Owens' phaser, but he resisted. As long as that smell was in the air, the weapon was a last resort.

He strained at the protrusion again, pulling and pushing, pulling and pushing. Finally, he felt it budge.

"Eureka," he breathed.

Putting all his strength into the effort, he hauled on it. And without warning it gave itself up to him, tearing loose of its moorings like an old-time sailing ship in a gale.

Easing the rock to one side, the captain couldn't help but groan with the exertion. The thing was as big as hell, but that was good. It would leave a big hole.

As he straightened his back, he heard the rasp of another stone coming loose. A moment later, it made a cracking sound as it landed on one of the other boulders they'd unearthed.

Kirk felt the gap again. It was the size of a watermelon back on Earth, nearly big enough for a full-grown man to fit through, head and shoulders. And certainly big enough for Karras.

"Ensign," he said.

"Sir?" the woman replied.

"You're going through."

A moment of hesitation. "What about the rest of you?"

"We'll join you soon enough," he told her.

"Sir, I can—"

"Move!" he barked. He had no patience for heroics right now.

Without another word of protest, Karras moved past him to the wall. With the captain's help, she found the hole and inserted herself into it.

There was a wriggling sound—the scrape of her uniform fabric against earth and stone. Then she was gone.

The captain had already set to work again, when he felt a shower of dirt on his neck and shoulders. It didn't stop, either. In fact, it got gradually worse.

There was no point in underlining the urgency of their situation. Autry was at it again too—straining as hard as he could, judging by his grunts and growls. Silently, Kirk shoved at yet another rock, sweat running down the sides of his face.

But nothing was happening. And somewhere in the cavern, something else collapsed resoundingly.

Finally, the captain had to throw caution to the winds. "Stand back," he told Autry. "I'm going to use the phaser." Drawing the weapon, he set it by feel alone. Then he aimed it at the gap, or where he thought the gap would be, and pressed the trigger mechanism.

There was no flash of phaserlight—and certainly no disintegration of the rocks around their escape hole. Hell, there wasn't even a hum.

The damned thing had no juice. The powerpack must have been damaged in the ground collapse!

Cursing, Kirk put away the phaser. "It doesn't work," he said, doing his best to make himself heard over the insistent hiss of falling dirt. "Come on— we're going to get this done if we have to *chew* our way out!"

Attacking the hole again with his bare hands, the captain found something to latch onto—the same thing, perhaps, that he'd failed to move before. He gave it his best shot and failed again. Worse, the air was full of airborne debris now; it made him cough, robbing him of precious oxygen.

"Autry," he said, gasping for breath, "let's try this together." Finding the crewman's arm, he guided him to the right place. Then they combined their efforts.

Still nothing. Not even a hint that the rock was going to budge.

"Captain . . ." Autry sounded faint. No wonder— he'd been unconscious only a little while ago, and he hadn't stopped pushing himself since. Any moment, he might succumb to the injury that had knocked him out in the first place.

Kirk's teeth ground together. He wasn't going to give in. He wasn't going to let them get crushed in here.

Dirt fell in his eyes and he dug it out as best he could. It was getting harder and harder to breathe; he coughed twice, explosively.

*C'mon, Kirk,* he exhorted himself, just as if he were some instructor at the Academy. *You've got a problem here. How're you going to solve it?*

Suddenly, he had an idea. Kneeling, he felt among the rocks they'd already torn out and found the biggest one he could. Then, arm and neck muscles straining, he lifted it chest high.

And hammered it into the region of the hole.

Again.

And again.

And *again*—as he felt a piece of wall break away! Letting the stone down, the captain scrabbled to check the size of the gap.

It was bigger. But was it big *enough?*

Only one way to find out. "Owens," he said.

A cough, another. Finally: "Aye, sir."

"Get up. We're getting you out of here."

The injured man didn't argue, not after hearing Kirk's conversation with Karras. He just got to his feet and lurched toward the wall.

The captain felt Owens fall against him and helped him straighten himself. "Autry," he said.

"Here," the crewman shouted back past the rush of dirt.

"Give me a hand with Owens."

"Aye, sir."

Together, they began to push Owens through, as careful as they could be—under the circumstances—not to abuse the man's knee. To Owens' credit, he continued to keep his discomfort a private matter. Or maybe Kirk just couldn't hear him over the din.

After a second or two, they felt Karras pulling from the other side, and then Owens slipped the rest of the way through the gap.

At least they knew now that the hole was big enough. "You're next," the captain bellowed in Autry's direction.

The stocky crewman didn't argue any more than

Owens had. He just climbed into the hole. Kirk got hold of Autry's boot and gave him something to push against. A couple of kicks and then he was gone.

By then, however, the shower of dirt had become a waterfall. The captain was weighed down by it, knee-deep in it. He tried to concentrate on maintaining his bearings, to keep his hands on the edges of the hole. If he lost track of his escape route, *he* would be lost.

But it wasn't easy. He was gradually bending under the burden, finding it harder and harder to breathe. *Drowning.*

The way out was so close, yet so far. A blackness more profound than the mere lack of light was eating away at the edges of his consciousness, threatening to consume him.

*No. No!* With what strength he had left, he pushed toward the gap in the wall, managing to get his head and shoulders into it.

But that was it. The tide of dirt offered nothing for him to kick against. Slowly, inexorably, it was burying his lower body.

Then he felt hands gripping his wrists, tugging on him, and someone—Karras, he thought—was yelling to him. He shook his head. He couldn't hear her worth a damn; the blood was pumping too loudly in his ears.

But Kirk was still aware enough to know what it meant when the rock all around him started to shudder. The remainder of the cavern was breaking down, coming apart. And it would crush him as it did so.

Spurred by the knowledge, he kicked desperately, trying his best to free his legs from the weight of dirt on them. On the other side, his companions pulled as hard as they could—until he thought his arms would come out of their sockets.

Finally, with a jerk that seemed to stretch every bone in his body, he was pulled through from darkness into darkness.

Except in this darkness, he could cough out the detritus in his throat. He could breathe. He could recover his senses.

And he could be grateful when the deathtrap he'd just escaped closed down with deafening finality and a spray of debris.

A voice at his ear . . . a feminine voice. "Captain? Captain, are you all right?"

He coughed, nodded. "I'm fine. Just give me a minute," he wheezed, "to get the gravel out of my pants."

Karras laughed softly. It was like gentle music—a good sound.

# Chapter Five

SCOTTY LOOKED AROUND the conference table. McCoy, Sulu, Uhura and Chekov looked back at him. The doctor had calmed down considerably since his blow-up earlier in the day, when he'd been informed of Kirk's fate. Likewise, Sulu had more or less accepted the impossibility of continuing his search, now that he had some understanding of the reasons behind Scotty's decision.

But the engineering chief wanted *all* of his officers to understand. And to face the rather formidable task before them armed with as much information as possible.

Scotty cleared his throat. "I called this meeting," he began, "to tell you what Starfleet has told me. But before I get into that, I'd like to hear a progress report on Mister Spock's situation."

McCoy nodded. "All right, here it is in a nutshell: The poison that creature injected into Spock is creating a condition which we'd be tempted to diagnose as hyperthyroidism if we'd found it in a human. Basically, hyperthyroidism was a disease where the thyroid gland—which controls chemical reactions in the body—goes haywire, speeding up a whole slew of bodily functions. I say it *was* a disease because we found a cure a hundred and fifty years ago.

"Vulcans never found a cure," the doctor explained, "because they never had the disorder. But whatever this thing poisoned Spock with has simulated the symptoms of hyperthyroidism. His biological functions have been speeded up drastically, creating a terrible strain on his heart and his other internal organs. Of course, we've loaded him up with sedatives to ease that strain, but it's a temporary solution at best, particularly because it keeps Spock in an unconscious state."

"I'm no doctor," Uhura said, "but can't you just cleanse his body of the poison? You know—filter it out of his bloodstream?"

McCoy grunted. "We've tried. But our filtration systems aren't foolproof, and it seems that even trace amounts of the substance are enough to trigger the reaction." He shook his head. "It doesn't make a whole lot of sense, medically speaking, but there it is. What we're attempting to do now is find something that will nullify the effects of the substance, render it inactive. But when we're working with something so unlike anything we've encountered before . . ." He shrugged his shoulders. "It takes time."

They all looked at one another. Finally, Uhura asked the question that they really wanted answered: "What are Spock's chances?"

McCoy shook his head. "Hard to say," he replied. "No, make that impossible. But I will tell you this— the damage that will be done to Spock is progressive. It's entirely possible that we'll cure him, but not before he's been crippled in one way or another."

For a second or two, silence reigned in the conference room. Then Scotty dispelled it.

"You keep working," he told McCoy earnestly, "and we'll keep hoping." He changed tacks as best he could, though the captain would have done it a lot more smoothly. "In the meantime, we've got more than Spock to worry about. Admiral Kowalski has sent us to Beta Cabrini to stop what appears to be a raid on the colony's processed minerals."

Reaching for the controls on the display terminal that sat in the middle of the table, he called up a chart of the colony's processing results. They were impressive.

"As ye can see," he went on, "Beta Cabrini has quite a supply of dilithium, not to mention duranium, berynium, and dolacite. Certainly enough to make a tempting target for the Klingons or the Romulans. However, the colony is nowhere near either one of those empires, which is why security there has been minimal. As I understand it, they don't even have sensors in place."

"If it's not the Klingons or the Romulans," Sulu asked, "then who is it?"

Scotty leaned back in his chair. "Ever hear of the Merkaans?"

The helmsman shook his head.

"They're a race o' scoundrels—pirates—that we get reports about from time to time. The fact is, however, we came face to face with them only once, briefly, some ten years back." He eyed the others. "Would ye care to guess the name o' the ship that made this historical contact?"

"The *Enterprise,*" Chekov replied, answering Scotty's largely rhetorical question.

"Aye," the engineer confirmed. Leaning forward again, he readjusted the controls on the display terminal. The production chart was replaced by an image of three unidentified starships. "A decade ago, these vessels, commanded by a Merkaan named Hamesaad Dreen, attacked a Federation freighter carrying rare medicines to Gamma Catalinas. The idea, apparently, was to extort a price for the medicines from the Catalinans, who were in desperate need of them.

"Christopher Pike, then in command of the *Enterprise,* arrived as Dreen was starting to load the medicines onto one of his ships. There was no way that he could recover the cargo by force, not when it was one vessel against three, so he resorted to cunning. To make a long story short, he outmaneuvered the Merkaans and sent them packing."

"And that was the last we saw of them?" McCoy asked.

"It was," Scotty confirmed. "Until now. Suddenly, they've come out of the woodwork and taken over Beta Cabrini. We dinnae know for sure about casualties, but Dreen's nae above killing to encourage cooperation. Odds are he's already taken some lives. And Starfleet is afraid he'll kill more before he's done, nae to mention make off with what's nae rightfully his."

Uhura's brow wrinkled. "How do we know what's taking place on Beta Cabrini? Did someone manage to get off a distress call?"

The chief engineer nodded. "That's exactly what happened. Unfortunately, we haven't heard anything since. For all we know, the one who sent out the call is dead."

McCoy muttered under his breath. "What does Starfleet expect us to do? If Pike couldn't go toe to toe with this character ten years ago, what makes them think we can?"

Scotty sighed. "First of all, Doctor, they had to do *something*. They couldnae just sit back and see the colony raped." He threw pride to the winds. "Also, dinnae forget, they were callin' on Captain Kirk, nae yours truly. They must've figured that if Pike could outwit Dreen, the captain could too."

What they hadn't figured was that Jim Kirk would be lost planetside—and that they'd have to rely instead on the strategic skills of a simple engineer. Scotty recalled the look on Kowalski's face; it hadn't exactly been a vote of confidence.

"In any case," he went on, "that's our mission. I thought you should know—all of you—because I'm going to need your help."

"We'll do whatever we can," Sulu volunteered. "You know that."

"Aye," Scotty replied. "But it's good to hear it anyway."

"Vhat's your plan, sair?" Chekov asked.

Mister Scott laid his hands on the table. "Actually," he told the ensign, "that's the thing I'm going to need your help with."

Hamesaad Dreen stood by the window in the administrator's office, looking out into the colony's nearly deserted main square. As dispassionately as he could, he considered the implications of what had transpired just an hour ago.

The human had been caught. That was the good news. The bad was that he had been killed before his purpose was determined.

Of course, it was possible that the human hadn't really had any purpose in mind. It was possible he'd eluded Balac's security cordon out of fear, perhaps not trusting the acquisitor's reasons for gathering the colonists in the square.

But they would never know that now. They would never be certain, because Balac had been incapable of controlling his temper. And it irked Dreen that this should be so.

It was a loose end. He detested loose ends.

The door behind him whooshed open. He did not turn immediately, secure in the knowledge that this place was well guarded.

"Acquisitor?"

He recognized the voice as Balac's. With a calculated slowness meant to denigrate the other man, he glanced over his shoulder. "Yes?"

"I have implemented the new production schedule, in accordance with your orders." There was a new note of humility in Balac's voice. It seemed the seriousness of his security lapse—and certainly it was his lapse, no one else's—was not lost on him. He was aware of how slender was the thread from which his career now dangled. "By the time we are ready to leave, we should have nineteen tons of duranium. And close to half a ton of raw dilithium ore."

It was more than Dreen would have thought possible. But he did not let on that he was pleased; he wanted Balac to squirm a bit.

"Acknowledged," he replied. "And the level of . . . cooperation?"

"It has improved considerably, Acquisitor. The humans seem to better understand the range of acceptable behavior."

Dreen grunted. "That is good. And you, Balac, do *you* understand the range of acceptable behavior? With regard to the discharge of your duties?"

The Merkaan's brow creased. "I do."

For what must have seemed to Balac like a long time, Dreen let the warning sink in. Then he spoke again. "That is all."

His second-in-command inclined his head, then turned and left. Before the acquisitor returned his attention to the window, he noticed the looks exchanged between the guards outside the door. They were smiling as they watched Balac go, ridiculing him behind his back.

As the door slid closed, Dreen smiled as well. So much for Balac's ambition. Now his only problem was trying to figure out how he was going to store all those precious minerals.

Nurse Christine Chapel sighed, frowned, and adjusted Spock's silvery thermoblanket. Not that it was really necessary; it was just something to do. Something nurses had done for hundreds of years, in fact, to keep their minds off their helplessness.

If Chapel felt helpless right now, she was in good

company. M'Benga had been spending every waking hour working on a cure for the alien substance—the poison that was trying to turn the Vulcan's metabolism against him. And except for a few hushed conversations with Scotty at Spock's bedside, McCoy had been laboring right alongside his colleague—without a glimmer of success.

*So far,* she amended. In time, they'd find a cure. They always did.

After all the dangers Spock had braved, all the hardships he'd endured, he couldn't die at the hands of some—what had McCoy called it? *Some overgrown maggot with a taste for Vulcans.*

She might have chuckled at the doctor's description if she hadn't seen Spock lying there, his complexion two shades too dark, his skin drawn and waxy. She might have thought it funny, were it not for the subtle contractions of the skin around his eyes—a sign of discomfort that she'd seen in the Vulcan before.

How many people would have known that—to look at the skin around his eyes? Not M'Benga, and he was their resident expert on Vulcans. Not even McCoy.

But then, neither of them had spent as much time with Spock as she had. Neither of them had been at his bedside through crisis after crisis, checking his vital signs on the overhead monitor every five minutes, scrutinizing his every feature for evidence of his condition taking a turn for the worse.

That's why she'd insisted, yet again, that she be the one to monitor Spock while his physicians were occupied elsewhere. Because she knew him so well.

And of course, neither McCoy nor M'Benga had objected—for the same reason: because she knew the patient so well. If they were aware of her feelings for Spock, it hadn't entered into the equation.

Well, maybe a little. People—all people—tended to take better care of someone they loved. It was just human nature.

And if the one you loved wasn't human? Wasn't

able to return your love? That didn't mean you loved him any less, did it?

Besides, at least one very prominent Vulcan had taken a human wife. So there was at least a chance that Chapel's devotion would be rewarded.

But either way, she would be there for Spock when he needed her, just as she was there for him now. She would stand at his side, even if it was only to adjust his thermoblanket.

*Frenzy. Disharmony. Disorder.*

Instinctively, Spock recoiled from the chaos, withdrawing as far as he could, until he found a corner of his mind where the storm wasn't quite as bad.

He had never before felt such disarray, such unrelenting tumult. Was this what it was like to be insane?

But he *wasn't* insane—he was sure of that. How could he be insane and still consider the matter so clearly? If madness ruled him, how could he regard it as if at a distance?

No. This nightmare of unreason was externally imposed. An invasion of the carefully ordered mentality he had fought so hard to achieve.

Concentrating, enduring the torment, he tried to remember; to piece together the events that had brought him to these straits.

Images flashed before him: a cavern filled with darkness; the sudden emergence of a ghostly-pale tendril; the sensation of being lifted high into the air, the agony of ribs scraping against internal organs as his torso was horribly compressed—while the others . . . others? *Yes—Kirk, McCoy and three crewmen* . . . scurried below, firing their phaser charges into the thing that held him captive; the amplification of the pain to the point where he began to lose consciousness; a vague awareness of a life form—something huge and fishbelly-white—exploding from the jungle floor, and a concurrent recognition that the tendril was part of it; a perception of being drawn to the thing . . . the stinging touch of a smaller limb than the one that held him, followed by . . .

Bedlam. An anarchy of the mind. And a notion that his body, which seemed so distant and unreal now, was gripped in an anarchy of its own.

But his body was no longer a victim of the tumult—was it? He reached out for his physical reality and found it relaxed, still—apart from the horror that plagued his intellect.

Then he guessed why that should be. He had been medicated. Sedated.

And only now was the medication beginning to wear off, at least enough for him to regain his faculties, his sense of self. And along with them, the frantic storm of irrationality that had invaded him.

His task was clearly defined: He had to gain control of the chaos, impose order on it. Then and only then did he dare try to shrug off the effects of the sedative.

It was imperative that his mastery of himself be perfect, flawless. Because if at any time the confusion gained the upper hand, he might become a threat to the welfare of those around him.

Knowing this, fully appreciating the difficulty of the road he had chosen, Spock took the first step down that road.

But he'd hardly set out before he found himself stumbling, stumbling over a word, a single word—*Dreen*. Uttered by Scott, or McCoy? Or both, in harsh whispers, thinking there was no one close enough to hear them?

The word triggered something in him. An . . .

Image: Smiling in a decidedly conspiratorial manner, the acquisitor called Hamesaad Dreen places a hand on Spock's arm; the Vulcan tolerates the violation of his physical being. Dreen's eyes are hard, black and shiny, like ebony. "This way," he says, "is our main cargo hold." His tone is guttural; every word sounds like a curse.

They follow the dimly lit metallic passageway to a broad door, which opens as the acquisitor touches a panel beside it. Inside, Spock can see a swarm of yellow containers; the hold is bigger than he expected.

Dreen gestures to one of the containers. "Thenium," he explains. He indicates another: "Malanium." And a third: "Kendricite." He points to an empty patch of deck in the corner. "And this is where the dilithium from the *Enterprise* will go once it's been brought down from the transport hall."

In yet another part of the cargo area, the containers are larger, squatter. The acquisitor tells him they are filled with seeds stolen from the Gnessis, an unaligned race equidistant from the Klingon Empire and the Federation.

"From the seeds grow the Gnessis' sacred trees. But changing meteorological conditions have made most of the trees barren; only a few seeds may be produced, and at great cost. We have stolen these—nearly all the Gnessis own—because the planetary government will pay anything to get them back."

"Impressive," Spock comments.

"Yet," Dreen says, "your captain tells me he can give me access to riches that dwarf these—to wealth I've never dreamed of." A pause. "I did not expect to find such greed in an alien. It is admirable. Are all humans possessed of such a quality?"

"Few."

"I see. And your captain is one of the few?"

"The captain is an unusual man."

Dreen chuckles, stops. "Tell me, how long have you served with Pike?"

"A year and a half."

"And when did he first express dissatisfaction with his role as captain of your starship?"

"Just a little while ago," Spock answers truthfully. "A few weeks, perhaps."

That seems to satisfy the acquisitor. He grunts and

changes tacks. "You are not human. You're Vulcan, I believe you said."

"Yes."

The acquisitor seems to roll the fact over his tongue. "How did you come to serve on a human vessel?"

"The Federation is made up of many races. Humans represent but one of them."

"Interesting. And is greed as rare among Vulcans as it is among humans?"

"It is," Spock tells him, "nearly unheard of."

"Then, like your captain, you are an aberration?"

Inwardly, Spock flinches. "I am different from other Vulcans in many ways," he replies. "The mere fact that I signed on to serve aboard a starship is evidence of that."

"I see." The light in Dreen's eyes seems to build for a moment; he seems on the verge of asking another question, perhaps a more penetrating one.

But he never asks it. They are interrupted by an intercom call from the acquisitor's second-in-command.

It seems there is some trouble in the ship's engineering facility . . .

Spock shivered. The dream sequence had finally released him.

With an effort, he found his road again. Clung to it, gathering himself.

And resumed his long, hard journey toward consciousness.

On Talos IV, Pike came awake slowly. It was some time before he felt the sun on his eyelids, bright and molten red, and turned away from it.

Instinctively, he reached out for Vina. And as always, she was there. Opening his eyes, he saw her sleeping the sleep of the righteous, her long lashes fluttering as if in the breeze. *Not a care in the world,* he thought.

Then he saw something moving up by the house. Some seagulls? Out of curiosity, he turned his head—and leaped to one knee, instinctively thrusting Vina behind him.

There was someone approaching them—someone tall and broad-shouldered, with gray skin and long, black hair. Someone who shouldn't have been here, not on Talos IV and *certainly* not in Vina's memory.

"Chris?" She tugged at him, awake now, startled. "Chris, what's wrong?"

"It's—" he began. And then he stopped himself.

No, it wasn't who he'd thought it was. The newcomer's features were too straight, too even. His skin, Pike saw now, wasn't even gray.

And that object in his hands—the one Pike had taken for a weapon at first glance—was nothing more than an exotic-looking pitcher.

Taking a deep breath, he expelled it. "Damn," he said, feeling his heart still racing. And again: "Damn."

Vina was standing before him now. "Chris, what is it?"

He indicated their visitor with an inclination of his head. "Him. I thought he was someone else—someone I had a run-in with some years back."

Vina turned and looked at the newcomer, who waved with his free hand. She waved back. Then she turned to Pike again. "You see? It's only Derret. He was my aunt's houseboy. I have to admit, I didn't expect him to be here either. But he's quite harmless."

He grunted. Every now and then, something or someone unexpected crept into the fantasies the Talosians created for them. It was because the details of the illusions were drawn from their unconscious minds, where their memories were often more complete.

As Derret got closer, he looked less and less like Pike's old adversary. Hell, he was just a *kid*.

"A runaway my aunt found on the street," Vina explained, by now knowing pretty well how her companion's mind worked.

"Right," he muttered.

She looked up at him. "He's a nice boy. I used to really like him when I was little."

He gave her a sidewise glance. "Don't worry," he said. "I won't ask him to get lost." He smiled. "Besides, he can't stay out here forever, can he? He's got to go back to the house sometime."

Vina looked at him with mock reproach in her eyes. "Yes," she replied. "I suppose he does." Then she left him to greet the pitcher-bearer.

Pike watched as she threw her arms around the youngster. And shivered a little.

Because even though he knew it was only the house boy, his mind couldn't help but see gray skin and black hair and come up with *Merkaan*.

# Chapter Six

KIRK GOT TO HIS FEET, wiped gritty, sweat-moistened mud off his face with the back of a relatively clean sleeve, and realized with a start that the ceiling here was high enough to stand under. He stood on his toes and raised his hands as high as he could. Still no evidence of anything above him, though there had to be something up there somewhere, or the place wouldn't have been so dark.

Though he still couldn't see worth a damn, the captain got the idea that this space was a lot more stable than the cavern had been. For one thing, there were no sounds of imminent collapse. For another, the air was clear.

And then, even beyond those facts, there was a *sense* about the place. A feeling of permanence.

Of course, now that he'd thought that, it would probably come crashing down around them. Which was a good reason for them to get a move on—to find out where that fresh air was ultimately coming from.

Just for kicks, Kirk decided to try communicating with the ship again.

"Karras?"

"Sir?"

"Let's try Mister Scott again, shall we? That is, if your communicator's still in working order."

He heard faint scraping sounds as Karras brushed the dirt off the device. "It seems to be in good shape, Captain." And then: "Mister Scott? Mister Scott, come in."

No response. Apparently, whatever had been blocking their signals before was blocking them still. Not exactly a surprise, Kirk mused.

"That's all right," he said. "I just thought it was worth a shot." The captain looked about him, imagined the bedraggled figures of his companions. "Owens?"

"Aye, sir." The reply had come from off to Kirk's right, and not very far away.

"Do you think you can walk, with some help?"

"With some help, sir, yes."

"You've got it, then. Autry—how do you feel?"

"Fit, Captain." But a slight tremor in his speech belied his bravado.

"Bull," Kirk concluded. "You're hurt worse than you're letting on. Karras?"

"Sir?"

"You and I will help Owens. Autry, find a wall and guide us to it."

It took a while for the captain, Karras, and Owens to locate one another in the dark. And even longer for them to hook up with Autry, who'd dutifully discovered a vertical surface.

Together, they followed the rough contours of the wall, Autry leading the way, the captain and Karras supporting Owens. They went on that way for some time, peering into oblivion, wondering if they were making progress or just going around in a circle.

They didn't talk much. What was there to say, other than to ask each other how he or she was holding up?

And even when anyone asked, the answer was always the same: Perfect. No problem. Even when they all knew that wasn't the case.

Then, at last, the dark seemed to become layered— less oppressive in some places than in others. It encouraged them to move a little faster. And before long, in one particular area, the pitch-blackness gave way to a shadowy gray.

There was light. And they were moving toward it.

"Captain," Autry said, "I think I see something. I hope my eyes aren't going."

"I hope so too," Kirk replied, "because if they are, mine are going as well."

Gradually, dark gray yielded to light gray, and light gray to something even lighter. For the first time since the ground collapse, they were able to see at least a little of what they looked like. And what they saw was quite ghastly.

Some months back, Scotty had lent the captain a book about Celtic mythology—one of the chief engineer's favorite subjects. The book had described the Firbolg, an ancient breed of "mud people."

Kirk was reminded of the reference now as he scrutinized his crewmen, their uniforms stiffened and caked with grime, their faces decorated with strange, whorling patterns, as if in deference to some pagan god.

And he was in the worst shape of all. A "mud person" if ever there was one.

It also became apparent what they'd been traveling through—a snaking series of caves, each connected to the next, forming a sort of crude tunnel. The configuration was punctuated at intervals with clusters of stalactites and stalagmites, which were mostly in the center of each cave, so they'd never known about them.

Nor was the passage as large as the captain had envisioned it. In fact, if he'd been just a little taller, he probably would have reached the ceiling back near their entry point.

Owens chuckled like a kid at the circus. "Damn. It really *is* light out there."

"Nicest thing I've seen in a long time," Karras remarked.

In a way, it was fortunate that their path was so crooked. Being exposed to the light in small increments, their eyes had a chance to adjust. By the time they actually saw a break in the craggy architecture of the walls, it was a good deal less blinding than it might have been.

"We're out of here," Autry announced, sounding relieved.

The break widened. It became an egress as wide and tall as the passage itself. They would have no trouble slipping out *this* exit, Kirk observed.

The plant life outside was much like what they'd seen at the beam-down site, except younger and spindlier. The captain recognized some of the trees he'd been cataloging with his tricorder when Spock was attacked. Inhaling, he was treated to a mixture of sharp jungle fragrances that dispelled the cloying earth-odor of the tunnel.

Savoring their good luck, the four of them emerged into the warm sunlight and looked around.

Kirk shook his head. It seemed they hadn't been quite so lucky after all. They *weren't* back on the surface. They were in a huge depression, separated from the true jungle floor by sheer, fifty-foot high walls of stone on every side, maybe the result of a collapse such as the one they'd been caught in earlier. Though if a collapse was responsible, it must have taken place some time ago, because the terrain showed no signs of having been disrupted recently. There were even trees growing here, if only small ones.

Karras spoke for all of them: "It was too good to be true." She shaded her eyes as she surveyed the upper limits of the smooth stone surfaces.

"Wait a minute," Owens said. "We're out in the open. We can contact the ship now and have them beam us up." He looked to the captain. "Right?"

Karras bit her lip. "It all depends. If these walls contain the same minerals that have been stymieing us so far . . ." She shrugged.

Autry finished the thought for her. "Then the *Enterprise* would have to be almost directly overhead for us to establish contact."

"Of course," Kirk said, "the ship may well *be* directly overhead. We can't have come out too far from the beam-down site, and Mister Scott knew enough to stay in line-of-sight contact under the circumstances."

Owens looked at the captain. "We can resolve this easily enough."

Kirk nodded. The crewman handed him his communicator.

The captain opened it. "Mister Scott," he said, "this is Captain Kirk. Repeat: this is Kirk."

They got no more response than they had back in the cavern. There was disappointment in their dirt-smudged faces.

Owens sighed. "So much for that."

"Not necessarily," Kirk insisted. "We'll keep trying. Eventually we have to make contact."

It was true, wasn't it? But it didn't do much to take the edge off their disappointment. He started to put the communicator away, then stopped. Gauging the weight of the device, he took another look at the cliffs that encircled them. "On the other hand, we may not have to wait for 'eventually.'"

Owens looked at him. "What are you thinking, sir?"

Kirk returned the look. "That we could toss a communicator up *there*." He pointed to a section of the cliffs. "Then we'd get a clear shot at the *Enterprise*, without having to worry about what's around us."

Karras nodded. "Bravo, Captain."

"Thank you, Ensign." Wandering out toward the center of the hollow, Kirk searched for a relatively open area up top—and found one almost directly above the tunnel mouth. Stepping back a couple of paces, he wound up and—keeping his eye on his target—pitched the communicator high in the air. As he'd intended, it just cleared the cliff and landed silently somewhere beyond.

"Nice toss," Owens remarked approvingly.

"We should check to make sure it wasn't damaged," Autry pointed out. He looked at Karras.

Taking out her communicator—the last one left to them—she flipped it open and attempted to make contact with its twin. They could hear a faint beeping from above. "There doesn't appear to be any problem," she observed happily, closing her device again.

Autry seemed pleased as well. "So much for . . . for . . ."

Suddenly, the man's knees buckled and he lurched into the captain. Kirk caught him before he could fall to the ground.

"I'm all right," Autry murmured.

"Sure you are," the captain told him. Easing him to the turf, he looked to Karras. "Help me get him out of the sun."

Together, they dragged Autry into the shade of a short, broad-leafed tree. That done, Kirk looked at her. "Ensign, you're the one with the back-up med kit."

"Aye, sir," Karras agreed. Dropping to her knees beside Autry, she took out her tricorder and scanned him. "Nothing serious," she concluded. "Mostly heat exhaustion." Then she noticed something. Brushing aside Autry's dirt-matted hair, she uncovered a bloody gash in his scalp.

"Must've happened when he got knocked out," Kirk observed.

"Uh-huh," the woman said absently, taking out

some sterile gauze and a disinfectant. Pouring a little of the disinfectant onto the gauze, she used it to clean Autry's wound.

The crewman flinched, but only a little. A moment later, Karras took out a second gauze pad and applied healing ointment to it. Placing it gently on the wound, she picked up Autry's hand and laid it over the gauze.

"Just hold it there for a while," she told him.

The crewman said he'd do that.

"Nice work," the captain commented. "I think Doctor McCoy would have approved."

The ensign smiled as she began to put her supplies back in the medkit. "Thank you, sir."

Owens sat down heavily on a pile of large stones. "Now what?"

Kirk looked at him. "Now we exercise some patience, Mister Owens." He paused, remembering that Autry didn't have a monopoly on injuries around here. "Also, we take a look at your leg."

Karras didn't have to be asked. She was already headed in Owens' direction.

The captain made use of the time to scan the surrounding barrier again, this time approaching it to get a better look. Closer inspection showed that what had appeared to be rock wasn't rock at all, or at least part of it wasn't. It was something coarser, with tiny holes shot through it—something brittle-looking. He touched it; the appearance had deceived him. It was no more brittle than the hull of the *Enterprise*.

Whipping out his tricorder, he analyzed the stuff and was surprised at what he found. The tricorder showed it to be the fossilized remains of some sort of plant life. The floral equivalent of coral, except much stronger.

Kirk tried to find something to dig his fingers into—a notch or two he could use to hoist himself up. Nothing.

He'd always been a pretty good climber, but not so

good that he could operate without hand- and foot-holds. If he'd had the right equipment, it would have been a different story. Without it . . .

There weren't even any tall trees around with which to make a ladder. Even if every tree here was stacked one on top of the other, they wouldn't reach the top of the cliffs. Nor were they sturdy enough to be split in half and still support a man's weight.

It was a good thing they didn't *have* to climb out. It wouldn't be long before Uhura would record their communicator signal and realize it was nowhere near the beam-down site. And not much longer than that before Scotty would send someone down to investigate.

He smiled to himself. They were probably worried sick up on the ship, as if they hadn't had enough to worry about with the attack on Spock. He could see Sulu and his party digging furiously, trying to buck the odds and get them out before they suffocated.

No—by now, they'd probably have given up. They'd be sitting on the ground, shaking their heads, caught between grief and bewilderment, wondering what had happened to their comrades' bodies.

Imagine their surprise when they'd get word from Scotty that their captain might have turned up, though not where they were looking. His smile broadened. It would seem like a miracle, wouldn't it? An honest-to-goodness—

"Captain Kirk!"

Kirk's nerves still frazzled from their ordeal in the cavern, he whirled. And saw Karras kneeling beside Owens, beckoning to him.

There didn't seem to be anything wrong, but she sure as hell had sounded agitated. Casting a glance at Autry, Kirk made sure the man was resting comfortably. Then he jogged over to join the others.

As he approached, he saw both Karras and Owens running their fingers over the stones on which Owens had deposited himself. The sight puzzled him. What could be so damn interesting about a bunch of boulders that it required his immediate attention?

That's more or less what he asked Karras and Owens as he pulled up before them. They seemed oblivious to the undercurrent of irritation in his voice.

"Look," Karras told him. She pointed to a place high on one of the boulders. Frowning, the captain got down beside her and examined the indicated area. Instantly, he understood what his people had been so excited about.

"Lord," he whispered.

The rock was incised with a series of hieroglyphs— something like the pictorial symbols found in the tombs of ancient Egyptians. Playing devil's advocate in his own mind, Kirk tried to see them as something else—as chance markings that just appeared to be hieroglyphs.

No dice, he decided. Someone had made these.

Someone intelligent.

Was this what Sulu had been so excited about when he referred to Ellis' discovery? Had Ellis found glyphs like these as well?

"You know what this means?" he asked his companions. When he saw the expressions on their faces, he was sorry he'd phrased it that way. "Yes," he muttered. "Of course you do."

Owens said it anyway. "This planet had sentient life at one time. Maybe even some kind of civilization."

Karras nodded. "Though it doesn't seem they're here any more." She regarded the captain. "Unless they're underground, where our sensors can't find them."

Kirk shrugged. "It could be, Ensign. But every underground civilization I've ever encountered had a reason for being underground, and a damn compelling one at that."

He took in their surroundings with a glance. "Except for the creature that attacked Mister Spock, this seems to be a pretty friendly environment, within the comfort range of most Federation life forms." He turned back to the hieroglyphs, running his finger along the edge of one. "Of course, it's possible that *this* life form found it *un*friendly—say, after some cataclysmic event drastically altered the weather or the mix of elements in the atmosphere, making it what it is today. But a society will usually bend over backwards—way backwards—before it'll give up the sun and the stars in the sky."

Owens grunted, still fascinated by the glyphs. *"Something* happened to the people who made these. If they didn't go underground . . . where did they go?"

The captain considered the matter. "A good question, crewman. Maybe if we understood what's written here, we'd have the answer."

Karras looked up at him. "Sir, would it be all right if I recorded the glyphs with my tricorder? It shouldn't take long."

Kirk nodded. "Go ahead. We came here to study the place. Until someone shows up to get us out of here, we might as well do what we came to do."

The ensign took out her tricorder and started making a record of the engravings. Owens watched her.

As intrigued as the captain was, he had other responsibilities. Getting up, he made his way to where Autry was stretched out.

En route, he couldn't help but glance at the cliffs. The sooner he saw somebody up there, he thought, the better.

# Chapter Seven

THE KEEPER STOOD beside Pike and smiled. Behind the diminutive, robed figure, the sun was setting in a miasma of golds and grays.

"Sure you don't want to sit down?" the human asked. He himself was seated on a smooth rock that was a lot more comfortable than it looked.

The Talosian shook his massive head. Veins rippled and writhed in the vicinity of his temples.

"No, thank you. I prefer to stand." The Keeper's lips didn't move; Pike only heard the words in his head. "Why did you ask me here?"

Occasionally, the former starship captain wondered where "here" was, exactly, underneath the illusion. Somewhere in the Talosians' warren, of course, but—

No matter. That wasn't what he'd wanted to talk about.

Pike looked in another direction, considering another part of the sunset and the sea that mirrored it in slow, rolling waves.

"Are you not happy here?" the Keeper asked.

The human grunted. "No, that's not it. I'm very happy here. Happier than I have a right to be." He frowned. "And grateful."

"Then what troubles you?"

Pike turned back to his companion. "I was just wondering, that's all. Wondering about my friends. The people who served with me."

The Talosian nodded. "I see. You wish to know what has happened to them since you saw them last."

"Yes, that's right. Particularly Spock. I want to know what's happened to *him.*"

The Keeper seemed interested in the remark. "Why Spock in particular?"

Pike thought about it. "Because he's so vulnerable. So easily hurt."

"I do not understand," his companion informed him. "Spock appeared to be the most durable member of your crew—or, for that matter, of Captain Kirk's. We observed in him greater mental capacity as well as physical capacity. Was that observation in error?"

"No. It was accurate, as far as it goes."

"As far as it goes? Please explain."

The human shrugged. Across the water, the sun was spreading out, losing its definition as it merged with the horizon. "Spock is half-human and half-Vulcan. But most humans see him as a Vulcan, because he *looks* like a Vulcan. And most Vulcans see him as a human because—" He stopped. "Hell, I'm not even sure why, but they do. So, for all intents and purposes, he's an outsider. A man apart."

The Talosian's eyes narrowed. He was listening.

"That's hurtful to Spock, even if he never says so. You wouldn't know it, he seems so damn aloof and all, but he craves love and acceptance more than anyone I've ever known. Of course, most times when he reaches out for it, he gets his fingers burned. Not because anybody wants to injure him in any way, but because they misunderstand him. They figure that someone so dignified, so intellectually absorbed, can't really give a fig about something as mundane as companionship. So, as great as his need is, it's hardly ever fulfilled."

"Unfortunate," the Keeper commented.

"You bet it is." He paused. "On the other hand, it's part of what makes Spock such a great friend. When he does find someone he can trust, someone he can depend on . . . he treasures them." Pike sighed. "If need be, he'd travel halfway across the galaxy for them. Risk his career, even his life, just to see them happy."

"You speak of yourself," the Talosian realized. "You are his friend."

"I am proud to be his friend." Pike looked at his hands—not his real hands, but those provided by the illusion. "That's why I want to know how he is, how all my friends are. Because I can't forget about them any more than Spock forgot about me."

The Keeper regarded him. "I believe I understand now. However, it will not be a simple matter to obtain the information you seek."

The human nodded. "I know. Talos Four is off-limits to Starfleet personnel. But you communicated with Spock, didn't you? Reached out with your minds somehow?"

"We did," the Keeper agreed.

"Then, why can't you do that again? Why can't you touch my friends, or someone who knows them, and see how they're doing?"

"Perhaps we can. It is only that our abilities have physical limitations. And not every mind is as receptive to contact as Spock's was. However, we should be able to tell you at least part of what you wish to know."

Pike smiled. "Thank you," he told the Talosian.

The Keeper tilted his head slightly. "There is a reason you make this request now, correct?"

"Correct," the human conceded. "I saw someone the other day, at the beach, who looked like an old enemy of mine. An individual named Hamesaad Dreen."

"An enemy," the Keeper repeated.

"I know it sounds stupid. It was only a kid who worked for Vina's aunt. But for a moment, he looked just like Dreen." He shook his head. "Just a case of mistaken identity."

"And this gave rise to concern?"

"It started me thinking about the past, and before you know it . . . hell. You know what they say: once a captain, always a captain."

The Talosian had never heard the expression before, but he nodded anyway. "I will comply with your request to the best of my ability."

A moment later, Pike was alone on the bluff. He listened to the wind and inhaled its faintly sweet scent as it rode in off the sea.

It was kind of stupid, wasn't it? Even if it had been Dreen he'd seen the other day, it was all an illusion. It had no connection with the real world whatsoever.

Nevertheless, he couldn't help but feel, even now, that it had meant something. That it had been a premonition of some kind, warning him his friends were in trouble.

Then he remembered something the Keeper had once told him: "There are no coincidences, Christopher Pike. Not in *this* universe."

He pondered that for a little while, until he noticed Vina coming up the trail. She was wrapped in a gaily printed sheet.

"Here you are," she said. "I was wondering what happened to you."

Pike smiled. "I couldn't sleep. I decided to have a talk with the Keeper."

Suddenly, she looked concerned. "With the Keeper? Whatever for?"

She was positively alluring in the last of the light. He embraced her. "I'll tell you in the morning, all right?"

Vina nodded. She'd become adept at knowing when to give him his space. "All right," she agreed.

Together, they made their way down the trail and back to the beach house.

As Doctor M'Benga tried to concentrate on his analysis of the substance in Spock's blood, he couldn't help but be a little distracted by the figure of the ship's surgeon pacing behind him.

McCoy shook his head. "I still can't believe we left them behind. I just can't believe it." He shook his head again. "If they had any chance at all, it's gone now. There's no way they could have survived."

M'Benga paused to glance over his shoulder at his superior. "The captain is a resourceful man," he said. "I wouldn't be so quick to count him out."

But he didn't say it with as much conviction as he would have liked. Truth to tell, M'Benga didn't believe the captain and his party had survived, either. But outwardly, he was determined to keep up the same front as Sulu and Chekov and most everyone else on the ship.

No one—except McCoy, apparently—was going to pronounce the missing crewmen dead before there was proof of it.

The older man stopped his pacing, eyed M'Benga and grunted. "Come on," he said. "Even if they managed to live through the collapse itself, even if they managed not to get crushed under some hunk of rock, where are they going to get air to breathe?" He cursed. "If we'd gotten to them immediately, we might have kept them from suffocating. But as it is . . ." His voice trailed off.

M'Benga decided to change the subject. If he had to have a conversation while he was studying Spock's blood samples, they could at least talk about something less depressing.

"Anything interesting in Mister Scott's briefing?" he asked. "Or can't you tell me about it?"

McCoy puckered up his face and shrugged. If he was aware that M'Benga was trying to distract him, he didn't resist. "No, I can tell you. It wasn't restricted information or anything like that." He slumped onto a nearby stool. "It seems the mining colony on Beta Cabrini's been taken over by some kind of space pirate—or more accurately, someone from a race of space pirates. Name of Hamesaad Dreen. He's after the rocks the colony's processed and he's not above killing a few colonists to make sure he gets what he wants."

McCoy had barely finished his thumbnail report, when a shadow fell through the open doorway and crawled across the bulkhead behind him. The ship's surgeon didn't see it, but M'Benga did, and something about it drew his attention.

"What?" asked McCoy, his eyes narrowing. "Is something wrong?"

The shadow didn't move. Neither advancing nor retreating, it just seemed to hang there. And was it M'Benga's imagination, or was it bent over as if in pain?

"Dammit, man, this is no time to be fooling around." McCoy must have followed the direction of M'Benga's gaze, because a moment later, he turned around and saw what his colleague had been staring at. "What in blazes," he breathed. "Who's out there, anyway?"

But just as he posed his question, the splash of darkness disappeared. M'Benga moved to the doorway and looked into the next room.

It was empty. Before he knew it, McCoy was beside him.

Puzzled, the chief medical officer grunted. "That shadow . . . it did look like a person, didn't it?"

M'Benga nodded. "Very much like a person." But who would be lurking around sickbay, appearing and disappearing like that? One of the other doctors? A nurse? Not Christine—McCoy had ordered her to get some sleep.

And definitely not a patient. They only had one, and he was too heavily sedated to be moving around.

Or was he?

M'Benga looked at McCoy. Judging by the look on the older man's face, it seemed he'd come to the same conclusion at the same time.

Together, they headed for the critical care area.

Uhura watched as Scotty sat in the captain's chair, turning the Beta Cabrini situation over and over in his mind. Every now and then his eyes screwed up as if he were onto something promising—and then unscrewed as he swore softly and shook his head, rejecting the idea.

The communications officer wished she'd had more experience in formulating action plans. But Captain Kirk seldom seemed to need such suggestions from his officers. Information yes, strategies no. Kirk always seemed to have a trick or two up his braided sleeve that was better than anything his officers could possibly have devised.

The last time Uhura had been called on for tactical advice, she'd been a senior at the Academy, taking part in battle simulations. And even then, she hadn't been as skilled a schemer as some of her classmates.

It was just as well that her interests had run toward technical matters, and eventually toward communications systems in particular. She would never have made a very good captain.

On the other hand, Sulu and Chekov—now sitting with their backs to her—had both trained in the Academy's command curriculum, hoping to become starship captains themselves one day. And they hadn't been any more successful than Uhura in coming up with a workable gambit.

In all fairness, it was an extremely delicate situation. According to the computer files, this Hamesaad

Dreen was capable of almost anything. He had no compunctions about killing. The slightest provocation might encourage him to start taking human lives en masse.

There had to be a way of dealing with Dreen, of stopping him without running up the death toll. There had to be. But how?

Uhura had barely completed the question in her mind, when the doors to the turbolift opened and someone walked out. She hadn't been facing that way, so she didn't notice at first who it was. But as the figure approached the captain's chair, she couldn't help but recognize it—and let out a cry of surprise.

"Mister Spock!" Scotty bellowed. He leaped to his feet, looking for all the world as if he'd seen a ghost. "What th' divil are *you* doin' here?"

The Vulcan seemed nonplussed. "I am the ranking officer on the *Enterprise*. It is my responsibility to inspect the bridge."

Uhura couldn't help but stare. It was a miracle. When they brought Spock back from Octavius Four, he was supposed to have been under heavy sedation to counteract the poison that was destroying his body. Now he showed no signs of either the poison or the sedatives.

"I dinnae understand," Scotty said. "If ye were up an' about, why was I nae told?"

Spock cocked an eyebrow. "What was there to tell? I am here."

The chief engineer mulled it over, grunted. "So ye are." He smiled. "And dinnae think I'm nae glad of it. I take it ye've been briefed on Beta Cabrini?"

The Vulcan nodded. "Yes. I am somewhat familiar with the situation."

Uhura grinned. Leave it to Spock to understate everything. She felt better already. She had a confidence in the first officer that ranked second only to her confidence in Kirk. Spock's style was a little different, but that wasn't important.

Somehow, she felt, they would save those poor colonists. Somehow they would carry it off.

"Well," Scotty said, "I guess ye'll be wanting the conn now, eh?" He moved over to make the captain's chair available.

But Spock didn't move to accept it. "Actually, Mr. Scott, I would appreciate it if you would retain command for now. There is some research I need to carry out regarding our current mission."

Scotty looked surprised, but he was obviously willing to help in any way he could. "Certainly, Mister Spock. I'll stay here as long as ye like."

"Thank you," the first officer told him. Then, without another word, he withdrew in the direction of the turbolift. A moment later, the lift doors closed behind him.

As Scotty settled back into the captain's chair, he happened to glance at Uhura. Their eyes met and they smiled at the same time.

It was good to have Spock back.

McCoy was livid as he and M'Benga entered the turbolift. Not caring who knew it, either, he reeled off a string of curses.

"Easy," M'Benga told him. "We'll find him, sir."

The chief medical officer glared at the lift doors, willing them to open. "Bad enough," he snarled, "that he got up and left sickbay without a word. Then he has the gall to visit the bridge and pretend he doesn't have a care in the world. And now he's leading us on a merry chase through the whole damn ship!"

M'Benga sighed. "I don't think that was his intention."

"Intention or not," McCoy railed, "he's doing it, isn't he? Just wait till I lay my eyes on him. I'll—"

Abruptly, the doors opened, revealing the corridor beyond. The library entrance was at the far end of it.

McCoy stalked the length of the curving corridor, completely prepared to find that Spock wasn't in the library at all. He pictured himself a minute from now, venting his anger on an empty room.

When the library doors opened and Spock was sitting there in the first cubicle, the doctor was almost shocked. Turning his head as if nothing out of the ordinary had transpired, the first officer acknowledged the doctors with a glance and resumed his scrutiny of the cubicle's computer terminal.

Controlling himself, McCoy strode up to the Vulcan, M'Benga right behind him. He glanced at the terminal screen, which displayed a detailed layout of the Beta Cabrini colony complete with architectural and engineering details.

"You lily-livered coward," McCoy spat.

Spock paused to look up at him. "Are you referring to me, Doctor?"

"You bet I am," Bones told him, warming to the subject. "You snuck out of sickbay like a thief in the night—and for one reason: you didn't have the guts to confront me."

The Vulcan shrugged easily—actually, McCoy thought, more a movement of the facial muscles than the shoulders. He'd seen Spock shrug enough times to know how it worked.

"It did not seem logical to remain there any longer than I had to," Spock began. "Clearly, I was no longer in need of your services."

"Like hell, you weren't. Maybe I miscalculated the dosage it would take to keep you under. But that doesn't give you the right to go traipsing out of bed like you're all cured."

Spock considered him coolly. "Perhaps you underestimated the Vulcan physique in more ways than one. Is it not a possibility that I am indeed cured? That I have cured *myself?*"

McCoy scowled. "Come on, Spock. Give me a little more credit than that. I've seen you hide physical distress before."

M'Benga chose that moment to join the fray.

"Vulcans don't exactly hide physical distress," he said, "they manage it. Of course, in this case, Mister Spock is doing more than that—he's regulating his entire metabolism." He regarded Spock. "But Doctor McCoy's point is still valid, Commander. You're afflicted with a very serious illness, and no amount of mental discipline can change that."

"I am fit for duty," Spock insisted.

"In a pig's eye," McCoy countered.

The Vulcan's features hardened. "Doctor, I *must* proceed with my research."

"Sure," said the chief medical officer. "And when you're all studied up, you're going to go back to the bridge, right?"

"That was my intention, yes."

McCoy shook his head. "Nothing doing, my friend. As far as I'm concerned, you're unfit for command. And we both know you can't sit in the captain's chair unless you've got my blessing."

Spock took a breath, then let it out. Finally he asked: "What is it you require of me?"

"Require?" The chief medical officer chuckled dryly. "Just a complete physical, that's all. But it would be a waste of time. As long as you've got that alien substance in your system, I can't let you take on any additional stress. For all I know, a good brisk walk might be enough to kill you."

The Vulcan frowned ever so slightly. "Very well," he said. "I concede it requires an effort to control my metabolic functions."

For the first time, Bones caught a glimpse of what it cost Spock to maintain that control—but only a glimpse—and then the facade of normalcy was perfect again.

"Even so," the Vulcan went on, "I must remain in command of the *Enterprise.*"

"And why is that?" McCoy asked, cocking his head to one side.

Spock's nostrils flared. "I was serving on the *Enter-*

*prise* under Captain Pike when Hamesaad Dreen was first encountered." A pause. "I know him, Doctor. I know the range of behavior of which he is capable. And I know his race's technology, having once visited one of their ships."

"You visited one of their ships?" M'Benga asked, astonished.

The first officer nodded. "Yes. It was a necessary component of Captain Pike's plan. In fact, I was Dreen's guest."

The chief medical officer regarded him. "Explain."

Spock explained. He told them the whole story, from beginning to end.

When he finished, there was silence. And McCoy was forced to consider the matter in a new light.

He hated to let a patient dictate his own treatment—or lack thereof. But there were nearly three hundred people in that mining colony. And there was just one of Spock.

If the Vulcan knew the marauders' ships, the way they thought . . . the way *Dreen* thought in particular . . .

"All right," he said. "You win, Spock. If you want to command the ship, I won't stand in your way." He grasped the back of the first officer's chair and leaned forward. "But if I see that your control is faltering—that this thing inside you is taking over again—I'll have you back in a biobed so fast it'll make even *your* head spin. Got it?"

Spock nodded. "You need not be concerned, Doctor. I have no desire to become a martyr."

McCoy had his doubts about that. But for now, he had to take the Vulcan at his word.

"One request," the first officer added. "I would prefer the crew was not made aware of my . . . problem. It is important they believe I am equal to the task assigned us."

The doctor saw the logic in Spock's wish. Grudgingly, he agreed.

# Chapter Eight

SOMETHING WAS WRONG. Kirk could feel it in his bones.

There was no way it should have taken Scotty this long to respond. As much as half an hour had passed since he had tossed Owens' communicator up into the jungle. By now, they should have been back on the ship, enduring a round of Doctor McCoy's physicals, as he made sure they weren't worse off than they seemed.

The captain sat with his back against a sapling, surveyed the cliffs, and sighed. Why hadn't Scotty gotten that signal? Was there something Kirk had missed? Some element he'd failed to take into account?

He tried to put himself in Scotty's place. What would he have done, step by step, starting with the realization that the captain's party had been lost?

He'd have sent Sulu's group to investigate the beam-down site, whereupon they'd have found a pit full of rocks and dirt and broken trees.

They'd have excavated with their phasers, if for no other reason than to find the bodies. How deep? Deep enough to—

He cursed softly. Deep enough to disturb the creature—or another just like it? Could that be it? Had Sulu's bunch been attacked the way Spock was? And had their rescue monopolized the bridge contingent's attention, distracting them from detecting the communicator signal?

The captain shook his head. It didn't make sense. Even if something had happened to Sulu, say, just before Uhura could have noticed the signal, that would have been a while ago. By now, the crisis should have been over, one way or the other. And someone should have figured out they were down here.

Something else, then. Something in the atmosphere that was preventing communication? The long-range survey hadn't indicated anything, but . . .

There were other possibilities, of course, not the least likely of which was that the ship had been called away. Directed elsewhere to handle a catastrophe of some sort, despite the fact that its captain and three crewmembers were missing. It wouldn't be the first time something like that had happened.

He wished he knew what was going on. He surely wished he knew.

In any case, they weren't going to find out by sitting in this hole. If there were any answers to his questions, they were on the surface. Up there, in the jungle. Somehow, they'd have to find a way to reach it.

For the time being, however, he'd keep his concerns to himself. If it turned out his fears were unfounded, there was no sense in panicking the others. Hell, they'd been through—

"Captain?"

Kirk turned in response to Owens' call. The injured crewman was still sitting beside Karras. "What is it?" he called back, starting off in their direction.

"Karras has found something," Owens reported. "Something pretty interesting."

"Oh?" the captain said, stopping beside the ensign.

Karras looked up at him. She seemed a little distracted. After a moment, however, she snapped out of it.

"Ensign?" Kirk prompted.

"It's the glyphs," she explained at last. "After I recorded them all, I used the tricorder to do some analyses. You know, nothing complicated. Just some basic comparisons with other primitive-culture data on file—for translation purposes. But I couldn't come up with anything even remotely like them." A pause. "Then I started comparing them to modern-culture data. And I found a match."

Owens was right. This was interesting. "With whom?" the captain asked.

"The Dombraatu," Karras said. "An ancient spacefaring civilization. We've found evidence of them on at least a dozen class-M planets, but none within thirty light years of this system."

Kirk was familiar with the culture. "No one's ever been able to pinpoint the Dombraatu homeworld, have they?"

The ensign shook her head. "But if these are really primitive Dombraatu relics . . ." Her voice trailed off meaningfully.

The captain scrutinized the inscriptions, this time with an entirely different level of appreciation. "Then this may be the birthplace of Dombraatu civilization," he finished.

"That's right," Karras told him.

"But the Dombraatu were spacefarers," Kirk pointed out. "Why isn't there any other evidence that they lived here? Evidence of technology, like on other Dombraatu worlds?"

"That's a good question," Karras agreed. "People don't become spacefarers overnight." She looked at Kirk. "But I don't have the answer."

The captain heard the hint in the crewman's voice. He decided to take it. "We don't have the answer *yet*," he amended. He ran his fingers over the glyphs. "But maybe these can tell us."

Karras eyed him hopefully. "Does that mean I can attempt some translations?" she asked.

"That's what it means," Kirk affirmed. "In fact," he went on, "you can consider this your assignment until I notify you otherwise."

She grinned. It was one of the most beautiful grins the captain had ever seen. "Thank you, sir."

He got to his feet. "If you want to show your appreciation, Ensign, show me some results."

Karras nodded. "Yes, sir."

Kirk looked past her at the encircling cliffs. Now if he could only find a way out . . .

The library doors slid aside and Spock swiveled in his seat to face the opening. A moment later, Mister Sulu entered the room.

"You called, sir?"

"I did indeed." The Vulcan indicated a chair in the cubicle directly opposite his. "Please, sit down."

The human crossed to the chair and sat. Folding his arms over his chest, he looked expectantly at his superior officer.

"When Mister Scott and I spoke earlier on the bridge," Spock said, "he asked me if I had been briefed on Beta Cabrini." He lifted his chin slightly, even now uncomfortable with the near-lie. "I may have understated my grasp of the situation."

Sulu smiled, understanding. "I see, sir. Would you like me to fill in the gaps?"

"Since Mister Scott is needed on the bridge, and he tells me your command of the pertinent data is as complete as his . . . yes, I would be most apprecia-tive."

The helmsman complied. It took a while, but he described the colonists' plight in minute detail.

"That's probably more than you wanted to know,"

he apologized when he was finished. "But I didn't want to leave out anything important."

Spock nodded. "In this case, I prefer to have as much information as possible. Thank you."

He'd already begun to turn back to his computer monitor, when Sulu said: "Begging your pardon, sir, but can I ask something of *you?* I mean, the computer was a little sketchy when it came to how Captain Pike outwitted Dreen."

The Vulcan made a sound of agreement. "That is true," he agreed. "You would like me to expand on the computer's account?"

"I would, sir."

Spock considered the helmsman. "Very well," he said, leaning back in his chair. "It began then, as now, with a distress call. However, it came from a vessel rather than a colony—more specifically, the Vegan ship *Lisander,* bound for Gamma Catalinas with a much-needed supply of rare medicines. It was surrounded by a trio of Merkaan raiders—a triad; it appears they frequently travel in such configurations. The Merkaans had already begun their seizure of the *Lisander's* cargo when the *Enterprise* arrived.

"Captain Pike established a private communication with the triad's leader, Hamesaad Dreen. Giving signs that he was tired of his career and out to make himself wealthy, the captain offered to provide Dreen with an insider's knowledge of easy targets in the Federation in exchange for a share of the proceeds. But first, the Merkaans would have to set the *Lisander* free. Otherwise, the captain would have a difficult time explaining to Starfleet his failure to engage Dreen's ships in combat.

"This, apparently, made sense to Dreen. The prospect of a larger profit in the future cooled his desire for immediate gain. However, he was not about to let the *Lisander* go, not without some evidence of Captain Pike's intentions."

"He wanted him to put his money where his mouth was," Sulu offered.

"In a manner of speaking, yes." Spock focused on the past. "To prove to the pirate where his priorities lay, the captain promised to beam aboard the *Enterprise*'s dilithium stores—which, of course, were measurable by Dreen's sensors. All the marauder had to do was lower his shields and Captain Pike's accomplice would beam aboard with the dilithium."

The helmsman looked at him, his brow creased in disbelief. "Not *you*, sir?"

Spock nodded. "None other. Who is more trustworthy than a Vulcan? Nonetheless, Dreen was leery of the offer. He proposed that his people would perform the transport—an arrangement which would have required the *Enterprise* to drop her shields. The Merkaan must have known that was an action the captain would not take lightly.

"However, Captain Pike was nothing if not a risk-taker. In the end, he went along with Dreen's demands. When the pirate saw the *Enterprise*'s shields go down, he believed the captain was sincere and beamed me aboard along with the dilithium. But Dreen failed to reckon with the skills of our ship's transporter chief, a fellow named Abdelnaby. While Dreen was showing me around his vessel, prodding me for information on Captain Pike, Abdelnaby simultaneously beamed our first officer and a team of security officers to the Merkaan flagship's engineering center, where they were able to seize control of the vessel.

"By the time Dreen discovered that the dilithium I had brought was not dilithium at all, but common carthite, it was too late. The captain was calling for his surrender. In the end, the Merkaans had to return to their homeworld without the *Lisander* or their shipboard weapon systems, which Captain Pike disabled before letting them go."

The human shook his head in unabashed admiration. "That Pike was something of a rogue, wasn't he?"

"I have heard that said," Spock conceded. But he offered nothing else. A conversation like this one was a luxury when they had work to do and plans to make.

Sulu seemed to take the hint. "Quite a story, sir. But I really should be getting back to the bridge."

"Yes," the Vulcan concurred. "Thank you for your help."

Sulu just shrugged. And as Spock turned back to his terminal, the helmsman departed.

Colony administrator Bradford Wayne was normally an easygoing man. But the sight of Hamesaad Dreen made his throat constrict with anger.

As Wayne entered what used to be his office, Dreen had his feet up on the administrator's desk. His long, black boots had displaced a picture of Wayne's wife and children. The frame now lay cracked in two on the floor.

At the approach of the administrator, who was sandwiched between two tall Merkaan guards, Dreen looked up from the desk's computer monitor, where he'd no doubt been perusing the colony's production figures for the umpteenth time. Dreen considered Wayne with his dark, uncaring eyes and swept a lock of hair back behind his ear.

"Ah, the administrator. You may come closer."

One of the Merkaans nudged the human forward. Setting his teeth against an outburst, Wayne took another couple of steps on his own.

"What is it?" he asked.

Dreen tilted his head to one side, causing his long, black hair to fall about his shoulder. "Tell me," he said, his cadaverous features screwing up in a display of curiosity. "Have I not made my intentions clear? Have I not been as explicit as I can possibly be?"

It was a game, and a cruel one. Wayne knew it because they'd played it before. But if he tried to diverge from the routine, Dreen might decide to take it out on his wife and kids. So he humored the Merkaan and played the game.

"You've been *quite* explicit, Acquisitor. Am I to understand there's been an incident?"

Dreen grunted. "You might call it that. It seems a couple of your people were reluctant to aid in the acceleration of the processing schedule." He turned to the monitor and tapped a command into the keyboard just below it. "At the duranium plant." The Merkaan looked up again at Wayne. "Needless to say, they were eliminated."

The administrator kept himself from barking out a choice retort. He kept himself from leaping over his desk and digging his fingers into Dreen's neck. But he couldn't keep his face from turning dark red.

Fortunately, the Merkaans didn't notice. They never noticed. They had gray skin—what did they know about being red-faced?

"Acquisitor," Wayne began, "all this violence is unnecessary. You need only contact me when you believe there is resistance, and I will see to it that the resistance ends."

Dreen's mouth snaked up at the corners. "Really, Administrator. Do you think I have the time for such nonsense? If you wish to avoid violence, you must do a better job of getting your people to cooperate."

Turning to one of Wayne's guards, he spat out a sequence of sounds in their own language. Both guards laughed.

"They *are* cooperating," the human insisted. He hadn't intended to say it, it just came out.

Dreen's eyes found Wayne again and narrowed. "I suppose that is a matter of interpretation," he said. His voice was a little weightier, a little more charged with meaning. "In this case, however, the only interpretation that matters is mine." He paused. "You agree, yes?"

Wayne bit his lip. If he pressed his case, he'd just get

himself killed, and maybe others as well. With Starfleet alerted to their plight, they needed time more than useless bravado.

He looked Dreen in the eye. "I agree, Acquisitor."

The Merkaan nodded. "Good. Now go and do your job."

Inclining his head, Wayne turned and allowed his guards to lead him out. Patience, he told himself. Bide your time.

Wasn't that what Chris Pike had always told him, back in the days when he served on a starship? To lull an enemy before striking? Hell, wasn't that how Pike defeated Dreen the first time?

The mere thought of his former captain was a calming influence as Wayne left his office and strode down the corridor outside it.

There has to be a way, Kirk told himself. There *has* to be.

He'd been sitting in the same place for what seemed like hours. The sun had disappeared some time ago past the rim of the cliffs, but the sky had remained an intense, searing blue. Now the heavens were starting to darken a bit, leaning toward indigo, and he still hadn't made any progress in the getting-the-hell-out-of-here department.

The captain prided himself on his ingenuity, his ability to make something out of nothing. But so far, his resourcefulness seemed to have met its match.

Once again, he considered the stand of spindly trees that grew in the center of the hollow. If they were cut lengthwise in quarters, they could perhaps be tied together and used as a rope.

That might be useful if they had someone up at ground level to haul them up. Or something at the cliffs' edge to hook their rope around. Or some sort of anchor, light enough to heave fifty feet in the air but heavy enough to stay in place once it got up there.

Unfortunately, they had none of these advantages.

Right now, a rope was about as much good to them as Owens' chargeless phaser.

There were rocks here, but not enough to make a pile fifty feet high. And even if there were, it would be nearly impossible to scale them.

Kirk had even thought about retracing their steps along the tunnel that had brought them here. By now, the debris involved in the collapse might have settled; the place might be reasonably stable. And given enough time, they might dig their way to the surface.

Then again, it might still be worth their lives to go back there.

And if Sulu was for some reason still excavating the place, burrowing up from the bottom might get them caught in a deadly phaser blast. The captain wanted to be found, but not that way.

"Sir?"

Kirk turned and saw Autry standing next to him. He looked a lot better; the only evidence of his head wound was a slight, purplish swelling near his hairline. Apparently, all he'd really needed was a little rest after what they'd gone through in the cavern.

Autry was holding out a pale green stalk—something that looked somewhat like sugar cane. The captain took it and looked up at him.

"Something edible, I trust?"

The crewman smiled. "Owens' tricorder seems to think so."

Kirk bit into it. It not only looked like sugar cane, it tasted like it. He glanced past Autry at Karras and Owens, who hadn't moved from the spot where they'd found the hieroglyphs. They were munching on the same kind of stalks that the captain held in his hand.

In fact, just to one side of the science officers, there was a small pile of the stalks. It had the neat, crisp look of a phaser cache about it.

"I guess you're the designated forager," Kirk remarked.

Autry shrugged. "I don't mind that, sir. Not at all. It

keeps me busy." He scanned the hollow and shrugged. "There's not a whole lot for a security officer to do around here."

The captain nodded. A light breeze ruffled his hair. "I know what you mean, crewman. Listen, if you find you've got some time on your hands, you can always think of a way to get us out of here."

Autry regarded him as if it were a joke. It took him a moment to realize Kirk was serious.

"Is that necessary?" he asked. "I mean, won't they just beam us out once they find us?"

"Call it a hypothetical problem, then. And a wicked one at that. Lord knows, it's got *me* stumped."

"Begging the captain's pardon," Autry said at last, "but if James T. Kirk can't come up with a plan, I don't think anyone can."

Kirk frowned. "That's very complimentary," he replied, "but not what I want to hear. Where would I be today if I'd decided I could never live up to the exploits of the legendary Garth of Izar? Or those of Matthew Decker and Christopher Pike? On a commercial freighter, more than likely, trying to reconcile bills of lading with receipts."

Autry grunted. "I see what you mean, sir."

"Good. Now tell me—if you were the captain, how would you get us out of this mess?"

The security officer thought for a second or two. He shook his head. "I don't know. I guess I'd—" He stopped himself. "No, that's not a very good idea."

"What isn't?" Kirk prodded him. "I want to hear it. That's an order."

Autry sighed. "Well, I was going to say we could stand on one another's shoulders. You know, make a human ladder, up against one of the cliff walls." He screwed up his features in an expression of disgust. "But that would only get us halfway—not even. We'd still have another twenty-five to thirty feet to go."

The captain gazed at the walls, nodding his agreement. "But a good try," he told Autry, "especially on short notice. That approach hadn't even occurred to me until you mentioned it." He turned back to the security officer. "Which goes to show you, even James T. Kirk can use some help now and then."

Autry seemed to stand a little taller. "I get the message, sir."

Kirk nodded again. "I thought you would. Carry on."

The man smiled. "Aye, sir."

The captain smiled too. Of course, he had thought of the standing-on-each-other's-shoulders idea as well. But if he'd said so, he'd have passed up a chance to build Autry's confidence.

He tried not to miss such opportunities. One never knew when a crewman's confidence—or lack thereof —might mean the difference between life and death.

# Chapter Nine

FOR A MOMENT, as Kirk opened his eyes, he thought that he was on Earth. The slanting rays of the sun, the warm air, the exotic fragrances—it all seemed to be part of a tropical paradise he couldn't quite put a name to, but was sure he had visited sometime before. And it was nice to be back. So nice to stretch out his arms and—

"Captain!"

Kirk bolted upright at the sound of his name. That's when reality drenched him with all the weight of a Tetracitian rainstorm, dispelling his dreams of Eden, planting him firmly in a deep and frustrating hollow on Octavius Four.

"Captain!"

This time, he followed the call to its source. It was Karras. And she was bending over those stones again —the ones with the Dombraatu carvings in them.

He remembered now. Just before he bedded down on the soft, brown turf near the tunnel mouth, he'd glanced in Karras' direction—and she'd been working on translating the glyphs in the last of the failing light.

Apparently, she'd resumed her studies as soon as she woke up. Judging by the angle of the shadows on the western face of the cliff wall, that could have been as much as an hour ago.

Kirk waved to let Karras know he'd heard her. Then, gathering his feet beneath him, he stood—and immediately regretted it. Every muscle in his body was stiff and sore, some muscles a good deal more than others. He felt as if he'd been ground up and spit out—which, now that he thought about it, wasn't so far from the truth.

Owens and Autry were still sleeping on the moss, which stretched on for a good thirty feet. Seeing no reason to wake them, the captain hiked over to where Karras had stationed herself.

"Progress?" he asked, as he approached the ensign and her stones. Funny how he'd come to think of them as her possessions.

"Progress," she confirmed. "Here, look. You see this symbol?"

Kirk sat a little awkwardly, trying not to abuse his weary body any more than he had to. If Karras was sore as well, she didn't show it. He took a look at the inscription to which she was pointing.

It was an upright line with six half-circles growing out of it, three on each side. If the glyph resembled anything, it was a tree—something in the weeping willow family.

He voiced his observation. Karras grunted.

"That's what I thought," she said, "at least, at first. It turns out I was wrong. Not that there aren't plenty of references to flora here." She touched a few of the other glyphs. "Like this one and this one, and I think this one too. But," she went on, returning to the symbol she'd first pointed out, "this one signifies something else."

The captain regarded her. "All right, I give up."

Karras smiled with the pleasure of a schoolchild who's just stumped her teacher. "It's a creature.

The kind that attacked us before the ground collapse."

Kirk scrutinized the glyph more closely. It *could* have been a rendering of the creature, he decided. On the other hand, he still thought it looked a lot like a tree. "That's interesting," he told the ensign. "But—"

"I know," Karras interrupted. "It's not exactly a surprise that they'd have a symbol for the creature. After all, in the primitive society that produced these stones, something that big would have gotten its share of notice—even, quite possibly, been revered as a god."

The captain nodded. "You took the words out of my mouth."

"But even deities don't get *this* much attention." Having said that, Karras proceeded to point out other appearances of the glyph. As Kirk followed her finger from one place on the boulder to another, he had to concede that the creature was an incredibly pervasive influence on whoever had carved the thing.

"What if there was a temple here?" he suggested. "A place where the primitive inhabitants worshipped the creatures? That would explain the frequent use of the creature-glyph, wouldn't it?"

"Yes, it would," Karras replied. "If the carvings referred to this site alone. But I don't think that's the case."

He regarded her. "You don't?"

The ensign shook her head. "I think every symbol represents a different location. Unless I miss my guess, sir, this is a map."

"A map," the captain found himself repeating.

"Yes. A guide to all the places in this region where the creatures are likely to appear, probably so they can be avoided. It would certainly come in handy for someone traveling from one place to the other."

"But that would mean the creatures always stay in the same places, Ensign. Even highly territorial lifeforms roam to a certain extent, which would make a map of their sightings pretty useless."

Karras shrugged. "Not if they were—are— basically stationary. You know, capable of only very limited excursions—say, fifty meters in any direction."

Kirk reflected on the possibility—a good one, he had to admit, given the creatures' bulk and the inherent difficulty of moving underground. Something else occurred to him: "If they are relatively stationary, the key could be their food supply. The attack on Spock suggests they're carnivorous. But their main supply of sustenance may be something buried deep in the earth. And unless the stuff is fairly common . . ."

"It would be a pretty compelling reason for a creature to stick around," the ensign said, completing his thought.

The captain considered Karras. There was a flush of excitement in her cheeks that made her rather alluring. He tried to ignore the fact as best he could. "Quite a job you've done here," he told her. "You ought to write a monograph. In fact, I think it's unavoidable, considering you're now the Federation's at-large expert on the primitive Dombraatu."

She looked up at the cliffs. Out of embarrassment? He didn't think so. Karras didn't seem the sort to be easily flustered.

"Before I write any papers," she reminded him, "we've got to get back to the ship." The ensign looked at him frankly. "And even if you're not saying so, there's some doubt about that, isn't there?"

Kirk could have lied, but she would have seen through it. "Yes," he said, "there is. At least, in the near term." He smiled wistfully. "It's starting to look like we're on our own for a while. If someone were going to rescue us, they probably would have done so by now."

Karras seemed to accept his response with equanimity. "What do you think happened?" she asked.

What indeed? "I don't know," he told her. He picked up a small stone and tossed it sidearm into a clump of yellow, prickly ground cover. "The only thing I can think of is that we're not their only problem. Maybe something called them away. Some kind of emergency."

She sighed. "I hope that's it, sir. I hope—" She stopped, thinking better of whatever she was about to say.

The captain saw it in her eyes, though. Starships were prone to all manner of disasters, even in an apparently safe orbit. And while it was unlikely that Scotty had let anything happen to the *Enterprise*, there was no way to rule it out completely.

Still, his theory was the more likely one. Or so he told himself.

He dusted off his hands, wincing a little as they complained about the punishment they'd taken in the cavern. "Until we know for sure," he declared, "we've got to do the best we can."

Karras set her jaw. "Aye, sir."

Kirk stood. "That's the spirit, Ensign." He tilted his head in the direction of the stalks Autry had gathered the day before. "I think I'll have some breakfast. Care for some?"

She shook her head again. "No, thank you." Her mouth pulled up amiably at the corners. "I think I'm going to get back to my research. You know, for that monograph."

He looked at her askance, feeling more like a mother hen than he liked. "You've got to eat, Ensign."

Her smile deepened as she thought about it. "All right," she said at last. "I appreciate it, sir."

"No trouble at all," he told her, heading for the impeccably organized pile of stalks. Halfway there, he noticed that Owens and Autry were waking up.

118

Both of them would need some medical attention. And Karras, while willing, was by no means a doctor. It would have been nice to have McCoy with them.

Then again, maybe it wouldn't have been so nice. The captain could hear him now: *"Sugar cane, eh? That's great. By the time anyone gets around to finding us, all our teeth'll have rotted out of our mouths!"*

Maybe it was just as well the doctor was somewhere else—up on the ship, taking care of Spock. Kirk paused. *Spock* . . .

When he beamed up, he was in stable condition. That's what Bones had said: stable. And that was half the battle, right?

All McCoy would have to do is get that poison or whatever it was out of the Vulcan's system. A piece of cake. The captain had seen him do it a hundred times before, with a hundred different alien substances. He gnawed on his lip. Definitely a piece of cake.

But what if Karras' fear was on the money? What if something *had* happened to the *Enterprise?* His throat tightened.

No. They'd been called away. *That was it,* he insisted silently. *That had to be it.*

And either way, there was nothing he could do to help. His job, his only job right now, was to find an escape route from this hole.

Abruptly, he realized that he'd stopped in front of Autry's food supply and remembered why he'd come this way in the first place: breakfast. Getting down on his haunches, he picked out a couple of succulent-looking stalks. Then, defying his still-aching legs to straighten, he started back toward Karras and the stones.

"The usual, Pavel?"

Chekov looked up, saw Sulu on the other side of the rec cabin and wondered how he'd gotten there so quickly. Am I that oblivious? he wondered. "Please," he called back.

Sulu turned to Beaumont, who was practicing his considerable cooking skills this shift, as he did every week at this time. Dressed in the traditional white garb of a chef, Beaumont stood behind a battery of gas-powered burners covered with pots and pans. Though Chekov couldn't quite hear what they were saying, he knew what his friend was asking for.

Ham and pierogies—the ham thick and savory and crispy around the edges, the potato-filled pierogies smothered under generous dollops of cold sour cream —exactly in accordance with the recipe Beaumont had gotten from Chekov. A moment later, the chef began preparing the requested fare. And not one portion, but two. Lately, the navigator noted, Sulu had taken a liking to Chekov's Russian version of a good, hearty breakfast.

A few minutes later, the helmsman lifted two well-stocked, steaming trays complete with coffee and made his way back to their table. But even the prospect of such a mouth-watering treat didn't take the edge off Chekov's anxiety.

At a time like this, his place was behind the navigation console, not a dining table. Granted, there was no immediate need for him to be on the bridge, considering he'd finished plotting their course a good ten hours ago. But what if something unforeseen came up? What if a course correction were required on short notice?

Not that DeSalle wasn't capable. He was *very* capable. In fact, until the Russian had gotten his long-hoped-for berth on the *Enterprise,* DeSalle had been the main figure at the navigational controls. It was only in the last couple of months that the lieutenant had opted for a wider spectrum of duties.

No, ability had nothing to do with it. It was simply

that Chekov felt that in a crisis, he belonged on the front line. Hell, he'd always felt that way—even as a youngster, when he'd been the pluckiest striker on the primary school football circuit. Not necessarily the most skilled, he conceded, but always the one who wanted the ball when his team was on the attack and time was running out.

It was that very quality—the desire to assume responsibility in a pinch, without fear of what would happen if he failed—that had endeared him so to his football coach. And it was the suggestion of his coach, an ex-Starfleet security officer, that first got Chekov thinking seriously about a career in space. Before long, he was following the exploits of the fleet's boldest captains—a select group which in time came to include a daring American named Jim Kirk.

That was another reason Chekov wanted to be on the bridge. With the captain missing and maybe—no. He wouldn't finish that thought even in the privacy of his own head. With the captain missing, he felt that he and the others on whom Kirk depended had to step up and fill the breach.

"Pavel?"

As the Russian's eyes focused, he realized that Sulu was sitting across the table from him and that his plate was already half-empty, in contrast to Chekov's, which was full and losing the last of its steam.

He smiled apologetically at his friend the helmsman. "How long have I been sitting here like this?"

Sulu smiled. "Well," he said, "I've seen you chart a course through an asteroid belt in less time."

Chekov shook his head. "Sorry. It's just that—"

"I know. You want to be where the action is." The helmsman leaned forward. "So do I. But right now, the best thing we can do is try to relax. Pretty soon, Mister Spock's going to need us. And we won't be doing anybody any good by showing up hungry and tired. You agree?"

The ensign grunted. "How can I not agree when you put it that way?"

"Good. Then dig into those pierogies and try to relax."

With an effort, Chekov forced himself to clear his mind and start eating. His first forkful made him wish he'd taken Sulu's advice sooner.

"These are terrific," he said.

The helmsman smiled. *"Vive la différence."*

Chekov's eyes narrowed. "Vhat did you have Beaumont do to them?"

"I know," Sulu remarked. "It's sacrilegious to experiment with the ancient Chekov family formula. But it seemed to me that a little cinnamon was in order."

The ensign took another forkful, and mulled it over. He had to admit it was an improvement. "Vell," he said, "I suppose my mother von't mind your tampering vith her recipe, as long as you added a Russian spice."

Sulu looked at him disbelievingly. "Pavel, cinnamon is not a Russian spice. If I'm not mistaken, it was introduced by the ancient Greeks. Or maybe it was the Romans. But definitely not the Russians."

"Nonsense," Chekov said. "The czars used to flavor their drinks with it. It was a big favorite in the royal court."

Sulu groaned—just as Lieutenant Leslie appeared at their table with a tray full of food. They looked up at him.

"Mind if I join you?" Leslie asked.

"Not at all," the helmsman replied. "In fact, I wish you would. Unless, of course, you're going to tell me soy sauce was invented in Topeka."

The brawny security officer just stared in that stony way of his. "Topeka?"

"Oh," Sulu said, "I forgot. You weren't born on Earth. Topeka's a city in the American Midwest."

Chekov regarded the newcomer. "Pay no attention to my colleague here. He is just a little confused."

"Whatever you say," Leslie responded, putting his tray down between the helmsman's and the navigator's. Pulling out a chair, he sat.

"So," Sulu prompted, "what's new in security?"

Leslie shrugged as he assaulted his breakfast. "Not much. How's Mister Spock doing? Still hanging in there?"

Sulu's brow creased. "What do you mean?"

The security officer looked up. "You know, with that poison inside him. The one the doctors can't seem to find an antidote for."

Chekov glanced at the helmsman. "I thought Spock vas cured."

"Me too," Sulu added. "When we saw him on the bridge, he seemed fine."

Leslie shook his head. "Not from what I understand. Annie Ferrara—you know, the new nurse we took on at Starbase Nineteen—told me that Mister Spock is still hurting. He's just hiding it with some kind of Vulcan discipline."

"Come on," the helmsman said. "You're pulling our legs, right?"

"Sairtainly," Chekov joined in. "I bet if ve asked Nurse Ferrara, she vouldn't know vhat ve vere talking about."

Leslie shrugged again. "Go ahead," he told them. "Ask."

For a couple of seconds, no one spoke. Then Sulu leaned back in his chair. He looked grim as he turned to Chekov.

"He's not kidding, Pavel."

The Russian nodded. "I know."

Chekov thought about Spock, keeping his pain locked up inside while he pretended to be fully fit in mind and body. How long could he keep up the pretense? A couple of days? A week?

And how much of a distraction would Spock's problem be when they got to Beta Cabrini? How much of himself could he devote to helping the colonists? How much would his sickness affect his judgment?

"Maybe that's why Spock went to the library," Sulu muttered. And then, in a stronger voice: "Maybe he couldn't stay on the bridge without giving himself away."

It made sense, didn't it? Chekov cursed in his native tongue.

More than ever, he wanted to be up on the bridge. If Mister Spock was truly in bad shape, he was going to need all the help he could get.

But Sulu's point was still valid. It was better to rest now and be ready when they reached Beta Cabrini.

Frowning, he pushed his plate to one side and hoped he could sleep better than he'd eaten. Damn, but he hated rest periods.

# Chapter Ten

HIS CONTROL WAS SLIPPING.

Spock leaned back in his chair and closed his eyes. He had to concentrate, regain mastery of his metabolic functions. Fortunately, he was alone in the library. There was no one to see him gritting his teeth, the tendons in his neck cording, the blood vessels in his temples bulging out like tiny green snakes.

Memories began to rise to the surface of his consciousness like great, slow bubbles. As they had when he lay in sickbay, trying to shrug off the weight of his sedative. Not daydreams, but rather the emotional residue of his contemplations, freed by his inner turmoil . . .

Image: Christopher Pike, naked from the waist up, his skin glistening with sweat in the light of the overheads as he pounds away again and again at a large, stuffed bag suspended from the ceiling. He is working hard. Abruptly, he senses he is not alone. A glance—blue-eyed, intense, angry. Then a relaxation of the dark brows as he recognizes who has entered the gym.

"Sorry to glare at you that way, Spock."

"It is I who must apologize, sir. I should have apprised you of my need to see you beforehand."

"No problem. What is it?"

The captain's bare knuckles are red and bleeding. It is difficult to ignore—even more so because red blood is still such a novelty.

"I believe I have discovered what—or more to the point, *who*—killed the crew of the *Telemakhos.*"

Pike steps away from the bag, massaging his hands without thinking about it. "You found something on the wreck?"

"Yes, sir. A virus, still living in the captain's quarters."

The human is interested. "The only part of the *Telemakhos* where life-support was still functioning."

"That is correct. To the best of our knowledge, this virus exists on only two worlds—Mercenam Four and C'tinaia Seven."

The captain digests the information. His eyes brighten. "And Mercenam Four was destroyed a year ago in a supernova. Which means that the C'tinai were behind that slaughter."

"It would appear so, sir."

Pike smiles. It is not an indication of joy. "Excellent, Lieutenant. I'll contact Admiral Penn. He'll want to know that the C'tinai are on the warpath again." A pause. "Good work, Spock."

There is no answer near at hand. On Vulcan, it is simply expected that one will do his utmost to produce the desired results. Among humans, it seems, that is not always the case.

"Don't be embarrassed, Spock. You've probably saved hundreds of lives. The next time the C'tinai show up, we'll be ready for them."

There is no ready answer for that either, but he manages one. "I am glad you are pleased with my efforts."

"It's just a pity," the captain says, "that we couldn't

have known about them in time to save the *Telemakhos.*" He shakes his head. "With its crew of two hundred and ninety." His features harden. "And a captain who knew all the best watering holes on Anacarthaginia."

Without warning, he whirls and kicks savagely at the bag. There is a muffled thud and the heavy object swings backward. Before it has swung back, Pike has grabbed his uniform shirt off a wall hook and is on his way out the door.

There is nothing else to do but to follow.

Image: The woman called Number One, intent on a control console full of blinking lights, her expressionless visage caught in their amber strobe effect. Her long, slender fingers fly over the console as if with a life of their own.

She seems oblivious to the amount of time that has passed since their transport to the Elarnite station, as well as to the chain reaction in the station's engine core that will soon destroy the long-abandoned facility and everything in it. All that concerns her is that they download as much of the data stored in the station's computer as possible.

Normally, this could be accomplished with a preset transmission. However, the Elarnite computer is not in good repair. It is necessary to maintain the link manually.

"Approaching maximum load," he tells her.

There is only the slightest flicker of movement in her face. "Let me know when we *reach* it, Mister Spock."

Was that a rebuke? "Yes, Commander."

Besides Spock himself, Number One is the closest thing to a Vulcan on the ship. It is difficult sometimes for him to remember that she is human.

"We have reached maximum load. The magnetic bottle may break down at any moment."

"Thank you, Lieutenant." Her voice is without

inflection. She is mesmerized by the possibility of preserving Elarnite experience, though it will probably do little or nothing to advance Federation sciences.

Knowledge for the sake of knowledge. It is, he recognizes, a distinctly Vulcan point of view.

"The bottle is breaking down. No breach as yet."

This time, the only response is a distracted grunt. If anything, Number One's fingers are moving more quickly now, fighting to maximize the flow of data to the *Enterprise*.

On the other side of the Elarnite bridge, a panel comes flying out of place amid a geyser of white sparks and blue flames. A small piece of fiery metal lands near the first officer's boot. She appears not to notice.

"Energy reversal," he tells her, speaking above the hissing sound that comes from the area where the panel blew off. "Life-support is failing."

"Implement back-up," she calls out. There's an urgency in her voice that belies her calm exterior.

"Implementing." But there is no response. Perhaps the back-up mechanism was damaged by the same thing that damaged the primary system. Perhaps it went down a long time ago, before the *Enterprise* ever discovered the station. "There *is* no back-up, Commander."

She curses, never taking her eyes off the controls in front of her. There is another explosion, worse than the first, and a second panel comes loose. It hurtles into what appears to be the Elarnites' main viewscreen. A smell of carbon fills the air; black smoke billows.

Their communicators beep. Number One ignores hers. He does the same, wondering if he is making a mistake.

The bridge shudders. He sees why. "There is a breach in the shields. An explosion is imminent." Then louder: "We must go!"

She looks at him, her eyes red and stinging with smoke. *"You* go, Spock."

"No. We go together—or not at all."

Still she hesitates, but for only a moment. Flipping open her communicator, she says: "Two to beam over. Energize."

As they dematerialize, he believes he sees the panel in front of him burst into blue-white flame, enveloping him. But he cannot be sure.

The next thing he knows, he is on the transporter platform. Number One is standing beside him.

"Are you all right?" she asks.

He nods. "And you?"

She shrugs. And faints.

As she falls, he sees the bloody, smoking rent in the side of her tunic. He looks to Abdelnaby, the transporter chief. The man is already calling for help.

But Spock cannot wait. Gathering the first officer in his arms, he carries her to sickbay.


Image: Philip Boyce, ship's surgeon, at his birthday party. Slight and silver-haired, he stands before a small crowd of well-wishers in the ship's rec. He frowns as he swirls some Saurian brandy around in his glass. "You shouldn't have," he says. "And I mean it."

"Come on," someone remarks. "If we hadn't, you'd never have forgiven us." There is laughter.

Boyce shakes his head. "That's what you think. I'd just as soon be nodding off in my quarters, poring over wild memories of my misspent youth."

More laughter. The individual who called out makes his way through the throng. It turns out to be Captain Pike. With deadpan seriousness, he puts his arm around the older man and proposes a toast: "To my chief medical officer. May he never feel as old as he claims he does."

Cheers follow. Glasses are raised and drained. The doctor's pale blue eyes seem to sparkle. For once, he is speechless.

A voice comes over the intercom system, requesting the presence of a crewmember on the bridge. It seems there is a minor emergency, though the captain is assured it's nothing requiring his presence. An officer is dispatched, though Spock does not take note of who it is. He is too intrigued by Boyce's behavior.

"I don't suppose I could get the rest of you to go with him?" the doctor suggests.

The very idea is met with a resounding negative.

"And now," Pike goes on, "the *pièce de résistance.*" All eyes follow as he gestures toward the open doorway. "All right, Garrison. Haul away."

A moment later, Garrison and Pitcairn guide a sickbay gurney into the room. There is a huge birthday cake sitting on top of it, aflame with more candles than one could easily count.

"That's my gurney!" Boyce complains, mock-indignant. He glowers at the captain. "You'd better lug that monstrosity off and feed it to someone quickly. Starfleet doesn't take kindly to the misappropriation of medical equipment."

"Don't worry," the captain assures him. "I cleared it with Admiral Penn. He gave it his official seal of approval, providing we save him a piece with a flower on it."

Most of those assembled don't hear the exchange, however. They are too intent on making room for the cake.

"So how old are you?" Garrison asks the doctor, peering at him through the conflagration of candles.

Boyce grimaces. But before he can reply, a strange smell permeates the rec cabin. People look at one another questioningly.

"I hope that's not the cake," someone remarks.

Yeoman Colt points to the ventilation grate. "Look."

Thick, yellow gas is billowing slowly out of the opening. Obviously, this is the source of the odor.

There are shouts of alarm and the room begins to empty out.

"You know," the captain says to Boyce, "if I didn't know better, I'd think you planned this, just to get out of admitting your age."

The doctor smiles. "No. But now that you mention it, it wouldn't have been a bad idea."

It is only later that the origin of the gas is discovered: an accident in the cargo hold, where an acid accidentally spilled over some mineral stores.

Image: Navigator Jose Tyler, looking red-faced over the brim of his coffee cup. His blush is accentuated by the golden-brown color of his hair and brows.

At the next table, Garrison and Sellers are speaking louder than they need to. It appears that their comments are actually intended for Tyler more than for each other.

"*The* princess?" Sellers asks.

"Damned right," Garrison answers.

"The one from Kalajia Seven?"

"That's her, all right."

Sellers sits back in his chair. "I just find it a little hard to believe. I mean, that lady is *gorgeous.*"

"I know how crazy it sounds." Garrison glances at Tyler, though Tyler doesn't seem to notice. "Hell, I didn't believe it at first either. But Mancuso swears he was a witness."

Tyler winces and sips at his coffee. He does not seem to enjoy the conversation between Garrison and Sellers, but he stays in the mess hall anyway.

A Vulcan would have walked away some time ago. It is difficult to see the logic of subjecting oneself to unnecessary abuse.

"Lieutenant?"

The navigator looks up. "Yes, Spock?"

"You seem uncomfortable."

Tyler laughs. "Whatever gave you that idea?"

"Your complexion. I have observed that humans turn that color only when they are experiencing some form of discomfort."

The navigator puts down his coffee cup. "Well," he says softly, "you've got me there. I guess I am a little uncomfortable."

"Then why do you remain here?"

Tyler leans forward. "It's been my experience that these things die down more quickly if you take them like a man. You know, show everybody you're not going to let them get to you."

"By 'these things,' you mean romantic liaisons?"

"Not exactly. I mean *rumors* of romantic liaisons."

"Rumors."

"Yes."

"Then they are not liaisons in truth?"

The navigator shrugs. "I didn't say that."

Indeed, he did not. Spock concedes the fact.

"You see, Lieutenant, where I come from, you don't kiss and tell."

"Kiss and tell?"

"Engage in one of those liaisons you were talking about and comment on it afterward. It's just not chivalrous."

"I understand. You are protecting the privacy of the other party."

"That's right."

"But if the rumors are untrue, why not say so? Would that not be the simplest way to protect the other party's privacy?"

"Not necessarily, Spock. Some people won't believe you. And the harder you claim nothing happened, the more they believe that something did." A pause. "Besides, if I protest only when the stories are untrue, then when I'm silent, it's tantamount to a confession."

"It is a more complex subject than I would have suspected."

"You're telling me," Tyler says.

Behind him, the door to the mess hall opens. The Kalajian princess—bound for home after having conducted successful trade negotiations with a number of Federation member worlds—enters the room. All eyes come to rest on her—except Tyler's. After a while, he turns around too.

She is indeed beautiful. That is difficult to avoid noticing. It is a beauty that seems to transcend cultural differences.

For a moment, her eyes search the room. Then they alight on Tyler.

The princess walks over to the navigator and without a word of explanation, bends over and kisses him full on the mouth. Their eyes meet, and the nature of their exchange is quite plain. Finally, the princess departs.

No one moves. No one even seems to breathe.

It is Tyler who breaks the spell at last. His face a darker red than before, he turns back to the table that separates him from Spock, picks up his coffee cup and, loud enough for everyone present to hear, says: "Okay. You got me this time."

Image: Yeoman Colt, catlike, slinking silently past the Dindamorii rebel she's just disabled with a well-aimed phaser blast. Her sandy-blonde hair is tied back into a ponytail, her green eyes exhibiting nothing of their usual good humor. Colt's every movement is focused, purposeful as she makes her way down the palace corridor.

The yeoman's feelings for Captain Pike are no secret, not even to Spock, though neither he nor anyone else actually discusses them. When she learned that the captain was in danger, taken captive along with the planetary governor by Dindamor's militant anti-Federation faction, she was the first to volunteer for the rescue team.

Circular forms being powerful symbols in Dindamorii myth, the palace is set up like a wheel, with the governor's office at the center and the main hallways radiating outward like spokes. They are proceeding along one of those spokes, trying to disable the perimeter guards and reach the captives without alerting the rest of the rebels. In the meantime, on the opposite side of the complex, another team consisting of Number One and Lieutenant Tyler is trying to do the same.

They must move quickly. If the rebels in the governor's office try to contact the guard Colt just knocked out, they will know that something is amiss. Spock pelts after the human female, his senses alert.

Colt stops at a joining of the main passage with a perpendicular one and he catches up to her. They listen; there is silence. She pokes her head around the corner, finds no one there, and waves him on. Again, they proceed with as much haste as they can muster.

Another joining—unpatrolled, like the first one. They are within a stone's throw of the governor's office. They will have to practice more caution here, so close to their objective.

But luck is with them; no one challenges them. They reach the office and peer inside through the transparent upper portion of a door, Spock to one side and Colt to the other.

The governor's workplace is set up like the palace itself, but in miniature. Pie-shaped floor plans of computer terminals and medialink units are separated and defined by six open paths, each one leading from a door like the one behind which Spock and Colt are hiding to an open area in the center of the room.

There is only one item in that open space: the governor's desk. It is surrounded now by a small crowd, which is in turn surrounded by half a dozen of the medialink devices.

Pike is not difficult to spot. The Dindamorii are ruby-red and covered with fishlike scales. There are five of them in the room, including the governor. So far, it seems, no one has noticed Colt and Spock.

Early on in the crisis, the notion of simply trying to beam up the captives was discarded. The captain, being human, would have been easy to distinguish from the militants, but that would not have been true of the governor. And it would have taken too long to get a fix on him in the midst of his rebel captors.

Hence, the idea of beaming down two teams at different points in the palace. If one did not make it, the hope was that the other one would.

It appears that Number One and Tyler have not made it—not yet, at least. Have they merely been detained by the presence of too many guards? Or has something happened to them?

Suddenly, Spock and Colt hear something from within—agitated voices. The Vulcan peeks through the transparent part of the door and sees the rebel leader waving his arms about. He catches a phrase: the Dindamorii equivalent of "rescue team."

Colt has caught it too. They look at one another. Number One and Tyler have been encountered; their presence is known to the rebels. She points to herself, then uses her forefinger to cut a semi-circular shape in the air. He understands. She is going to enter the office, circle around and try to reach the other side of the room. This way, the rebels will have two targets to worry about. He nods in agreement.

Opening the door as quietly as they can, they slip inside. Despite their care, their entrance does not go unnoticed. A narrow, blue-white stream of energy devours the door, bathing Spock in its bright, hot backlash.

He fights to maintain consciousness. He fails.

After an indeterminate amount of time, he recovers—only to see Colt's flushed, anxious face hovering over him. "Spock," she says, "are you all right?"

Taking stock of himself, he nods. "I merely lost consciousness." He licks his lips, which seem terribly parched. "Did we succeed?"

Just then, the tall figure of Captain Pike looms

behind her. "Did you *ever*," he chuckles. "You and Colt here took down everybody except the ring-leader."

Colt doesn't bother to say she did it on her own, her partner being unconscious the whole time. She just smiles at Spock, then turns to look up at Pike. "We wanted to leave you *something* to do, sir."

The captain smiles back. "Yes, Yeoman, I'm sure you did."

As Spock sits up, he sees Tyler and Number One standing with the governor on the other side of the room. They are guarding an open door.

"Sir," the first officer says, "I don't think we should linger here. The other rebels . . ."

"Of course, Number One." Opening his communicator, Captain Pike says: "Six to beam up, Mister Abdelnaby."

The memories faded and Spock opened his eyes. He had regained command again. But it had weakened him to such an extent that if he'd had to stand up just then, he didn't think he could have managed it.

*Strange,* he remarked inwardly. Of all the events he had recalled from his days under Captain Pike, not one of them concerned the man he *wanted* to remember—the man he might need before this was over. The man whose file was still displayed on Spock's library monitor: Bradford Wayne, administrator of the Beta Cabrini colony.

# Chapter Eleven

IN THE SOUTHERN TIER of the hills that surrounded the colony, four-and-a-half kilometers from the main square, Wayne sat in the cabin of a many-legged mobile extraction unit and worked the controls. The night-black shaft before him seemed to descend forever, illuminated only by the vehicle's forelights.

Ever since Dreen had decided to accelerate the production schedule, Wayne had been hauling loads of duranium-rich rocks to the surface. Though he was far from skilled in this sort of thing, the Merkaans were putting everyone to work, trying to pull as much more out of the ground as they could before Starfleet caught on to their presence here.

Fortunately, however, the Merkaans knew nothing about mining. They had to rely almost completely on the administrator and his assistants to direct things, which had given Wayne the opportunity to ride with just about anybody he wanted to, barring the processing experts.

This morning, he'd arranged to partner with Ron Gross. Of course, the geologist hadn't talked much since they'd left the surface behind, but Wayne didn't find that difficult to understand. In fact, he'd felt the same way once, the time he'd lost his friend Daniels to the Halriccian on Elzibar Seven.

The administrator slowed down for a particularly tricky set of turns. He grunted. "Two days, Ron. That's how long it's been since you and Green sent out that call for help. By now, a ship might be approaching the outskirts of the system."

Gross looked at him. His features were taut, wary. "That was the idea, wasn't it? To attract some help?"

"Sure. But you know how seldom Starfleet passes through this sector. Odds are that we'll get a single ship at first. And a single ship isn't going to be enough against Dreen's triad, not if it's anything like I remember."

The geologist swallowed. "So?"

"So we've got to help whoever answers the call. We've got to let them know they can depend on us. And to do that, we've got to send another message. Something clear and concise, like before, so it'll get past the Merkaans' monitors."

Gross swallowed again, harder. "I can't do it, Brad."

"Ron—"

"Don't even ask, because I can't do it." He turned to the administrator, and there was unconcealed fear in his eyes. "Not after what they did to Green." His eyes opened even wider. "I thought I could do it, but when I saw how they—" He shook his head. "Please don't ask."

Wayne regarded the man sympathetically. "You did fine, Ron. You got that first message off."

"Once. But I couldn't do it again. My knees would turn to soup." His hands were shivering in his lap now, holding tight to one another. "For the love of god, Brad—"

Wayne took his right hand from the steering mechanism, put it on the man's shoulder, and gripped hard. "Ron, don't worry. I'm not asking."

The geologist looked surprised. "You're not?"

"No. That's not why I wanted to get together." He smiled gently. "I just needed the key back."

Gross stared at him for a few seconds, then started to relax a bit. "Damn. Sorry." He thought for a moment, then said: "Hell, I think I've got it right here." Searching his pockets, he stopped at the one by his left shoulder and took out the key. "I left it in my coat and forgot all about it, till you reminded me just now."

Wayne accepted the key and tucked it away. "Thanks. And don't be sorry, Ron. I've seen men go completely to pieces over a lot less."

The geologist grunted. "I just never want to—" He halted in midsentence. "Who's going to do it then? I mean, if not me, then who?"

Wayne negotiated a bend in the shaft. "Me, Ron. I'm going to take care of it myself this time."

Gross regarded him. "But that's crazy. You've got a wife. Kids."

The administrator felt the muscles in his jaw tense. It was an argument he'd used on himself, back when the necessity for another transmission was just becoming clear to him. But it didn't hold water.

Sure, he had a family. But he was responsible for this colony as well. He'd already risked the lives of others in an attempt to discharge his responsibility— because at the time, that seemed like the surest way.

But the situation was different now. He wasn't in a position to create a distraction. And he had no excuse for asking someone else to do his dirty work.

Captain Pike came to mind again, as he had so often in the last few days. Never—not once—did Chris Pike ever lead the charge from the rear. If there was danger, he was the first one to expose himself to it.

Could Bradford Wayne do any less?

"It doesn't matter," he told Gross. "You did your part. And Lord knows, so did Green. Now it's my turn."

The geologist didn't press the matter any further. He just sat there and stared into the shaft as they descended deeper into the earth.

The closer the captain studied the cliffs, the more insurmountable they seemed and the more frustrated he became. He'd always believed that nothing was impossible, that there was a way around any obstacle. But this one was starting to loom as the exception that proved the rule.

*No use hitting my head against the wall—literally or figuratively,* Kirk told himself. *Not when I could be doing something useful.*

Hell, sometimes it helped to take a break. Some of his grandest strategies had come to him while he was working out in the gym or raising a glass with Leonard McCoy. With any luck, he'd discover a solution to their present problem while cataloging the local shrubs.

Taking out the tricorder he borrowed he set out for a clump of green-and-white speckled bushes. The sun was hot on his neck as he stepped out from the shadows—hotter even than it had been the day before in the jungle above. A change in the weather, or just the absence of any wind?

As he was wondering, he saw Owens walking stiffly in his direction, his bad knee immobilized between two splints. Like the captain, he had a tricorder in his hand. In the other he grasped a long, smooth stick, which he used to help himself along.

"Feeling better?" Kirk asked.

Owens smiled and shrugged. "Actually, my leg's throbbing like the dickens. But I just couldn't sit there anymore. I felt like I was starting to take root."

The captain nodded. "I know the feeling. Welcome aboard."

Owens glanced at the green-and-white thicket, which seemed to have grown out of a shoulder of exposed rock. No, not rock—the fossilized material that covered the cliff walls. "Looks like as good a place to start as any. Unless you had plans for it, sir."

Kirk shook his head. "No plans, crewman. I'll find some other specimen on which to feast my tricorder."

The captain spotted another thicket just a few meters away. Somehow, it didn't look as interesting, but one never knew. Approaching it, he lowered himself onto one knee and extended his tricorder toward the nearest clump of narrow, pointed leaves.

But he'd barely begun to analyze the plant before he heard a shout. Spinning about, he saw Owens stumbling backward and finally sprawling. A moment later, he saw why.

There was a thick, white spiral of vapor coming from the shrub the man had been examining. Or not exactly from the shrub, Kirk saw at second glance, but from the ground beside it, where a tiny pool of bright, red liquid had gathered and was bubbling fiercely.

The captain didn't blame Owens for being startled, though he didn't seem to be in any danger. As Kirk thought that, in fact, the bubbling ceased and the vapor stream dissipated. The injured man looked up at him, no doubt feeling a little foolish.

"Frightened by a bush," Owens remarked ruefully.

The captain smiled. Apparently, neither Karras nor Autry had noticed. "I won't tell a soul," he promised. As the crewman gathered himself and stood, Kirk recovered his walking stick for him. "Exactly what happened?"

Owens shook his head. "I was examining the bush when I found some berries. I mean, they sure looked like berries. Come on, I'll show you."

Avoiding the red liquid, which was starting to seep into the ground, they approached the bush again. Then, with the help of his stick, Owens eased a couple of branches aside.

"You see?" he said. "There's a couple more."

The captain saw. They looked like berries all right —large, succulent berries the color of rubies. Good enough to eat, he'd have said, if he hadn't seen the bubbling and the vapor. He could only imagine the havoc that stuff would wreak on a man's stomach.

"Interesting," he told Owens. "But it might be a good idea to keep them at arm's length from now on."

The crewman nodded. "I hear you, sir." Gently, gradually, he let the branches resume their normal position.

As the captain started for the object of his own study, he took a last look at the red stuff and thought he noticed something strange. He knelt beside the bush to get a closer look.

"What is it, sir?" Owens inquired.

Kirk grunted. He looked about, found a flat stone and used it to sweep aside what was left of the liquid, revealing a series of irregularly shaped pockmarks in the otherwise smooth stone surface.

The crewman gasped. "The berry juice did that? To solid rock?"

The captain shook his head. "Not rock," he replied. "At least, I don't think so." He searched the immediate area, found some more of the fossilized material and pointed to it. "See this? I found it all over the cliff walls. It's some kind of long-dead plant life." He rapped his knuckles on it. "Hard too." Next, he traced the outlines of the pockmarks with his finger, careful not to actually touch the liquid. "I noticed some of the stuff around the plant before. But in the area the liquid got to, there's none left."

Owens looked at him. "So it didn't consume the rock, but it ate away everything else."

Kirk nodded. "Looks that way. It must break down organic compounds." He trained his tricorder on the remains of the liquid. "If it was simply a variety of acid, it wouldn't have eliminated just the fossils. As I said, they were pretty—"

And then it hit him. For the moment, he forgot about his tricorder analysis and peered through leafy branches at the cliff walls.

If those sheer surfaces were covered with fossils, and the berry juice *ate* through fossils . . .

"Damn," he muttered.

"Sir?"

The captain looked at Owens. "Hang onto your tricorder, crewman. I think we may have discovered a way out of this place, charming as it is."

When the message came from the direction of Beta Cabrini, Uhura was as surprised as anyone.

Up until now, they'd all assumed that one call for help was all the colonists had dared to send—before the Merkaans made it impossible. Apparently, they'd assumed wrong.

"Mister Scott?" she said, turning to the captain's chair, where the chief engineer was firmly entrenched.

He swiveled to look at her. "Aye, Lieutenant?"

"Sir, I've got a communication from the mining colony."

He leaped up from his seat and came around to her station. "From the mining colony? What is it, lass?"

Uhura read it directly off her display: "Here daily this time. Await instructions; will confirm."

Scotty looked at her. "This could be helpful—extremely helpful. Mister Spock will want to know about it."

She nodded. "I'll relay it to the library."

As McCoy entered the room, he saw Spock sitting, leaning forward with his elbows planted on one of the tables, the palms of his hands pressed together mere inches from his face, his eyes closed. If the human didn't know better, he'd have said the Vulcan was praying.

Which, of course, was ridiculous. Vulcans didn't pray. But they did meditate on occasion, particularly when confronted with a problem which defied casual analysis. And the crisis on Beta Cabrini certainly seemed to fit that description.

It took a couple of seconds for Spock to acknowledge McCoy's presence. And even then, the first officer didn't turn around. He just opened his eyes.

"Can I help you, Doctor?"

McCoy chuckled. "Actually, Spock, I was going to ask you the same thing."

Apparently resigned to the fact that this would not be a momentary interruption, Spock sat back in his chair and let his hands settle on the surface in front of him. Finally, his head came around—slow and almost lizardlike, his eyes dark and piercing.

"I beg your pardon?"

"The poison, remember? That serum in your blood?" With an effort, he bit back the combativeness that Spock always seemed to provoke in him. "I wanted to make sure you were still in control—"

"I am," the Vulcan said quickly.

The doctor frowned. "Dammit, Spock, I'm not trying to drag you back into sickbay." And then, in a softer voice: "Not anymore. I've had some time to think about it, and maybe you *are* those colonists' best hope. I just thought you could use a helping hand. You know, some medication to—"

The first officer shook his head emphatically. "No. No medication, thank you." A pause. "It would only dull my thinking."

McCoy grunted, not having thought of that possibility. The effect on a human would be negligible. But on a Vulcan . . . "I suppose it might at that," he conceded.

Spock regarded him. "You agree with me?"

The doctor nodded. "Surprised?"

"I did not expect it," the first officer remarked. "Though I harbor no fantasy that it will serve as a precedent."

McCoy smiled. "Touché. Nothing I like better than a feisty Vulcan."

Shooting him a withering glance, Spock turned away again. "If that is all, Doctor, I would like to resume my contemplation of the matter at hand."

The chief medical officer took a long look at his colleague. Something was wrong, something beyond the matter of Spock's sickness. He said so.

"I do not know what you mean," the Vulcan replied.

"Come on, Spock. You think a doctor can treat someone—even someone like *you*—and not get to know that person even a little? I've been your physician long enough to see you're not yourself." He stopped for a moment, considering the best way to put it. "Listen, if there's nothing wrong except what I already know about, or hell, even if I'm just plain out of line, tell me, and I'll take a walk. But if—"

"A plan," the Vulcan blurted. He sighed. "I am unable to formulate a suitable plan for taking back the mining colony."

"Ah," McCoy breathed. "So that's it."

"I asked myself what the captain would do in this instance," the first officer went on. "It occurred to me that he would employ a bluff—that is, a deception, a show of apparent strength intended to deter or frighten. The strategy is used in the Terran game of poker, where a player will place a bold bet on an inferior hand with the intention of encouraging an opponent to withdraw a winning h—"

"Spock," the doctor said, "I know what a bluff is. And I think you're right—that's *exactly* what Jim would have done in this case."

The Vulcan looked at him. *"Jim?"* His features took on an odd cast—one that almost suggested guilt. "Actually, I was referring to Captain *Pike.*" His eyes found McCoy's. "But of course, you are correct. Captain Kirk would have attempted a bluff as well. In many ways, he and Captain Pike were cut from the same cloth." A subtle quirk of his mouth. "However, *I* am cut from an entirely different one. For some time, I have been sitting here trying to devise a bluff. But I am not practiced at deception. It is not something that comes easily to me."

McCoy understood. Lying—especially the preconceived variety—didn't fit in easily with the current mode of Vulcan philosophy. Though he'd have bet that hadn't been the case hundreds of years before, when Spock's people were cutting each other's throats at the drop of a *lirpa*.

"You know," the doctor replied, "I think your problem is you're just trying too hard."

Spock's eyes narrowed. "Trying too hard?"

"Yup. If you think back, the captain's best bluffs weren't complex, or even particularly credible, in and of themselves. But he sold them. He made the opposition believe that he was ready and willing to execute an option he never had in the first place. And that, my friend, is the key to a good bluff. You've got to be convincing."

The Vulcan thought about it. "I do not believe I can be convincing."

McCoy snorted. "No? Ever hear the expression 'poker face'? Well, if you haven't got one, I don't know who has." He leaned forward, planting one hand on the desk in front of Spock. "Don't y'see? Everybody knows Vulcans don't lie—can't lie. That worked to your advantage ten years ago, when you beamed aboard Dreen's vessel. Hell, why do you think Pike sent *you* and not someone else?"

"That was different. I was merely a pawn. There was little for me to do besides walk with the acquisitor and nod."

"Still, you did it. You pulled it off. And you can do it again. You've just got to allow yourself to, well, 'omit' the truth a little . . ."

Spock raised an eyebrow.

"Don't give me that look," the doctor said. "Do you want to help those colonists or don't you?"

The first officer's expression of doubt gradually dissipated. "You know I do," he answered.

"Then bend a little, for godsakes. Give a little good, honest perjury a chance."

McCoy would have loved to hear Spock's response. However, the intercom chose that moment to beep.

"Commander Spock?" It was Uhura.

"Yes, Lieutenant?"

"I've just received a communication from Beta Cabrini, from the mining colony."

The skin between the Vulcan's brows crinkled. "What kind of communication?"

"Just eight words." She told him what they were.

Spock leaned back in his seat. "Thank you, Uhura."

"Of course, sir."

The doctor was cheered by the news. "How 'bout that? I guess our subspace correspondent is still open for business."

"It would appear so," Spock concurred. "Though the brevity of his—or her—message indicates that the Merkaans are monitoring communications. Perhaps not so much expecting the colonists to contact us as vice-versa."

McCoy rubbed his chin. "Then that Dreen fella might not even know we've been called in, assuming both messages slipped by unnoticed."

"That is correct."

"And if we want to keep it that way, we've got to send a return message with the same brevity in mind." He harumphed. "It's going to take a lot of back and forth to come up with a coordinated effort, even assuming one of us had something in mind."

"Not necessarily," Spock countered. "I know one of the colonists. Or at least, I used to. I have not seen him in six or seven years."

"You know someone? Who?"

"The colony administrator. A man named Bradford

Wayne. He was one of Captain Pike's helmsmen." A beat. "I was not as well acquainted with him as with some of the other officers on board. But we had a number of experiences in common. If I can mine those experiences for references . . . "

"Interesting choice of words," the doctor noted, "under the circumstances. *Mine* those experiences indeed."

Spock looked at him. "An unintended double entrendre," he said. "In any case, if I can draw on our common history, I believe I can not only abbreviate individual messages, but minimize the need for communications overall. Though as you say, my acquaintance with Wayne is useless if I do not come up with a—"

Suddenly, right before McCoy's eyes, the Vulcan's entire demeanor seemed to change. He was clicking on all cylinders now—the doctor could see it in his eyes.

"What is it, Spock? What are you thinking about?"

The first officer met his gaze. If McCoy didn't know better, he'd think Spock was about to break out in a grin. "A plan, Doctor. A logical, workable scheme— one with a reasonable possibility of success. And one which you yourself brought to mind."

McCoy was intrigued. *"Me?"*

Spock nodded. "Yes—when you pointed out my unintentional pun."

The human grunted. "Care to fill me in on it?"

Spock hesitated, apparently still working out the details. But after a second or two, he began describing it to McCoy. And damn it, he was right—it *did* have a reasonable possibility of success.

"The tricky part," McCoy decided, "is going to rest with the colonists. We don't know how difficult it's going to be for them to hold up their end of the bargain. The Merkaans are bound to be watching them like hawks."

The Vulcan nodded. "True. However, the message

we received asks for instructions. Does that not imply an ability to carry them out?"

The doctor mulled it over. "All it implies is they *think* they can do it. They may not know what's in store for them if they try."

"Bradford Wayne would know. He was serving on the *Enterprise* when we encountered Dreen the last time; he would not discount the danger."

McCoy shrugged. "I hope you're right. In the meantime, you've got an entire day to come up with a message. Our friend won't be receiving until this time tomorrow."

Spock shook his head. "It will not take me a day, Doctor. I have already contrived an appropriate communication."

McCoy considered the first officer. "Already?"

"Yes."

"And it's concise?"

"It could hardly be *more* concise."

The doctor scowled. "Well? What is it?"

Spock told him. It was pretty damn concise, all right.

Kirk wiped his brow and considered the fruits of their labor. *Fruits indeed,* he mused, smarting at the unintended pun.

At his feet lay a harvest of some twenty red, juicy berries. Some were larger than others, of course, and a few had funny shapes. But they'd all come from the same kind of bush, which, fortunately for the humans, grew in some abundance down here.

It hadn't been easy to pluck the things and transport them to where they needed them: this open spot perhaps five meters from one of the cliff walls. As careful as they were, they'd lost a couple on the way. No great tragedy, though it might've been one if any of his people had been splattered in the process. As it was, they'd come through the job unstained and unscathed.

Even as he thought that, Karras carried over another one, holding it by its short stem, and as far from her body as possible. Concentrating, she slowed as she approached the accumulation. Then, getting down on her knees, she put the berry down beside the others.

Looking up at the captain, she breathed a sigh of relief. "Maneuver completed," she quipped.

"Well done," he told her, coming round to offer her his hand. She gave him hers in return. He took it.

That time before, in the dark of the cavern, he'd found her hand small and cold. It still felt small, but no longer cold. It felt as warm as anyone could wish a hand to be.

If the situation had been a little different, if they'd been somewhere else besides this hole in the landscape of Octavius Four, if he were someone other than her commanding officer . . .

But circumstances were what they were. As tempting as it was to speculate, Kirk had more immediate matters with which to contend.

"Thanks," she said, getting to her feet.

"Don't mention it," he told her. And then, more as a way of wrenching his thoughts back to reality than anything else, he asked: "How's your research going?"

Karras shrugged. "I've been able to interpret some more of the glyphs, but they're not telling me much I don't already know. For instance, there are symbols of sickness next to each of the creatures. But having witnessed what happened to Mister Spock . . ."

The captain nodded. "I see what you mean. But then, that's the nature of this kind of work. Most of the surprises are in the beginning. The rest is just fine tuning."

Before she could respond, they were joined by Owens and Autry. Autry was carrying a berry; his companion was empty-handed.

Owens smiled crookedly. "I know what you're thinking. But I didn't drop another one. I didn't get the chance—there was only one left, and Autry was in better shape to handle it."

The security officer nodded, though he kept his eye on his burden. "That's the truth, sir. As far as we can tell, this is the last one." Gingerly, he deposited it at the fringe of their supply.

"No problem," Kirk assured them. "This should be all we're going to need."

Removing his makeshift throwing apparatus from his belt, he tested its integrity. The device passed with flying colors.

It was just a forked stick with a broad leaf wrapped around the prongs and secured with strong, slender vines. But if all went well, it would send the berries hurtling toward their targets, without submitting them to the pressure of the captain's grasp.

After all, he didn't want one of those things coming apart in his bare hands. The very thought made his teeth grind together.

"Karras," he said, "will be helping me. Everyone else, stand back."

"Sir," Autry interjected, "I can—"

"I know," Kirk told him. "But I've been watching you, and Karras handles these berries better than do any of the rest of us. Now, give me a wide berth. I've never done this sort of thing before."

As Owens and Autry retreated, the captain took up a position to one side of his ammunition. He held out his throwing contrivance and looked at the ensign. "Well?"

Frowning with concentration, she picked up a medium-sized berry—one of the sturdier-looking ones—and placed it on the broad-leaf part of the device. Then she fell back to where the others were already standing.

Kirk hefted the projectile. It felt secure in the V-shape.

For a brief moment, he had a vision of himself as he

must have looked to his companions: a grown man, a starship captain, holding a big berry in a toy made out of sticks and leaves and vines.

But this was no joke. This was serious. If he whipped his payload forward too quickly, he could wind up his own target. Hell, he could wind up deceased.

No, he had to forget about what he looked like and focus on what he had to do. Eyeing a large, fossil-covered area about halfway up the cliff wall, Kirk shifted his weight onto his back foot, paused, and let fly.

He could have done a lot worse. Though he missed the spot he was aiming for by a good couple of meters, the berry struck another sizable patch of petrified flora. On impact, it exploded, its bright red juices hissing and bubbling over the sheer surface for a meter or more in every direction. Then, as if the rock itself were bleeding, the stuff dripped in slender rivulets almost to the very ground.

White vapors rose from the affected area as the liquid did its corrosive work. After a little while, they stopped.

By then, Karras had come back to help him reload. "So far, so good," he commented, taking a little pride in his accomplishment.

She nodded. "Just watch your release point."

He regarded her. "My release point?"

"Yes. You let it go too soon. Take your time. Follow through."

"Follow through," the captain echoed, as Karras placed another berry in his throwing apparatus. This one, though a bit smaller, weighed noticeably more. It also felt more fragile, somehow.

Nonetheless, he took the ensign's advice. As he brought his arm forward, he was careful not to release his missile too soon. And he made a conscious effort to follow through.

The berry struck its target right on the nose. And

like its predecessor, it erupted in a helter-skelter burst of ruby fluids. Scalded, the fossil stuff yielded a rippling, ghostly haze.

*Follow through,* he thought. *Not a bad idea.*

And so it went. For nearly half an hour, Kirk threw the deadly fruits at the cliff wall. Thanks to Karras' care and his own concentration, not a single piece of ammunition went awry. And by the time they were done, the barrier looked like the victim of an angry god—or a very persistent vandal.

Only the very top of the sheer surface, perhaps a couple of meters altogether, was untouched. The captain had simply not been able to fling his organic bombs hard enough to send them that high.

No matter. He'd cross that bridge when he came to it.


Pike sipped at his tea, put it down on the small, wooden table beside him. His bare feet felt cold against the planks of the rugless wooden floor.

It was the middle of the night; the living room was dark, its furnishings forming a dark and mysterious terrain all around him. Outside, seen through the beach house's bay windows, the white of the surf was barely visible, the sky dense with low-hanging clouds the color of iron.

Vina was in the next room, sleeping. If she knew he was out here, she hadn't made any move to bring him back to bed. Pike was grateful for that.

He shifted his weight in his big, soft easy chair, listening to the slow, distant rumble of the incoming breakers. It seemed to give voice to his thoughts. His doubts.

After his meeting with the Keeper, the undercurrent of anxiety that plagued him had gotten worse. It had kept him tossing in his bed. And finally driven him out here, where he could at least make an attempt to understand it.

But really, what was there to understand? It all

came down to one question: How good a captain had he been? Not in the sense of carrying out his missions, because he'd certainly done that better than any of his peers. Or even in the sense of bringing his crew home alive—though for a while, toward the end of his stint on the *Enterprise,* that had been the standard against which he'd most often measured himself.

None of that was at issue now. What he was really asking himself was: What kind of *leader* was Chris Pike? What kind of example did he set for his crew?

He sighed. What kind indeed?

Pike had been too involved in the day-to-day regimen of running a starship to think about such things at the time. To project far enough into the future to realize that his every word and deed would stand as a model for his officers, who might go on to command starships of their own.

He put himself in the place of Spock or Tyler or Colt—or even Number One. Tried to look at himself through their eyes. And what he saw was someone who was too wrapped up in his duties, too burdened with his own sense of guilt and responsibility to teach anyone anything.

What kind of example? Not a very good one, he was afraid.

He was certain Boyce would have disagreed with him. The doctor would have said Pike was worrying too much—that he'd been a fine teacher, a shining example of how to handle oneself among the challenges offered by the stars.

But then, at least half of what Boyce used to tell him came under the heading of therapy, not heartfelt opinion. So even if the doctor were here, he would hardly be a reliable authority.

Pike sighed again, this time with a little more vehemence. What was the point of all this soul-searching anyway? What was done was done. If he'd given his people a few good tools, a few tricks to trot out in a pinch, great. And if he'd failed to give them *enough* tools, enough understanding of the way people and things worked . . . well, it was too late to do anything about it now.

Still, it was difficult not to harbor regrets. It was hard not to be concerned about them.

Pike wished he had it to do all over again. He'd have given them more. He'd have left them a better legacy.

# Chapter Twelve

BRADFORD WAYNE slipped through the narrow thoroughfares of the mining colony, alert for patrolling Merkaans. His goal, as on the previous night, was the administration building—the one that housed his office, or what used to be his office.

It was dark out. Dark and windless, and a little less cold than usual. Though both moons were up, they were occluded by a heavy blanket of clouds, the kind that sometimes came to hover over the colony and stayed for days, never quite lifting or breaking out into a storm. Just sitting there.

In this case, the cloud cover had overtaken them in midafternoon. As a result, the colonists had only been privy to the last bit of sunset—a sliver of reddish-orange glory visible between the gray blanket and the horizon—before the pale disc of Beta Cabrini dropped out of sight altogether.

Under normal conditions, there would have been complaints about that. Everybody looked forward to the sunsets here, and for good reason. They were truly spectacular, starting out with a mellow golden haze as the sun slid earthward, gradually igniting into scarlet here and there as wisps of clouds were caught in the deepening light, and finally exploding into a conflagration of oranges, greens, and purples.

However, Wayne had been willing to forgo the spectacle this time, if it meant that it would be more difficult to spot him on his nocturnal mission. The night before, he would have been easy to pick out in the moonlight; tonight, he wouldn't have that problem. He could merge with the shadows and feel a good deal more secure.

The administration building was only two blocks away. Not having seen any guards in the area the last time he made this foray, he didn't expect any tonight either. And so far, nothing had happened to thwart that expectation.

Of course, it still made sense to be careful. Wayne recalled the time Captain Pike led a landing party down to an ancient castle on Rigel VII—a castle that was supposed to be unoccupied, but was anything *but*. The price of discovering their error had been the lives of three of their comrades.

*Learn from your mistakes.* That was another lesson Pike had drilled into him, over and over again.

Except in the captain's case, he'd carried them around with him long after the learning process was over. Pike never forgave himself for the men he lost, even if it was through no fault of his own.

As a young helmsman, Wayne had been unable to understand that. If there was nothing one could have done, why blame oneself? But he understood now. Every colonist Dreen's men had cut down was a weight on the administrator's soul—a weight he'd probably carry to his dying day.

With any luck, though, the killing would soon be over. All he had to do was keep sending out his call at the appointed time, and before long someone would answer it. Someone, he hoped, who could—

Wayne cut short his reverie as he heard something up ahead. Freezing, he listened more intently. Yes, definitely something—the sound of distant laughter.

Clenching his teeth against his fear, the administrator pushed himself toward its source, creeping forward as silently as he could. The laughter seemed to be coming from around the bend—off to the right, he thought. Advancing carefully and quietly to the next intersection, he lowered himself onto his belly and peered around the corner.

It was hard to see—darkness being an impartial condition—but he managed to make out their silhouettes anyway. There were three of them. And if he'd harbored any doubts that the figures were Merkaan, they were dispelled by their postures and the length of their hair and the bulges of their weapons. Besides, who the blazes else would be out here?

". . . best time I ever had in my whole life," one said. "Of course, her family was due back pretty soon, so I didn't dare hang around. But before I left, she gave me a small token of her affection—a flowerstone ring she'd had since she was little."

"A good story, Marsal. So good I almost believe it."

"What? It's the truth, I tell you."

"Come on, now. A high-and-mighty lord's daughter took in the likes of *you?* Not likely."

"Damn it, it happened—every bit of it."

"Right. And you've got the flowerstone as proof, or did you manage to conveniently lose it?"

"Lose it? Not me. The damned thing was worth six months' pay."

"So you've still got it?"

"Hell, no. I sold it to a court fop for twice what it was worth. He said he could use it to blackmail the young lady. Served her right for socializing below her station!"

More laughter. The space between the buildings rang with it.

"You're a gallant one, Marsal, I'll give you that!"

Wayne withdrew a bit and sat with his back against the wall. The Merkaans seemed occupied. Possibly, he could slip past the intersection without their noticing him. Possibly.

He'd resolved to try when he saw movement in the street up ahead—a silent parting of shadows. The administrator grew cold with the fear that he'd been spotted. His heart started pounding against his ribs so hard it hurt. But just as he was about to give in to his panic and make a run for it, the newcomers—two of them—reached the intersection and turned abruptly to their left, in the direction of the first group.

"Uh—Second Balac! We stand ready, m'lord."

"Do you, Marsal? It didn't sound like it just a minute ago."

"A minute ago? We were right here, m'lord, watching the streets, just as you told us to."

"I don't doubt that you were here, Expeditor. My ears can attest to that. But watching the streets? I doubt it. How intently could you have been watching, when you were having such a good time telling your story?"

Wayne understood the situation now. The one called Balac—the acquisitor's right-hand man—was checking up on his people, making sure they were alert.

Why? Did Dreen expect the colonists to try something? Or was it just a routine precaution, the kind of thing they did as a matter of course?

In any case, security was likely to get tighter. Marsal's bunch was going to be on its toes. Wayne cursed silently.

He had a decision to make. He could try for the building now, while the Merkaans were still distracting one another . . .

But he might find it a lot more difficult to get out than to get in. And if he was caught, all their efforts would have been for nothing. The Merkaans would know that help was on the way and prepare accordingly. Dreen would destroy the communication device. And when a Federation ship arrived, it would be on its own, with no possibility of an assist from the colonists.

On the other hand, he could retreat and hope he'd have more luck the following night. Hell, it might not even matter. The rescue ship might still be a couple days' journey away, in which case tomorrow was plenty of time in which to contact them. But if the ship was close, hovering just out of sensor range until it could get in touch with him, and colonists died in the next twenty-four hours, colonists who might have lived if their rescuers had acted sooner . . .

Of course, there was a third option: He could withdraw into one of these buildings, sit tight, and hope the situation would change somehow—that Marsal's group would go off duty or leave to patrol another sector. And when they did, he would move in. But that assumed a lot. And every moment he stayed in the vicinity, he risked being nabbed by the Merkaans.

A tough choice. And he didn't have a whole lot of time in which to make it, considering the conversation between Balac and Marsal seemed to be winding down, and quickly at that.

Suddenly, Balac turned and began to retrace his steps. Frowning, Wayne scampered back down the alley. And he didn't stop until he was safely around a corner and into a storage building—one filled with canisters of maledoric acid, the stuff they used in extreme dilution to kill the nastiest strains of native bacteria.

Settling down, resting his back against one of the canisters, he took a deep breath and tried to relax. He decided he'd wait half an hour before going out to see if the Merkaans were still out there. If they were, he'd try again a half hour after that.

And again and again, all night long if need be.

Though even then, there was no guarantee he'd find a clear path to the communications unit.

The berries had done all it was hoped they'd do and more. It still wasn't exactly an easy climb, but Kirk now had projections around which he could wrap his fingers, and niches in which to lodge his boots. He just had to be careful to not slip on the red stuff that still clung to the wall.

"Ready, sir?"

"Ready, Mister Autry."

Kirk waited until the security officer had interlocked his fingers, then placed the sole of his boot in Autry's grasp. Finally, boosting himself as high as he could, he reached for a cavity formed by the corrosive action of the berry juice. His fingers probed and clung.

Fortunately, the juice lost its potency after a few seconds. Otherwise, the captain's idea of using it to eat out pockets of the fossil stuff might not have been a workable one.

Satisfied that he had a secure handhold, the captain sought a place for his free foot. After a second or two, he located one—a little farther to his left than he would have liked, but he was hardly in a position to complain. After all, he'd gotten his wish: they had a fighting chance of getting out of here, didn't they?

Taking his weight off Autry's hands, he clung to the wall. There was a second foothold just where he wanted it to be.

The next priority was another handhold. Scanning the cliff wall, he found one just above him. It seemed a bit too high, but he stretched and reached it.

"Damn it, Captain, you're doing it!" It was Owens' voice.

"Don't sound so surprised," Kirk told him. "You think I was *born* in a captain's chair?"

Laughter. "I don't think I ever thought about it, sir." More laughter.

*Foothold, handhold. Step up. Foothold, handhold. Slide up a little farther.*

It was going even better than the captain had hoped. And the berry juice wasn't slick at all. If anything, it was sort of tacky.

*Foothold, handhold, pull, and push. A little higher. And higher still.*

Kirk glanced over his shoulder at the far side of the hollow. It turned out to be a mistake. The sun, which was sitting just on the brink of the cliffs, stabbed at him with blinding intensity.

For a moment, he felt a wave of vertigo come over him. But he didn't panic. He waited for it to pass. And when it did, he was still clinging to the barrier, every bit as secure as before. Resolving to keep his eyes where they belonged, the captain resumed his climb.

*Foothold, handhold. Slither. Foothold, handhold.* Scraping his way up along the rock, using muscles he'd forgotten he had.

He remembered the summer he'd learned to climb, he and his brother Sam, in the hills of northern Colorado. Sam had taken a couple of spills, one a bad one. But Jim had been an expert from the beginning. He remembered feeling so comfortable on those aspen-dotted cliffs . . . as if he'd been climbing all his life.

*Sam . . .*

Kirk still regretted the way his brother had died. It was so unnecessary. If only someone had foreseen the spread of the epidemic to Deneva . . . if only they'd arrived a little sooner . . .

He sighed. This was the wrong time to be pondering such things. It was the wrong time for his mind to be wandering.

He was halfway up now. A fall from this height wouldn't kill him, but it might disable him. And he was the only experienced climber in the group. If he got hurt, their chances of escaping this place were virtually nil—and they'd have squandered all the hard work and good luck it took to get them this far.

*Foothold, handhold. Inch up. Foothold, handhold. Keep going.*

None of his companions were making any noise. None of them wanted to distract their captain. But he could sense their presence, feel himself buoyed by their hopes.

*Foothold, handhold. Boost. Foothold—careful now —reach and haul.*

Kirk's breath was starting to come hard. Pressing his cheek against the smooth, hard stone, he stopped and rested, gathering his strength.

And went on.

*Foothold, handhold*—but they weren't as easy to find as farther below. He hadn't been able to hurl as many berries up here. And even if he had, he saw, it wouldn't have done much good. The fossilized areas were few and far between at this height.

The captain looked up. How much farther? Five meters? Perhaps even a little less.

But the niches he could see above him weren't too promising. Too far from each other. And in a bad configuration.

He scanned the wall to his right. *Damn.* There were even fewer opportunities than on his present course.

To the left, then. Kirk nodded judiciously. *All right.* This was a little more like it. There were pockets of dissolved fossil almost all the way to the top. Not a lot, but maybe he wouldn't need a lot.

The trick was to get there. The first thing he did was move his right foot in line with his left, so that they shared the same recess. Luckily, the space was big enough for that. Then he moved his left foot out until it encountered another recess.

Now it was a matter of repeating the procedure with his hands. The captain's right went to the pocket currently occupied by his left. Next, his left hand reached for—

Suddenly, his left foot slipped. Kirk caught a glimpse of the terrain forty feet below as he hung on desperately with his right hand, his fingers straining to maintain their grip on the scoured-out stone.

But despite his best efforts, they were sliding out of position. Another second, maybe less, and he'd be plummeting down the face of the barrier.

And falling from this height, he *might* get killed.

Fighting down his fear, the captain searched for the handhold he'd been reaching for when his foot came loose. Finally, he found it, stretched—and missed.

A second time, he cast his left hand out—and felt his fingers hook in. Nor was it a fraction of a second too soon, for no sooner had he found purchase with his left hand than his right lost its grip.

His left knee slammed into the rock, sending pain shooting up his leg. But he tolerated it.

After all, he had his balance now. His weight was evenly distributed, even if it all depended on one hand and one foot. A moment later, he re-established his right hand's grip, securing himself even better.

Only then did he allow himself to breathe. And to appreciate how close he'd come to falling.

Finally, shrinking his field of concentration, Kirk groped for a place to put his other foot. Finding one, he tested it, then placed part of his weight on it. It held fine. He was in business again.

*Foothold, handhold.* His limbs were starting to tremble with his exertions. But he was almost finished. Just a little farther to go.

The captain could feel the sweat collecting in the small of his back. It was streaming down his forehead as well, and along the sides of his face.

*Foothold, handhold. Hoist. Foothold, handhold.* His muscles aching, he snaked his way up the cliff wall.

And abruptly found himself bereft of options. He'd arrived at, and was about to exceed, the altitude to which his missiles had ascended. After this, he was on his own.

Kirk looked up again and frowned. From below, it hadn't seemed like an insurmountable task to negotiate this last couple of meters. But up close, it seemed nearly impossible.

The only thing he had going for him was a stray root that stuck out over the edge of the cliff. Not far out, probably less than a foot. But it looked sturdy enough to bear his weight—if he could grab it, he could wrestle himself over the top.

The problem was how to get close enough to get a hold of it. Measuring the distance between his present handholds and the root, the captain estimated it to be a little less than his height.

Which meant that if his feet were where his hands were, he could stand up and reach the root. Of course, he'd have no niches in which to anchor his hands at that point. No way of holding on if one of his feet should slip again.

But there didn't seem to be an alternative. Taking a deep breath, Kirk brought his left foot up to an unoccupied pocket in the cliff wall. Then, letting go of his handhold, he reached for flat, featureless rock. And pressing his hand against it, hoped for the best.

It was even harder to let go of his other handhold, but he did it. Forcing himself upward with the strength of his left leg alone, he found himself hugging the sheer surface of the barrier with both hands—his footholds his only tenuous link with survival.

The root was closer, temptingly close. But not close enough. The captain knew that if he reached for it, he'd only be flirting with disaster. Squelching the impulse to try, he brought his left foot up again—to the highest niche in the rock. Then, again lifting himself with his left leg, he brought his right foot even a second time.

Now the root was right above him. Slowly, with the utmost care, he extended his right hand toward it. He stretched it as far as he could, without upsetting his already precarious position.

And fell inches short.

Kirk clenched his teeth. There was no way he was going to fail now. Not after coming so far, not when so much depended on it.

Bringing his hand down again, he let it dangle at his side. By now, his trapezius muscle would be tight as a clam from the strain he'd put it through. If he could get it to relax, he might be able to reach a little higher.

After a moment, he brought his arm up again. More. More. Again, he found himself just inches from his goal. He willed his trapezius to stretch . . .

*Got it,* he thought, as his fingers closed around the root. Making sure of his grip, he flung his other arm up. And as his boots slipped free of their footholds, his left hand found the root as well.

The motion swung his body out, then back again. He waited until the swinging stopped and he was hanging straight up and down.

*One last maneuver,* he promised his aching arms. *One last maneuver and you're home free.*

Scrabbling for purchase with his feet, he lifted himself close to the root—almost as if he were doing a chin-up on his high school horizontal bar—and kicked his left leg up as high and far as it would go.

As tired as he was, as muscle-sore, he didn't know if he'd have the strength to do this a second time, so he put all he had into it. Fortunately, it was enough. His heel hooked over the brink of the cliff. Twisting and groaning, he managed to pull the rest of him up after it.

For a second or two, he just lay on the sweet-smelling jungle grass, gazing up at the depths of blue sky. Then he heard the sound of distant clapping.

Peering down, he saw the others. They were applauding his effort as loudly as they could. His hand trembling, he waved in acknowledgment.

All in a day's work. That's what he'd tell them— just as soon as he could find the energy to sit up.

\* \* \*

It was time. Uhura acknowledged the fact as she sat at her station and awaited word from the mining colony, poised to respond with the message that Mister Spock had pre-recorded for efficiency's sake.

She glanced at each of the officers hovering over her. Only the Vulcan himself was really needed, in case the situation called for a different kind of response than the one he'd prepared. McCoy and Scotty were merely interested spectators. No, more than interested—*anxious* would have been a better word.

Not that she blamed them. When an opportunity like this came up, one had to take advantage of it. Hell, she was a little anxious herself.

"Where the blazes are they?" the doctor muttered.

"Give 'em some leeway," Scotty told him. "It's nae exactly a perfect situation down there."

Spock said nothing. As usual, his expression was unreadable.

A minute passed. Another. No communication. Not even a hint of one.

"Something's wrong," McCoy concluded.

The engineering chief was tight-lipped. He glanced at Spock.

The Vulcan continued to reserve comment.

A third minute past the deadline, Uhura looked up. "Still nothing, sir."

Spock thought for a moment. At last, he spoke up. "Send the message, Lieutenant."

McCoy regarded him dubiously. "But there's nobody listening," he protested.

"We do not know that," the first officer responded. "It is possible," he said, "that our ally has lost the ability to transmit, but can still receive."

*True,* Uhura conceded inwardly. *Not likely, but definitely possible.*

And how could it hurt? The Merkaan's monitors wouldn't catch it anyway. She followed orders. Spock's message went out on subspace, aimed at the fourth planet in the Beta Cabrini system.

The Vulcan nodded approvingly. "And continue to transmit at irregular intervals."

"Aye, sir."

McCoy shook his head. "I don't know. I've got a bad feeling that the Merkaans found our friend."

Scotty sighed. "Aye. I've got the same feeling."

Spock turned to them. "Fortunately, intuition is often far removed from fact." And without further comment, he descended to the captain's seat.

But before he left them, Uhura had caught the shadow of doubt in the Vulcan's eyes. There was no question in her mind: Spock didn't disagree with his fellow officers, he just hated to concede that their best chance to defeat the Merkaans had probably been snatched away from them.

It was the kind of emotional response Uhura would have expected from a human, perhaps, but not from someone like Spock. And she found *that* more alarming than anything else.

# Chapter Thirteen

"APPROACHING THE OUTSKIRTS of the Beta Cabrini system," Chekov announced.

From his position in the captain's chair, Spock saw the ensign turn in his seat, awaiting instructions. The Vulcan leaned his elbows on the chair's armrests, formed a peak with his fingers, and forced himself to come to grips with the realities of their situation.

It had been hours since he'd asked Uhura to begin transmitting his encrypted message to the colonists. Hours since the prospect arose that their ally in the colony had been silenced.

At the time, he had preferred to play the optimist, to believe that whoever sent the earlier dispatch had only been delayed, thrown off schedule. Nor did Spock rule out that possibility now.

But as time went on and there was no response from the colony, it seemed increasingly likely that Doctor McCoy's intuitive assessment was accurate after all. More and more, Spock had to admit the logic of the conclusion that their correspondent had been caught.

And that, of course, put matters in an entirely different light. Gazing at the forward viewscreen, which showed him the outermost planets of the Beta Cabrini system, the first officer knew what he had to do.

"Slow to impulse," he said. "We will proceed with caution."

"Slowing to impulse," the ensign confirmed, turning back to his controls. A moment later, the *Enterprise* dropped out of warp.

"Mister Scott," Spock called, "inform me when Acquisitor Dreen's triad appears on our sensor scan." Since Merkaan sensor technology was more or less on a par with that of the Federation—or had been the last time the Vulcan had a chance to inspect it—the *Enterprise* and the enemy would probably record each other's presence at approximately the same time.

The engineer responded from his bridge post. "Aye, Commander."

"Lieutenant Uhura, be prepared to hail the Merkaan flagship."

Uhura sounded relieved at the temporary respite from her attempts to raise the colony. "Acknowledged, sir."

There was no longer any reason to delay their confrontation with Dreen. In fact, there was every reason not to.

If their correspondent had been caught, his life would be in peril. Knowing the Merkaans, so would the lives of others. Dreen was a firm believer in violence as a deterrent; he would not be inclined to limit punishment to the guilty. Nor would a single death assuage his anger.

Unfortunately, with no way to communicate Spock's plan to the colonists, he was forced to fall back on the strategy of the bluff to carry out their mission. It was still not a strategy in which he had a great deal of confidence, McCoy's exhortations to the contrary . . .

Just as he thought that, he felt his control slipping

away again. The foreign substance in his body was trying to reassert itself.

Clenching his fists, Spock fought it, driving it down —not all the way, but enough so that he could maintain his composure before those on the bridge. Not only because he was their leader and he needed their confidence, but because the idea of revealing his weakness in public was anathema to his Vulcan sensibilities.

Fortunately, the attack hadn't taken him by surprise this time. He'd felt it coming, and knowing what to expect, he was able to fend it off—to postpone it, at least for a little while.

"Mister Sulu," he said, hoping no one noticed the tension in his voice. "Estimated time of arrival within sensor range of Beta Cabrini Four."

It took the helmsman a couple of seconds to reply. "At our present speed, three hours and forty minutes."

Spock nodded. "Thank you, Lieutenant." Three hours and forty minutes was long enough to retire to his quarters, regain command of himself and still have ample time to apprise his colleagues of his plan. But first, he needed solitude—rest.

"Mister Scott," he said, rising, "you have the conn."

If the engineer knew anything was amiss, he didn't show it. "Aye, sir," was his only response.

Doing his best to conceal his infirmity, to maintain a semblance of self-possession, Spock rose and walked stiff-legged to the turbolift. It seemed like an eternity before it came, and before he could avail himself of the compartment's privacy to slump against the wall and moan in pain.

Gritting his teeth, he gave the lift its instructions. It began to move.

By the time it reached the deck he required, the punishment had gotten worse, much worse. Incredibly, no one saw him as he lurched out of the compartment, doubled over, and staggered into a bulkhead. Or as he made his way to his quarters, step by agonized step.

He could feel the alien serum claiming its due. He could feel its wild, throbbing insistence—its horrific call to every organ in his body.

To join in the mounting frenzy. To accelerate its function far beyond its flesh-and-blood limitations.

Finally, he reached the door and touched the panel beside it. He watched it give way and swung himself inside.

As soon as the metal panel whispered closed behind him, Spock took a deep, rasping breath and collapsed. He lay on the floor, shuddering, wondering how so brief a journey as that from the turbolift to his quarters could have wrung so much out of him.

Up on the bridge, he'd believed he could control the acceleration better for having experienced it before. His assumption was incorrect.

If anything, it had been more difficult.

Now, as he lay on the deck, he felt old memories rising again within him—brought to the surface by his recent preoccupations, taking on shape and substance as they broke into the light . . .

Image: Captain Pike, sitting on a bluff against a sweep of startling green sky. His arms are folded against the weather, the collar of his regulation-gray jacket pulled up around his ears.

He is overlooking a distant cluster of reddish-brown, animal-hide tents. Thin streams of black smoke climb from the roofs of the dwellings into the sky, finally dissipating on the winds.

The captain's expression is one of longing. He does not appear to notice Spock's approach, and then he turns to peer down at him, as if he had been aware of it all along.

"What is it, Lieutenant?"

"Sir, the others have all beamed up. Number One suggests that we do the same, before the natives catch a glimpse of us."

"The research files have all been uploaded?"

"Yes, sir. And the shuttle has been destroyed. There is no trace of it to give away our visit—or for that matter, the emergency landing to which the survivors of the research vessel were forced to resort."

Pike regards him with curiosity. "And why didn't Number One tell me any of this herself? Does she think my communicator's on the blink?"

Confusion. "The 'blink,' sir?"

The captain smiles. "Dysfunctional, Spock. Inoperable."

"I see. In that case, no. I do not think she believes that."

"Then why the personal service?"

"It was at my suggestion. You appeared to be meditating. I thought I could soften the impact of the interruption."

A pause. "I appreciate that. You know, Spock, you're getting more human all the time. And that's a compliment, so don't go getting all huffy on me."

"'Huffy,' sir?"

"Never mind." He turns in the direction of the tents again. "Damn, but I envy those people. All they do is hunt and fish, without a care in the world." He shakes his head. "I hate planets like this one. They remind you of how simple life can be."

"Simplicity is not always a virtue, Captain. There is much to be said for complexity . . . for subtlety. And for diversity."

Pike grunts. "I've had enough of those things to last a lifetime. Sometimes I wish I could just . . ." He doesn't finish the sentence. It's as if he's unable to, as if it would take him over a line he isn't ready yet to cross.

Abruptly, he curses. His eyes assume a new intensity. "If you could do anything, Spock, be anyone, what would you choose?"

It is a question to which Spock had not given much thought. Nonetheless, the answer is clear. "I would do what I am doing now, sir. And I would be what I am."

The captain casts a glance at him. "I should've known you'd say that. You were born to be in Starfleet, Lieutenant."

"I have heard the same said of you, Captain."

"Have you?" He seems to find that amusing. "Maybe once, I would've agreed with that." High above them, something very much like a bird makes circles against the sky. "But now I'm not so sure."

It is colder up here than in the woods below. Sir . . ."

The captain nods. "I know. I'm coming." He flips open his communicator. "But one day, Spock, one day . . ."

Image: Number One, her face paler than usual, her feelings more closely guarded. Her dark eyes are fixed on the three-dimensional chess set in front of her; she moves the pieces as if she is concentrating on the game, playing both sides. But even Spock can tell that her mind is elsewhere.

He has heard of her father's death. On his own world, it would be impolite for him not to express his sympathy. After all, they are colleagues, even if they have known each other for only a few days. But then, Vulcan and Earth are two different places, and he is not knowledgeable about Terran mourning protocols.

Slowly, deliberately, the first officer lowers her white bishop two levels and takes a black rook—a move she should have made a turn before, and Number One is an impeccable player. It is a further indication of how distracted she really is.

He wishes to approach her, to express his sorrow. But he decides not to do so until he is certain of the proper behavior. The last thing he wants is to offend her.

Transporter Chief Abdelnaby is on duty. Perhaps he will have some time to enlighten a non-Terran. Spock resolves to head for the transporter room.

And then Number One looks up at him. Apparently, she has become aware of his stare. Silently, her expression asks the reason for it.

He swallows. The opportunity for enlightenment vanishes. One way or the other, he must confront her now.

Spock walks over to where she is sitting. He stands before her. And while his mind races, trying to come up with a way to solve his problem, he stalls for time by pretending to be intrigued by her chess game.

"An interesting situation," he remarks.

"You think so?" The first officer gestures to the seat beside him. "Would you like to take a side?"

He nods. "Thank you." He sits down. "Have you a preference?"

Number One shakes her head. "No."

"Then I will be black," he decides, "which would make it my turn."

"That's right. Then, you were watching."

"Pardon me. It is only that I find the game familiar —we play it on Vulcan. And there is so little that is familiar to me here."

"No need for an apology," she tells him.

He looks at her, wondering if he should just come out and express his dilemma. But as before, he is concerned that he will give offense. Stymied, he turns his attention to the game.

He sees immediately that he is at something of a disadvantage. A moment later, he moves a black pawn up one level, placing it in the white bishop's path. It is an attempt to lure her piece into a slowly closing trap, and therefore achieve a balance of power.

Number One appears not to notice his scheme. She takes the black pawn.

Spock responds by bringing his queen up a level. The trap is set.

She cannot avoid it. No matter where she moves her bishop, the Vulcan will take him with one piece or another.

The first officer frowns. Accepting her bishop's fate, she maneuvers to make Spock pay a price for it. The piece that takes the bishop will itself be taken—though at this point, all the Vulcan need sacrifice is a pawn.

But he hesitates. It occurs to him that the situation presents an opportunity he had not anticipated.

After an unusual amount of time has passed, Number One prods him. "Make your move, Mister Spock. This is only a five-year mission."

He looks up at her. "My apologies. I was only considering the nature of your loss. The *magnitude* of it."

She returns the look—and understands, he thinks. The skin between her brows crinkles subtly. "It was . . ." She stops, then starts again. "It will be a significant loss. But the game will go on."

He nods. "Nonetheless, it is regrettable."

"Yes," the first officer agrees, "it is regrettable."

Spock notices that a tear has collected in the inner corner of one of her eyes. She does not wipe it away. Slowly, it draws a path down the side of her patrician nose.

"It's still your move," she reminds him.

Grateful for the opportunity fate handed him, Spock takes her bishop. But from that point on, Number One's game improves considerably.

Image: Abdelnaby, half a dozen rivulets of ale still clinging to his lips, his large, expressive eyes awash with sincerity. As he leans forward over the table, he holds a mug of what he described earlier as "Dinartian poison."

"You're a good man, Lieutenant." The background

noise is considerable, but Abdelnaby manages to make himself heard. "I mean a *damn* good man. I mean—well, hell, you know what I mean, don't you?"

Spock believes he does. "Thank you," he replies.

The transporter chief points with his chin to Spock's mug, which is still full except for the sip he took half an hour ago, which he found rather disagreeable. "And it's a good thing you decided to abstain. This stuff sneaks up on you like an Aldebaran horned serpent."

Not for the first time this evening, Spock finds he requires a translation. It seems to him he *always* requires an explanation. He wishes now his mother had made more use of English idioms during his formative years.

"Sneaks up?" he asks. "In what way?"

Abdelnaby turns to Pitcairn, the man who will soon replace him as transporter chief. He shakes his head. "In what way, he asks!"

Pitcairn chuckles, his blunt features spreading good-naturedly. He angles himself toward Spock in a decidedly conspiratorial manner. "What 'Naby means, Lieutenant, is that you can get plastered before you know it."

Over in a distant corner of the large room, a musical device of indeterminate origin begins to add to the din. The Vulcan wonders why anyone would want to come here at all, much less on shore leave.

He sighs. " 'Plastered?' "

Abdelnaby leans forward even more. "Inebriated, Mister Spock. *Drunk.*"

Understanding dawns. "I see," the lieutenant says. He regards the transporter chief. "Then why, may I ask, do you partake of it?"

Abdelnaby stares at him for a second or two. Then he straightens in his seat. "That's a fair question. A very fair question." He turns to the other human. "Mister Pitcairn, why *do* we partake of it?"

Pitcairn thinks, shrugs. "Because we . . . um . . ."

He shrugs again. "Now that you mention it, I'm not sure myself."

The waitress comes by. "Can I get you gents a refill?" she inquires.

Abdelnaby and Pitcairn look at one another. "No, thanks," the transporter chief tells her. She leaves—a little disgruntled, Spock thinks.

The musical device in the corner becomes louder than ever. The sound it makes is almost painful.

Silently, the Vulcan promises himself he will avoid shore leaves in the future.

Image: Yeoman Colt, grinning like a child, her eyes fairly dancing with delight. She drops to her haunches, reaches out, and stops just short of touching her half-meter-high duplicate.

The duplicate drops to its haunches as well. It peers up at her, smiles—even goes so far as to stretch out its hand, all in perfect mockery.

"It's so *cute*," she says.

Tyler grunts. "Yeah. Cute—and weird as hell. Sort of makes your hair stand on end." He looks around. "Damn! There's another one."

Spock follows his gesture and sees the replica of Sellers that emerges from the bushes. Sellers approaches it—and it him.

"Careful, all of you," the Vulcan warns yet again. "We do not know their intentions."

Sellers chuckles. "Come on, Spock. How much harm can they do? Hell, they're only about sixteen inches tall." He turns to the yeoman, and so does his tiny double. "Hey, Colt, can my kid play with your kid?"

She scowls at him. Her Doppelgänger follows suit. "Not if it means I've got to let you within twenty feet of me."

Tyler laughs. "Serves you right, Sellers. Subtle you're not."

"No need to get all self-righteous about it," Sellers

counters. He glances at Tyler. "I could tell a few stories about you too, old man."

"Wait a minute," Colt says. "Maybe Sellers has something."

"You mean like a disease?" Tyler quips.

"No," the yeoman continues. "Maybe these *are* supposed to be our kids, in a way." She considers the doll-like figure in front of her. "What if our likenesses are the equivalent of protective coloring? By assuming the appearances of small humans—children, if you will—these life forms are keeping us from wanting to eat them. I mean, few species eat their young, right?"

Spock nods. "A good theory, Yeoman."

Sellers looks at them. "It is?" He points to his replica, who points back. "You think these look like children, Lieutenant?"

"No," the Vulcan replies. "But many life forms are born almost identical to their adult counterparts, just smaller. Humanoids, of course, undergo significant physical changes as they mature, but humanoids need hardly be the rule when it comes to this planet."

"How about a little test?" Tyler suggests. He turns to Sellers. "You walk away from it and I'll walk toward it."

"What's that going to prove?" Sellers asks.

"It'll tell us if this is a proximity thing. I'll bet it turns into me once I'm the closest one to it."

"All right," Sellers says. "Let's try it."

As the humans approach one another, Sellers' duplicate begins to tag along behind him. Then, as his path crosses Tyler's, it stops. Its appearance seems to ripple for a moment, then re-stabilize. It now resembles the navigator.

"Ah-*hah*," Tyler exclaims. "You see?"

"Too bad," Sellers comments. "It used to be so much better-looking."

Tyler kneels. His double does likewise. "I have to admit," he says, "these things look a lot less weird when they're *you*." He reaches out, as Colt did before him. The replica responds in kind. "I guess they are kind of cute."

"Mister Tyler . . ." Spock cautions.

"I know," the human returns. "Be careful. But we're here to find out about this place, aren't we? So, in the interest of science . . ."

Reaching out a little further, he touches his finger to his doll-like counterpart's.

There is a flash of blue light and a crackling sound. Tyler is flung backward. He rolls as he lands and comes up clutching his forefinger.

"Yeow! What was *that*?"

Instinctively, Spock comes to his aid. He examines the finger.

"Second-degree burns," he concludes.

Leery now, Colt withdraws from her own duplicate. "I guess these things have more than one kind of protection going for them."

"So it would appear," the Vulcan remarks.

Tyler's replica just holds its finger and looks at them.

Image: Doctor Philip Boyce, the muscles in his temples working, his blue eyes fixed on his patient's sharply boned face as he runs his tricorder over him. He curses, shaking his head gravely.

Spock wonders what has gone wrong. The doctor's treatment of the Horidian monarch seemed to have gone so well until now. But the Horidian prime counselor, standing a couple of feet behind Boyce, asks the question before the Vulcan can.

"Doctor Boyce? Is something amiss?"

The doctor turns and glares at the Horidian prime counselor. "No. Nothing is amiss. Nothing at all." Frowning, he puts his tricorder away.

The Horidian approaches his lord's bedside. "He will live?" he asks Boyce, requiring clarification. "The treatment was effectual?"

"We were in time," the doctor explains gruffly.

"The patient is doing fine. He'll probably lead a very long and active life."

The Horidian nods. "His grandeur will be appreciative."

Boyce grunts. "Bully for his grandeur."

He stands up, glances one last time at the sleeping form of Harr Harath, undisputed ruler of three worlds, and curses again beneath his breath. Then he heads for the door, which has been watched by two of the monarch's burly, deaf-mute bodyguards since they entered Harath's quarters nearly an hour and a half ago.

At the time, Harath had been in great pain, afflicted with Bendal Fever, which he had contracted in an attempted conquest of the planet Bendalia more than a year earlier. The fact that Bendalia was a Federation member-world—and that Starfleet had to step in and thwart the invasion—had not stopped Pike from responding to Harath's request for help. Or more accurately, the request of Harath's prime counselor.

After all, it was a chance to establish friendly relations with the Horidians. And with Harath in particular—despite his penchant for conquest, not to mention the bloody domestic purges on which he'd built his long reign.

With time, Pike believed, the Federation might have a positive influence on the Horidians. And maybe even on Harath. In any case, it was better to have such an individual's gratitude than his enmity.

As Boyce leads Pike and Spock out of the room, the deaf-mute guards glance at them suspiciously. The Vulcan ignores them. He is much more interested in the conversation between his fellow officers, which begins as they emerge into the hallway.

"Damn it, Doctor, wait up," the captain says.

Boyce stops and glowers at him. "What?"

"I want to know what the hell you thought you were doing in there."

"Why?" the doctor asks.

"Because it's my duty to find out, that's why." More softly: "What's wrong, Doctor?"

Boyce shakes his head. "As I told that Horidian quack a moment ago, nothing is wrong."

Pike persists. "It doesn't sound like nothing."

"You mean the swearing? The expression of disgust?" Boyce looks like a man who has just eaten something extremely distasteful. "Why am I so fearfully angry?" His mouth twists. "Because the damn patient is doing *fine.*"

Pike doesn't back off. "And that rankles you?"

The doctor nods, his eyes still blazing. "Yes, it does." He chuckles bitterly. "Why? You think I'm letting my personal feelings get in the way of my oath? My promise to heal the sick, regardless of how hateful I may find the one I'm healing?"

The captain pauses meaningfully. "You tell me," he says.

"All right. I'll tell you." Boyce looks back in the direction of Harath's unmoving form, still visible through the open doorway. "I did want to kill him. I thought of all the lives that might be saved, the misery that might be avoided, if just this one time I injected the wrong medicine. Hell, I wouldn't even have to give him anything deadly. I could just let him wither away from his disease, and no one would be the wiser."

Pike swallows. "We're not gods, Doctor. We don't have the right to decide who lives and who dies."

Boyce explodes. "Don't you think I *know* that? Lord, Chris, it scares the hell out of me!" He is shivering with emotion. "A chief medical officer who lets his feelings get in the way of his duty . . . is a chief medical officer who should be considering some other line of work." He shoots the captain a desperate look. "Maybe it's a sign I've been at this too long, Chris. Maybe . . . ." He hesitates, confused. "Oh, hell. Let's just get back, all right? Let's just get back. I think I need to be alone for a while."

Without waiting for a response, the doctor turns

and resumes his march toward the main entryway and the courtyard beyond it, where they will have a chance to beam up without the interference of Harath's protective forcefield.

Pike looks at Spock and sighs. The Vulcan wonders if the *Enterprise* will shortly have a new ship's surgeon —either by Boyce's choice or the captain's.

For now, however, all they can do is follow the doctor out of Harath's palace.

Gradually, Spock emerged from the flow of images, of memories. Gradually, his mind cleared—and he became aware enough of his external self to realize he was completely drained and his uniform tunic was crumpled where he'd lain on the floor.

He would need to change his clothes. He would need to collect himself.

Most of all, he would need time to work out the details of the exceedingly difficult task ahead.

# Chapter Fourteen

KIRK MOPPED THE SWEAT from his face and neck with his uniform top and sunk down onto his haunches. It was still hot, though the sun was dying in the west.

It had taken longer than he'd expected to work out a way to bring the others up after him. A large tree would have helped, but there weren't any trees in the immediate vicinity, and those not in the immediate vicinity were too heavy to lug through the jungle on his own.

Vines had been their other option—an even better one, considering Owens' injury and the difficulty he'd have in trying to climb anything. But whereas thick, strong vines had seemed rather plentiful at the beam-down site, they were far from abundant around here.

In the end, Kirk had to explore the jungle around the hollow for hours before he found a suitable source of vines. Cutting them down with a sharp rock and hauling them back to the cliffs took nearly another hour. And then it had been necessary to tie them together—not an easy task, given their thickness and lack of flexibility.

By the time he anchored the end of his vine ladder to a short, stout tree, the sun was already approaching the horizon. And he had a decision to make.

They could set out now and try to find the beam-down site. Or they could spend another night here and wait until morning.

On one hand, he was eager to get a move on. He still had the feeling that there was something to be found at the site, some clue that would help them if they got to it in time.

On the other hand, it might not be prudent—or useful—to launch an expedition just before dark. After all, they had only a vague idea of where the beam-down site might be. Trying to find it at night wouldn't only be difficult—it could be dangerous as well.

Particularly if the creature was still around. And if Karras' theory about the creatures being stationary was correct, it wasn't going anywhere.

Then, of course, there was Owens' communicator, telling him he was wrong about the need for haste. Telling him that they had all the time in the world to get back to the area of the ground collapse.

For the fourth or fifth time since he recovered it at the cliff's edge, he pulled out the device and hailed the *Enterprise*. For the fourth or fifth time, there was no response.

The captain almost wished the damn thing had been broken when he'd found it—damaged when he'd tossed it up here the day before, despite Karras' findings to the contrary. It would have helped to explain why they hadn't been rescued yet.

But it was working fine, just fine. Kirk shook his head.

Down below, his people were preparing for the journey ahead of them. Owens was binding Autry's sugar stalks in bundles. Autry was testing the vine, making sure it would support his weight. And Karras, bless her scientist's heart, was making additional records of the glyphs with her tricorder, not knowing when she'd have a chance to see them again in person.

The captain stroked his jaw, where a distinct stubble was starting to emerge. Despite everything, he still wanted to return to the beam-down site, and quickly. But there was a limit to what kind of risks he would take in order to accomplish that.

Reluctantly, he made his decision. They would hold off until morning to begin their search. Kneeling at the brink of the pit, he called down to tell them.

At his place behind the navigation board, Chekov whistled softly. Nor was he the only one who expressed admiration for what he saw on the main viewer.

"Impressive," Sulu muttered. "*Very* impressive."

Of course, they'd seen the recorded image of a Merkaan triad in their briefing with Scotty. But that recording was ten years old. The ships it had showed them bore little resemblance to what confronted them now.

This triad was trim. Spartan. Lethal-looking. And while appearances could be deceiving, that was seldom the case when it came to starship design. Who would make outward alterations if they weren't part of an integrated technological overhaul? Why bother?

Unfortunately, there was no way to be sure what new technologies the Merkaans had embraced. Not without a violent confrontation—and that was, at best, a last resort.

Spock's voice brought the Russian back from the realm of speculation. "Mister Scott, is there any evidence that the Merkaans are scanning us?"

The chief engineer shook his head. "None yet, sir. But that's only if their sensors operate the same way ours do—and there's no guarantee of that."

Spock took the information in stride. If there was

something wrong with the Vulcan, Chekov thought, he certainly wasn't showing it. He seemed as much in command of himself as ever.

Perhaps Leslie's nurse friend had been mistaken. It wouldn't be the first time a newcomer had blown something out of proportion.

Finally, Spock came to a conclusion. "Lieutenant Uhura, hail them."

"Aye, sir," the communications officer responded.

Chekov and Sulu exchanged glances, but said nothing. Obviously, Spock was willing to give up the advantage of surprise. But why? For what greater benefit?

Then the ensign answered his own question. If the *Enterprise* initiated the contact, it would imply confidence. Particularly if that contact came as a surprise to the Merkaans.

But that would be useful only if Spock were going to—he stopped in mid-thought, and smiled. So *that* was his strategy.

Uhura's voice rang out. "The Merkaans are responding to our hail, sir. They have instructed us to stand by."

Before Uhura had finished, the Merkaan vessels began to move, to alter their configuration into one that addressed the *Enterprise*'s angle of approach.

Spock's tone remained matter-of-fact, unconcerned. "Inform them that we will do no such thing, Lieutenant. Can you give me visual contact?"

A pause. "Aye, sir."

"Please do so."

A moment later, the bridge of the Merkaan flagship filled the borders of their viewscreen. The chair in the center of the tableau was empty, but a rather officious-looking Merkaan stood beside it.

"I am Tezlin," he announced, "third in command. Who dares approach?"

Spock ignored the question. And when he spoke, his

manner belied the importance of not only Tezlin himself, but of any threat he might represent.

"Attention, Merkaan vessels. This is the U.S.S. *Enterprise* under the command of First Officer Spock. The planet which you are orbiting is a Federation colony. You have no authorization to be here. You will depart at once."

Yes, Chekov mused, definitely a bluff. Normally, he would have approved of the approach wholeheartedly. After all, it had worked for them in the past.

But that was when James T. Kirk had been sitting in the captain's chair. How well could a Vulcan—even one who knew Kirk's techniques as well as Spock did—carry off such a gambit?

The ensign steeled himself. Time would tell.

Leaning back in Bradford Wayne's chair, Dreen gnawed on the *nargah* egg that had been transported down from the *Clodiaan.* As he savored its simultaneously sweet and sour flavor, the egg's bright red yolk spilled down his chin in thick, slow gobbets.

Of course, he could have fabricated his meal in the humans' food processing units, just as his men had been doing since their arrival on Beta Cabrini. But the units were apparently incapable of creating Merkaan delicacies without a certain amount of reprogramming, and the acquisitor hadn't wanted to wait that long for a taste of home cooking.

Popping the warm, juicy remains of the egg into his mouth, he licked some yolk off his long, gray fingers. It wouldn't make sense to waste any of it, not when the ship's supply was so low.

Soon, however, the *Clodiaan* and its sister vessels would be returning to the homeworld in triumph. He would lay at their owner's feet the kind of haul few acquisitors ever managed. Nineteen tons of duranium, the dilithium, and perhaps a human slave or two, just for novelty's sake. Dreen's cut alone would make a tidy sum.

Then he could have all the *nargah* eggs he wanted. He could eat *nargah* eggs from dawn till dusk.

What's more, this expedition would make a name for him. Maybe some other owner would offer him a meatier commission—enough to buy a triad of his own, if only a modest one. Or at least an estate on one of the manor moons . . .

The buzz of his communicator interrupted his reverie. Wondering what his third-in-command might want, he reached across the desk for the device, pressed the appropriate stud, and answered: "Yes?"

"Acquisitor, we have a ship on our screens. A Federation ship."

Dreen leaned forward, trying to control the racing of his pulse. Bad luck, but he could deal with a single starship. That was the advantage of having three vessels at one's disposal.

In fact, he almost looked forward to testing the destructive capabilities of his triad. Until now, that opportunity had not presented itself.

On the other hand, it meant he could not linger here much longer. Given enough time, the Federation could muster a veritable armada. And he did not wish to endanger such a valuable haul—or, for that matter, his newly revived status as an acquisitor.

"Indeed," he said, stretching the word out. "Have they hailed you yet?"

"No. We have—your pardon—they have just this moment begun to hail us."

"Good. Initiate defense posture. And relay any messages to me. I want to hear them."

"As you wish, Acquisitor."

Dreen waited a few moments. Then a voice came over his communicator—a voice much too calm and fluid to belong to a Merkaan. Strange, he thought. It was almost as if he had heard it before, though all human voices sounded much alike to him.

". . . is a Federation colony. You have no authorization to be here. You will depart at once."

A bluff. He'd expected that. But he wouldn't fall for it. He knew only too well how wily human starship captains could be.

For a moment, there was silence. Then the message began all over again, from the beginning. "Attention, Merkaan vessels. This is the U.S.S. *Enterprise*—"

Dreen leaped to his feet. *Enterprise!* Had his ears deceived him?

"—under the command of First Officer Spock."

*Spock!* He pounded his fist on Wayne's desk. This was too good to be true! Spock was the Vulcan who had beamed aboard the *Mananjani* ten years before—the one who had distracted the acquisitor while a pack of humans invaded his engineering level.

"The planet which you are orbiting has been claimed by the Federation. It is a—"

Dreen's head was swimming. He cradled it in his hands, willed it to stop.

Fate had dropped this opportunity in his lap. He had to take advantage of it, but not too eagerly. He couldn't let the *Enterprise* slip off the hook.

"Tezlin!" he barked.

His third-in-command responded immediately. "Yes, Acquisitor?"

"Have me transported back to the ship—immediately!"

A pause. "Acquisitor, that will require lowering the shields."

"It's all right. The Federation ship will not attack; it's vastly overmatched and its people know it."

This time, there was no pause. "As you wish."

"And Tezlin . . ."

"Acquisitor?"

"Transport me directly to the bridge."

"Of course."

While Tezlin relayed the order to the transport hall, Dreen tried to put his thoughts in order. Spock seemed to be in charge now, though he had described himself as first officer, not captain.

Did that mean Pike was gone? Perhaps promoted to a headquarters capacity at some point in the last ten years? It was certainly possible.

Perhaps he'd just been killed. The acquisitor liked that possibility a lot better. In any case, he'd find out soon enough.

Suddenly, he was enveloped by the sizzling scarlet fog that presaged transport. The next moment, he was back on the *Clodiaan*, standing on the bridge beside Tezlin. The third-in-command raised his fist in salute, but Dreen barely noticed. He was too intent on the forward monitor that dominated an entire wall—and the image he saw there.

He smiled. It was *him*—it was the Vulcan.

"Spock," he hissed between clenched teeth, relishing the sound as if it were the homeworld's finest liqueur. "How good to see you again."

The first officer of the *Enterprise* regarded him, unshaken by his presence. Abruptly, Dreen was reminded of that most irritating of notions—that he would meet his enemies once again and they would fail to recognize him. But as it turned out, his fear was unfounded.

"Acquisitor Dreen," Spock replied. "I wish I could say the same, sir."

The Merkaan laughed. He was going to enjoy this.

"And where is your captain? The one called Pike?"

"He no longer serves on this vessel. However, that is not germane to the situation at hand."

"I see. Then you haven't come to reminisce, Spock? And here I thought you were paying me a visit after all this time."

"You know the reason we are here, Acquisitor. You have unlawfully seized a Federation colony. You must withdraw immediately."

"And if we do not?"

"We will have no choice but to use force."

Something in the Vulcan's tone gave Dreen pause. After all, it had been ten years since he'd last encountered a Federation ship. Was it not possible that the humans and their allies had devised some new tactical system that would tip the scales in their favor?

Yes, it was possible. But even if the acquisitor was wrong about Spock—even if the Vulcan was telling the truth—it really didn't change anything.

Dreen much preferred death to a return to the homeworld with his cargo holds empty. No manner of dying could compare to being shamed so a second time.

And as for his ships, his men—they were of no real consequence. If they went up in a blaze of glory, it was probably more than they deserved.

Dreen turned to face Tezlin and spoke softly, so those on the *Enterprise* couldn't hear. "Issue instructions to our sister ships. Surround the enemy. Do not permit them to escape. If they fire even a warning shot, disable them."

Tezlin's brow creased. "Disable, Acquisitor? Not *destroy?*"

"You heard me correctly. Under no circumstances is the *Enterprise* to be annihilated. I have a score to settle with the Vulcan."

Tezlin bowed slightly. "As you wish," he said, and went to carry out Dreen's orders.

When he turned around again, Spock hadn't moved from his place on his ship's bridge. Nor had his expression—or rather, lack of expression—shifted one iota. He was as impassive as ever.

"I sincerely hope," the Vulcan said, "that you are directing your ships to remove their personnel in preparation for departure."

Dreen shrugged. "I am doing nothing of the sort. If you would be so cooperative as to consult your instruments—"

He was interrupted by an exclamation from one of the *Enterprise*'s bridge officers. No doubt, the man had just picked up the movement of the Merkaan vessels. As the acquisitor watched, the information was relayed to Spock, who continued to face the viewscreen.

He finished his remark: "—you will see that you are surrounded. Be advised, we will obliterate you at the least provocation, so it is very much in your interest to not provoke us."

Now, Dreen told himself, they would see if Spock could back up his threat. He awaited the Vulcan's response with great interest.

"Acquisitor," Spock began—with not the least hint of fear in his voice—"the force to which I referred is not limited to this ship alone. As we speak, a number of other Starfleet vessels are converging on these coordinates."

"Ah," Dreen said, "I see." In other words, there was no secret weapon, no newfound technology. In short, as he had suspected, the Vulcan had been bluffing—and he had exposed the bluff.

"It would not be wise to take the prospect lightly," Spock advised him.

"No," the acquisitor declared mockingly, "I would never do that. But I must tell you, I have done some research on the dispersement of your Starfleet vessels. And I believe that by the time reinforcements arrive, I will be long gone. If I were you, First Officer of the *Enterprise,* I would be more concerned with the immediate future. For that is the time frame in which I will decide the fate of the colonists—and your crew as well."

The Vulcan frowned ever so slightly. "You must know I will not allow you to harm the colonists."

Dreen chuckled. "And *you* must admit—if only to yourself—there is little you can do about it." He paused as a tempting little scheme came together in his mind. "Unless, of course, you are willing to be my guest."

Spock regarded him. "Your guest?"

"Yes. Do you find that idea unappealing?" He felt his features tighten with unexpected anger. "That wasn't always the case, I remember. There was a time when you were only too eager to take advantage of my hospitality, though as I recall, your stay with me was cut short."

The Vulcan seemed to be considering the matter. "I do not understand," he said—though he understood perfectly.

"Here," the acquisitor offered, "let me spell it out for you. You and I have unfinished business. Surrender yourself and I will give you my word—before all my officers here—that I will harm neither the colonists nor your crew for the duration of your visit."

Spock's eyes narrowed. "And that you will leave Beta Cabrini with its mineral stores intact?"

Dreen shook his head. "No. The bargain is as I described it. Take it—and see your people safe—or reject it and accept responsibility for the consequences. The choice is yours, *First Officer.*"

The reply came sooner than the acquisitor had expected. "I will accept your offer," Spock said. He glanced at one of his officers—not the man who had apprised him of the Merkaan ships' maneuver, but another. "Mister Scott, you have the conn. I will be beaming over to the Merkaan flagship."

There was something in the Vulcan's voice that gave the acquisitor pause. An eagerness, and it made him wary.

It occurred to Dreen that transporting Spock to his vessel might not be such a good idea. After all, wasn't that how Pike had tricked him? By convincing him to momentarily lower his shields—so that the humans could take over the *Mananjani?* If one human transport technician could take advantage of that tiny window of opportunity, maybe another could as well.

"I've changed my mind," the acquisitor announced.

Hearing him, Spock turned back to Dreen. "I beg your pardon?"

"You heard me. I've decided that you will be my guest on the planet's surface. I'm sure your transport technician knows the coordinates for the colony's main square; you will appear there in exactly five minutes. Any deviation from my instructions will be construed as an act of treachery—and I need not tell you how I will respond."

The Vulcan nodded. "No, you have made yourself quite clear on that count."

"Good. Five minutes, then."

Showing Spock his back, Dreen eyed his communications technician. With a cutting motion just underneath his chin, he ordered the Merkaan to discontinue contact. A moment later, the technician complied.

Turning back to the screen, which now displayed an image of the hated *Enterprise* flanked by the *Clodiaan*'s sister ships, the acquisitor grinned. Tezlin came up beside him and was quiet, awaiting his superior's orders.

"Alert the transport technician," Dreen said finally. "I want to return to the administrator's office."

His third-in-command nodded. "As you wish." He began to withdraw.

"Oh, and Tezlin—"

"Yes, Acquisitor?"

"I want my beasts transported as well."

Tezlin looked at him. If he was puzzled by the instruction, he didn't ask for an explanation. Then again, perhaps he had an inkling of what Dreen was up to. "It will be done," he said, and went to see to it.

# Chapter Fifteen

As THE VIEWSCREEN REVERTED to a vision of Dreen's flagship, the Vulcan turned to make his way to the turbolift. However, Mister Scott was moving toward the lift as well. The engineer looked horrified.

"Mister Spock!" Scotty hissed softly. "Sir, are ye sure ye want to go through with this?"

The Vulcan cocked an eyebrow. "I appreciate your concern, Commander. It is, however, unnecessary."

Behind Scotty, the turbolift doors opened. "I dinnae like it, nae one bit. Lord knows what kind of torture that slitherin' Merkaan's devised for ye."

Spock straightened. "I have no illusions as to Acquisitor Dreen's intentions, Commander. However, I have been tortured before. And if I can keep him occupied long enough, it may aid our cause." He paused. "What is more, he does not make idle threats. If I do not beam down as he instructed, he will make the colonists pay with their lives."

The engineer scowled, leaning closer. "But in your present condition, sir . . ."

The first officer shook his head emphatically. "My condition," he breathed, "is not a factor here."

196

Mister Scott's point was quite valid, of course, though he declined to admit it. Under normal circumstances, he might have survived whatever revenge Dreen had in mind. However, with his mental and physical powers already taxed to the limit . . .

Scotty looked sympathetic, but not quite believing. "Aye, sir. Whatever ye say." His eyes glittered. "Good luck, Mister Spock."

Spock started to discount the concept of luck, good or otherwise, but he thought better of it. "Thank you," he said instead.

Then he slipped past the engineer and into the turbolift. A moment later, the doors closed, eclipsing Spock's view of the bridge and its personnel. He programmed a destination: the transporter deck.

As the compartment began to move, the Vulcan sighed. His bluff had failed. Doctor McCoy had been wrong; he was incapable of perpetrating a falsehood in the manner of Captain Kirk—or for that matter, in the manner of Captain Pike.

Perhaps there were some things one could not learn, no matter how capable his mentor. The legacy of his commanding officers—the men he'd admired and tried to emulate—had been, for all practical purposes, wasted on him.

At least he could take comfort in one thing: he was leaving his people with a plan. No matter what happened to Spock, Uhura would continue to try to convey it to the colonists. And with any *luck,* she might still succeed.

His thoughts turned to Captain Kirk again. Quite possibly, Spock told himself, he would perish at the Merkaan's hands without ever knowing what had happened to his friend. Of all his regrets—and he had his share of them—that would be the most difficult for him to bear.

With the most subtle of decelerations, the turbolift came to a halt. However, it had not yet reached the destination he'd indicated.

It was too bad. He had hoped for privacy, so he could marshal all his resources in anticipation of his meeting with Dreen. Apparently, he was to be denied that.

*Please,* he asked silently, *let it not be someone who knows what I am about to do.* Spock was not one for lengthy good wishes—or for that matter, lengthy goodbyes.

The doors opened, revealing the first officer's companion for the duration of his lift journey. If Spock were simply a human, he would have cursed.

McCoy smiled as he got in. The doors closed behind him.

"What's the matter?" he asked. "Did you think I was going to let you face that bastard on your own? Without your personal physician?"

"How did you hear so—"

"So quickly?" McCoy shrugged. "Let's say a little bird told me—someone who's concerned for your safety—and leave it at that."

Spock frowned. "What do you hope to gain by this?"

McCoy regarded him. "Look, Spock, it's pretty obvious this Merkaan bastard has more in mind than tea and crumpets. This is his chance to get his revenge, and he's going to milk it for all it's worth."

Spock raised an eyebrow. "Your point, Doctor?"

McCoy snorted angrily. "My point, you—" He stopped himself, touched the stud on the lift's control panel that halted its operation. "My point, *Commander,* is that you're sick, whether you want to admit it or not. And sooner or later, Dreen's going to realize that. He's going to see he's gotten damaged goods, and he's going to feel cheated. After all, how can he enjoy the full measure of his revenge if you're too weak to endure it?"

The Vulcan hadn't thought of that. However, it didn't change anything. Not really. He still had to accede to the acquisitor's demands.

Perhaps Dreen would renege on their agreement when he learned the truth about Spock's health. But in the meantime, he'd be giving Uhura a chance to contact the colonists, a chance to carry out his plan.

"I know what you're thinking," the doctor told him. "You're telling yourself it doesn't matter. All you want to do is buy some time." He swallowed. "Well, I'm going to expand your purchasing power—Lord help me."

Spock shook his head. "I fail to see—"

"I'm going to keep you alive," McCoy interrupted. "I'm a doctor. I can do that. And Dreen's going to let me—hell, he's going to demand I do it—because as surreptitiously as I can, I'm going to let him know what's ailing you. I'm going to make it plain that his revenge won't be as sweet as it should be."

The Vulcan felt his jaw muscles tighten. McCoy's arguments made sense, in a bloodless sort of way. But he still couldn't let the doctor place himself in deadly danger. He could—and would—do this on his own.

"I cannot let you do that, Doctor."

McCoy scowled. "Because it doesn't make sense?"

"No. Because it would involve placing yourself in jeopardy."

This time, the human's ire flared. "Damn it, Spock, you think you're the only one around here who's allowed to risk anything? You know, I may have to face Jim again some day. And I won't be able to do that if I let you beam down there by yourself."

McCoy sighed. "Besides, it's bad enough to have to face what you're going to face. Someone should be there with you. You know." He hesitated. "A friend."

Spock recognized what it had cost the doctor to utter those last two words. He nodded. "I appreciate the gesture, Doctor. However, you do not know what you are getting into."

McCoy grunted. "And you do?" His voice dropped an octave. "Look, Spock, you want to buy some time for your plan to work, right? I can help you do that. I can keep you going."

The Vulcan saw that it was no use arguing. Rather, he reached for the control panel and restarted the lift.

McCoy looked at him. "I don't hear any protests," he said. "Does that mean I've convinced you?"

As the lift came to a halt, Spock did his best to look resigned. The doors opened. "After you," he told the doctor, indicating the corridor beyond.

McCoy started out of the compartment—but didn't get very far before the Vulcan reached for the juncture of his neck and shoulder. A quick application of pressure, and the ship's surgeon went limp.

Spock caught him and lowered him gently to the floor. Then he reprogrammed the turbolift for a distant deck and stepped out. As the doors slid shut, he strode down the corridor toward the nearby transporter room.

He wondered who the "little bird" was—Uhura? Scotty? He was touched by their regard—and, of course, by McCoy's as well—though it bordered on rebellion. He would have to remonstrate with them for this behavior when—and if—he returned.

Before he finished the thought, he'd entered the transporter room. Lieutenant Kyle was waiting for him; he looked up at Spock's arrival, then hesitated, surprised.

The Vulcan paused before the transporter console. "Yes, Lieutenant?"

Kyle nodded. "I thought Doctor McCoy was going to accompany you."

"That was the plan," Spock explained. "But the doctor was unavoidably detained."

Kyle frowned, but dropped the matter. Relieved, the Vulcan proceeded to the transporter platform and mounted it. As he turned about, he saw the human making last-minute adjustments in his control settings to allow for orbital drift. Finally, Kyle finished.

"Ready, sir?"
"Ready, Lieutenant. Energize."

Spock had never before visited the Beta Cabrini colony, but he had seen others of its sort throughout the Federation. The blockish buildings, the thoroughfares all laid out at right angles, the barren and not-so-distant hills with their cornucopia of valuable mineral resources . . . it was all in agreement with his expectations as he materialized in the colony's main square.

Likewise, the armed Merkaans among whom he had arrived; unfortunately, they were also just as he had expected. Two of them had their weapons out, trained at his midsection. The others leered, glared, or peered at him with curiosity, according to their individual natures.

Dreen was nowhere to be seen—not that Spock had expected him to be there waiting for him. The acquisitor placed a high value on appearances. It would be much more dignified for him to be contacted when the prisoner arrived.

True to form, one of the Merkaans tapped a device on his belt. "The Vulcan is here," he announced, his breath issuing from his mouth in the form of vapor.

There was no response via communicator. But then, responses were for underlings, according to the Merkaan code of behavior. Spock had learned as much during his brief stay on the *Mananjani*.

He wondered if Dreen was still on his flagship, or if he'd already beamed down. The Vulcan didn't have to wonder long.

A door opened in what was probably the colony's administration building. Dreen emerged, followed by one of his officers, and walked slowly across the square. He was smiling, and the closer he got to his captive, the broader his smile got.

Finally, they were face to face. Without warning,

the acquisitor backhanded Spock across the face. *Hard.* The Vulcan tasted blood.

"That," Dreen said quietly, the calm in his voice belying the emotions he must have been feeling, "is just a sample of what I've got planned for you."

Spock met his gaze dispassionately. "You may do what you wish with me—as long as you adhere to the remainder of our agreement."

The acquisitor looked at him. "You doubt my word?"

The Vulcan shook his head. "I only wished to make certain we understand each other."

Dreen grunted—neither a confirmation nor a denial of his part in the accord. He turned to the officer who had followed him across the plaza.

"Balac, search him. Make sure he doesn't have any devices the *Enterprise* can use to trace his whereabouts."

The one called Balac did as he was told. Spock endured the examination stoically, trying not to let on how repulsed he was. If they'd known how Vulcans avoided physical contact, they would only have used the knowledge against him. And there were some forms of torture he dreaded more than others.

At length, Balac stepped back. "He has no devices," he told Dreen.

The acquisitor nodded—to Spock, not to his officer. "Good. And smart, Vulcan. *Very* smart."

At the far end of the plaza, a group of colonists in heavy coats appeared. At first, Spock thought they might have slipped into the vicinity of the square of their own volition—even that they might have come to intervene on his behalf.

But no. They were herded by armed guards, driven into the square like so many beasts of burden. The Vulcan stiffened as he saw how the humans were being treated.

He eyed Dreen. "You said you would not harm them."

"*I* don't see them being harmed," the acquisitor insisted. "But then, harm is such a subjective concept."

Spock saw it would do no good to protest. He remained silent, apparently unaffected.

"No response?" the Merkaan prodded. And when he saw that he couldn't get a rise out of his captive: "Just as well. You shouldn't waste your energy arguing; you'll need it all for what's ahead."

As the colonists were brought into the center of the plaza, Spock felt a small shiver of recognition. One of them was Bradford Wayne.

The man's shock of bright red hair had receded a bit from his forehead, and there were threads of gray mixed in with the red. Care lines had taken hold in his face where none had existed before, nor was he quite as slim as he used to be. But it was Wayne nonetheless. Their eyes met and the Vulcan knew that the administrator recognized him too.

It was good to see Pike's old helmsman. Reassuring, even, in an odd sort of way. Never mind the fact that he hadn't known the man well; Wayne was a piece of the past, a familiar element in a sea of uncertainty. The Vulcan imagined he saw the same feeling in the set of the administrator's jaw.

We have shared dangerous times before, they seemed to say to each other, and we prevailed. Why not again?

However, a moment later, Wayne turned away. And Spock guessed why. Dreen wouldn't necessarily know that the administrator had been part of Pike's crew. Giving that fact away would only put Wayne's life in jeopardy—and deprive the *Enterprise* of a valuable ally planetside.

"Ah," the acquisitor said, "my friends the colonists." He looked directly at Wayne. "I thought you would like to see this." He gestured in Spock's direction. "May I introduce Spock, first officer of the *Enterprise*. He is here to 'rescue' you."

The Vulcan remained silent, aloof. He would have to let Dreen entertain himself, no matter the cost to his dignity. The most important thing was that he not give away his relationship with the administrator.

Dreen came over to Spock, touched his chin with a long forefinger and turned his head gently to one side. "Heroic, is he not? Too bad his efforts were doomed to failure." He made a clucking sound with his tongue. "Just as any attempt to rescue you would be doomed."

Wayne frowned. Maybe their captors didn't know how much Vulcans hated to be touched, but *he* did. "Why," he asked Dreen, "are you showing us this?"

The Merkaan leveled a stare at Wayne. For a moment, Spock was afraid he would have the man killed. Then the moment passed, and Wayne was still standing there.

"Because," he explained amiably, "I want to disabuse you of any hopeful notions you may have harbored. I wanted you to see how limited your options really are."

Those weren't his reasons at all, Spock knew. He was just trying to maximize the Vulcan's humiliation, to get the most out of their bargain.

Abruptly, Dreen turned to Balac. "My *mesirii,*" he said. "What is the delay?"

The Merkaan activated his communicator again. *Mesirii?* Spock was unfamiliar with the reference. Nor could he glean anything from Balac's brief exchange with the flagship . . .

"The acquisitor wishes to know why his *mesirii* have not yet been transported." A pause. "I see."

Dreen looked at him. "Well?"

Balac returned the look. "It seems," he reported, "that there was a difficulty with the beasts. It occurred en route to the transport hall."

The acquisitor glared. "They've been hurt?" he barked.

Balac shook his head quickly. "No, not the *mesirii*.

However, those who were escorting them were mauled. One badly; he will lose a hand."

Dreen relaxed visibly. "Ah. Well, perhaps that was to be expected. After all, they were scheduled to feed."

Spock was beginning to understand what *mesirii* were—and what role they might play in the acquisitor's plans for him. It was not a pleasant prospect.

And there was still the possibility that his sacrifice would be for nothing. If only he could know for certain that Uhura would get through, that his scheme would be carried out.

It was a bitter irony; the man with whom he wished to communicate was standing not twenty paces from him, yet he could not convey even the brief message he'd formulated.

Then again, why couldn't he? The message was designed to be undecipherable. And if it didn't seem appropriate to just blurt it out, it was because Spock had a command of English idiom the Merkaans did not.

"Boyce's birthday," he said out loud.

Dreen looked at him. "I beg your pardon?"

"Boyce's birthday," the Vulcan repeated casually, fixing his gaze on the acquisitor. He didn't dare look in Wayne's direction, for fear that his intent would be divined.

Dreen tilted his head slightly. "And what does that mean, First Officer?"

Spock shrugged, trying to remember how Kirk had "sold" various deceptions in the past. The incident with the Fesarius came to mind, in which the captain had successfully put across the idea that the *Enterprise* had a self-destruct system based on corbomite—a non-existent material.

Drawing on Kirk's maneuver for inspiration, the first officer explained: "It is simply an expression."

"What kind of expression?"

The Vulcan didn't relish the prospect of outright lying. But it seemed inevitable, under the circumstances.

Then someone else spoke up. It was Wayne. "It's something we say when someone is badly hurt—in this case, the fellow who got mauled. It's a way of voicing sympathy."

The acquisitor didn't take his eyes off Spock. "I am speaking," he said, with a subtle edge in his voice, "to the Vulcan. Mister Spock, did you not know the one to whom you referred is a Merkaan, the same as those who hold you here at the point of our weapons? Does your sympathy extend that far?"

"My sympathy is not restricted to my friends," the first officer replied truthfully.

Dreen regarded him with what seemed like genuine curiosity. "Really. I didn't know that about you, Spock. Is this true of all Vulcans?"

"Most," Spock told him.

"And your expression—'Boyce's birthday'—this is a Vulcan saying? Or one the humans came up with?"

"On a starship, one picks up many expressions devised by other cultures." Again, quite true, in and of itself.

The acquisitor seemed inclined to pursue the matter further, until a scarlet mist appeared in the plaza. It gave rise to four material forms—two Merkaans and a pair of sleek white quadrupeds. The Merkaans appeared nervous, to say the least. And more than a little glad when the beasts started padding gracefully in Dreen's direction.

Balac tapped his communications unit. "They have arrived," he said simply. A second or two later, the animals' escorts vanished again.

The acquisitor lowered himself to one knee, obviously glad to see the *mesirii*. The feeling seemed to be mutual. For a little while, the Merkaan and the beasts nuzzled one another.

Then, Dreen looked up at Spock. He was smiling again, a hungry sort of smile. A *deadly* smile.

With a tilt of his head, he indicated the hilltops to the north, visible past the colony's one- and two-story buildings. "You see those highlands, First Officer?"

The Vulcan nodded. The hills seemed close, but that might have been the effect of the clear, cold air.

"In a moment, I will have you transported there—far from this square, far from any of the colony's facilities—to a place where no one can help you. An hour later, I will transport to the same place. Then, with the help of my fine beasts, I will hunt you down and slaughter you like an animal. Which, if you think about it, as I have had occasion to think about it, is no more than you deserve."

There were hushed reactions of horror from the colonists. Wayne protested: "You can't do that, Acquisitor."

Dreen stood suddenly and looked at him. "I can, Mister Wayne—and I will. And though I am inclined to be patient with you for all the help you have given me, you have tested that patience twice in the last several minutes. See that you do not test it again."

Wayne bit his lip. He dared not go any further, and Spock recognized the fact. "It is all right," the Vulcan said. "I knew what to expect when I struck the bargain."

"Come," the acquisitor told his pets. He urged them toward Spock. "This is the one. Familiarize yourself with him."

The *mesirii* approached him, flicking long, black tongues. They sniffed his trouser legs, scrutinizing him with their large, golden eyes, growling low in their throats. Their breath froze in billowing clouds.

The Vulcan could see their teeth—slender, sharp, and dangerous-looking. He recalled what Dreen had said about the beasts' having missed their last feeding.

"Careful," the acquisitor warned them. He looked

up at Spock. "I'd hate for the chase to end before it had a chance to begin, eh?" He slapped his thigh, and the *mesirii* returned to him.

By the way they moved, the Vulcan could tell they were fast. And probably long-winded as well. The kind of tracking beasts who could not only find their quarry, but run it to ground and finish it off.

"Now, remember," Dreen remarked, "our deal is only in effect for the duration of your visit. When you are dead, your visit is over, so if you truly care about the welfare of these humans, it is in your interest to remain alive as long as possible."

"I assure you," Spock replied, "that would have been my intention in any case."

The acquisitor grinned. "You say that now, Spock. But as the chase wears on, you may feel otherwise."

He gestured to Balac, and Balac made contact with their ship again. "Transport the Vulcan to the prearranged coordinates," he instructed.

As Spock felt a tingling—the side effect of the Merkaan transport process—a thought came to him: he was glad he had prevented Doctor McCoy from beaming down—or the *mesirii* might have been hunting two Starfleet officers instead of one.

"Doctor? Doctor McCoy?"

He opened his eyes. A pretty, young brunette was gazing into them.

*If this is a dream,* he mused, *I don't want to wake up. I just want to enjoy it.*

And then he remembered.

"Don't move," the brunette counseled. She was wearing the uniform of a security guard. "I've called for a doctor."

"Damn it," he croaked, getting to his feet. *"I'm* a doctor—and I feel fine." They were in an open turbolift. Stepping out into the corridor, he looked around. They were no longer on the transporter deck. And—

"Where the hell is Spock?"

The woman watched him reset the lift controls. She shook her head as the compartment doors closed and the lift began to move. "Mister Spock, sir? He beamed down to the colony a good fifteen minutes ago."

McCoy's eyes narrowed. "He did *what?*"

The security officer looked at him. "Is something wrong, sir? Something I should report?"

The doctor snorted. "Damn right there's something wrong. That son of a—" Choking on his own fury, he had to stop for a moment. "He gave me that Vulcan nerve-pinch of his and took off alone."

The woman seemed to reach a decision. "Maybe I *should* report this," she said.

"Report all you want," he told her. "I'm not going to let that pointy-eared computer get away with this." As the lift stopped and the doors opened, he started off purposefully in the direction of the transporter room.

The security officer hurried after him. "Doctor, you were unconscious. Wouldn't it be a good idea to—"

Abruptly, he rounded on her. *"Enough.* When I get back, I'll be glad to tell Mister Leslie what a fine job you're doing. But for now, leave me the hell alone. I've got to preside over a blasted suicide."

He left her standing there, confused. Striding the length of the corridor, he barely gave the doors a chance to slide aside before he entered the transporter room.

Mister Kyle did a double-take when he saw him. "Doctor McCoy . . . ?"

"I've no time for explanations," the doctor barked. "Have you still got Spock's coordinates?"

The transporter chief nodded. "Aye, sir. But Mister Spock said—"

"Never mind what he said. Beam me down—now." And for emphasis, he advanced to the transporter platform and stepped up.

Still a little hesitant, Kyle re-activated his equipment. "This'll take just a second or two," he advised. When he was finished, he looked up.

"Are you sure you know what you're doing?" he asked the doctor.

McCoy scowled. It was a good question. Nonetheless, he replied: "Damn right I'm sure. Let's get on with it. You know, energize and all that."

"Whatever you say, sir."

The doctor gritted his teeth. He hated transporters; if he could have walked down to the colony, he would have. But Spock needed him.

A moment later, he was caught in the transporter effect—and it was too late to turn back.

# Chapter Sixteen

SPOCK MATERIALIZED on the crest of a barren hill among other barren hills. The terrain seemed the same in every direction, all the way to the horizon.

It was colder here than in the plaza. But then, he had expected that. Taking a deep breath, he put his thoughts in order. The more thinking he could do now, while he had the chance, the better. Later, there might not be time for such luxuries.

The first officer knew he was north of the colony—he'd determined that back in the main plaza. By the sun's position in the sky and his knowledge of the planet's rotation, gleaned in the *Enterprise*'s library, the Vulcan reckoned that north was . . . *that* way. Which would mean the mining facility was in the opposite direction—due south.

A return to the colony, even by a circuitous route, was out of the question. Far better to head north, to lead Dreen away from the colonists, who could then implement Spock's plan without the acquisitor stumbling on them accidentally.

Of course, that presupposed that Wayne had understood his reference to Boyce's birthday. And that he could apply it to the problem at hand. And also, that Spock had not forgotten something which would prevent the scheme from being carried out.

However, the Vulcan couldn't worry about that now. It was out of his hands. All he could do was prolong the chase—in Dreen's words, "remain alive as long as possible." If nothing else, he knew that until he was brought to ground, the colonists were safe.

How much time could he hope to win for his cause? How long before the *mesirii* caught up with him?

It was difficult to say. It depended on too many factors. The amount of distance he could put between himself and this place in the next hour was crucial. But a bigger consideration was the degree to which he could maintain control over his metabolism, in the face of considerable physical exertion.

As Spock prepared himself for his trial—quite possibly the last he would ever know—it occurred to him that he might be setting out in the wrong direction entirely. He was relying on the Merkaan transport technician's having deposited him in the area Dreen had indicated. If he'd been beamed to some other area, south of the colony, or east or west—

No. It was unwise to engage in fruitless speculation. He had determined the most likely set of circumstances; he had no choice but to follow them to their logical conclusion.

Taking off at an easy lope to conserve his strength, Spock made his way north along the crest. The land crawled by on either side of him; up ahead, he knew, there had to be a slope.

In the days before Surak brought his philosophy of peace-through-logic to the masses, Vulcans had committed any number of atrocities in the name of conquest. To Spock's knowledge, however, they had not hunted one another. Even his most warlike, bloodletting forebears hadn't stooped so low as to treat their brothers like beasts.

But then, even in the blackest of ages, no Vulcan had ever lived who was quite as cruel as Hamesaad Dreen.

Bradford Wayne pounded the control console of his mobile extraction unit. "Damn. What was it Spock was trying to tell me?"

Gross put a hand on the administrator's arm. "Calm down, Brad. You want to get us killed down here?"

Wayne looked at his partner, then at the shaft ahead, and frowned. The man was right. Getting ticked off wasn't going to help matters any.

Paying more attention to the meanderings of the mining tunnel, he said: "All right, I'm calm."

"Then let's go over it one more time," Gross suggested. "From the beginning."

The administrator nodded, glad that he'd decided to partner with the geologist again today. Gross had an active mind, and that was what he needed right now.

"One more time." He took a deep breath. "Boyce was the chief medical officer on the *Enterprise*. We served together for a number of years. Three, I think. But there was only one time we celebrated his birthday."

"Because he didn't like to make a big deal of it," Gross added. "He hated to draw attention to his age."

"That's right. Anyway, this was a surprise— Captain Pike's idea. Great party. And Boyce had a good time, even if he didn't want to admit it."

"And that's it?"

The administrator shrugged. "That's all I remember. As I said before, I couldn't stay for the whole thing. I had to get up to the bridge."

As Wayne guided the vehicle around a turn in the shaft, the cab tilted. Out of the corner of his eye, he could see Gross shaking his head.

"Baffling," the geologist remarked. "And yet, it must mean something, or why would your friend have ventured so much to say it?"

Why, indeed? The administrator concentrated, but nothing came to him.

Here Spock was risking his neck out in the hills, no doubt trying to give them time to carry out his plan. And Wayne was dropping the ball.

"You mentioned a cake," Gross went on. "Was there anything written on it?"

Wayne shook his head. "Just 'Happy Birthday,' or something like it." He sighed. "Nicest-looking cake I ever saw, though. I remember that much. And I never even got a taste."

Gross sat back in his seat. "Did anything significant happen after you left?"

The administrator shrugged. "I don't think so. Why?"

"It occurs to me," the geologist replied, "that Spock may not recall your leaving early. He may be referring to something that you were never present to observe."

Wayne grunted. "There's a rosy prospect."

Gross turned to him. "Or maybe he *does* recall that you had to leave. And that's what he's talking about— the circumstances of your departure." His eyes narrowed. "Was there anything unusual about it?"

Actually, there was, now that the administrator thought about it. "It wasn't my regular watch. It was an emergency of some kind. The helmsman on duty had gotten sick."

"From what?" the geologist prodded.

Wayne thought some more. Abruptly, he remembered. "There was gas in the ventilation system. It was thick and yellow, and it had temporarily disabled a couple of the bridge officers." He nodded, visualizing it. "I recall now. A container of durochloric acid had spilled over some of the cargo—some raw turacite we were carrying. The combination of the acid and the mineral had produced the gas." Suddenly, as their vehicle came in sight of the surface, it hit him. He knew what Spock wanted them to do.

"Brad? What is it?"

"I've got it figured out, damn it. I *know* what Spock was telling us." Wayne bit his lip, formulating a method of attack even as he spoke. "Listen, we're going to need some help. Johansson, Piniella—maybe some of the others delivering ore to the processing plants." He smiled grimly. "The Merkaans are so bloody eager to get their hands on our goods. Well, we're going to give them a little more than they bargained for."

Kirk reached down and took hold of Owens' hand. Bracing himself, he pulled the man up onto the jungle floor.

As the captain and Autry stood back, Karras helped Owens extract himself from the sling they'd made for him out of vines. Getting to his feet as best he could, the crewman caught a glimpse of the hollow from above.

"Damn," he said. "It looks like an even longer haul from up here."

Autry rubbed vine bark off his hands. His palms were red and a more than a little raw from helping to hoist Owens up.

"Longer than you want to know," the security officer jibed.

Kirk nodded in agreement. "Next time, Mister Owens, you might want to consider not damaging your leg. As a favor to the rest of us."

Owens grinned ruefully. "Believe me, sir, I'm going to take your advice. Next time, that is."

"That's good to hear," the captain told him. "In the meantime, make yourself comfortable. Barring any unforeseen circumstances, we'll be back before too long."

Owens looked at him. "I beg your pardon, sir?"

Kirk had expected the man to be unhappy, of course. But he'd thought about it the night before and it didn't make sense for Owens to come along. He'd only slow them down.

Besides, someone had to remain in the area. They'd been signaling the ship from this place for nearly two days now. If Scotty did send a rescue team, he'd more than likely send it here.

The captain explained as much. And Owens had no choice but to accept it.

Autry turned to Kirk. "Sir, request permission to stay behind as well. If anything happens—another ground collapse or something—Owens has got that bad leg and—"

The captain held a hand up. "Enough said. I was going to ask either you or Karras to keep Owens company." He clapped Autry on the shoulder. "Since you volunteered, it makes the choice a little easier."

Autry nodded—and with that settled, the captain looked to Karras. "Let's go, Ensign. The day's not getting any younger."

She returned the look. "Aye, sir."

And they started off through the jungle, heading west—which was, according to their best estimate, the direction in which they'd escaped from the ground collapse.

Sunlight filtered through alien branches. Sharp and pungent fragrances wafted to them on the wind. Even with all the uncertainties that nagged at him, it was difficult for Kirk not to notice the languid beauty of the place.

"Captain?"

He turned in response to Karras' questioning tone and tried not to dwell on the way the shadows played on the bones of her face. "Yes, Ensign?"

She appeared to have something on her mind. Something serious. "I went over those hieroglyphs again last night." A pause. "You remember how you said that in this kind of work, most of the surprises came in the beginning?"

"I do."

"Well," she told him, "I think I found another one. A surprise, I mean."

Kirk pushed aside a low branch that hung in their way. "And?"

"I may have found a way of helping Mister Spock."

That got his attention. He stopped dead in his tracks. "Go on, Ensign. I'm listening."

Karras held out her tricorder, showing him a record of some glyphs on the device's screen. "You remember these?" she asked.

The captain took a closer look. "The creature-glyphs, right?"

"Right. Now look at *this.*" She bumped up the magnification. "See those marks? Right beside the creature symbols?"

Kirk nodded. "What are they?"

"Those are the sickness glyphs—the ones I told you about yesterday. If you notice, every sickness glyph has a companion—another character right beside it, that looks like the sickness glyph on its side."

The captain saw what she was talking about. "I'm with you so far."

"At first," Karras said, "I thought those companion characters might just be a different kind of sickness glyph—you know, for emphasis. Then I dug a little further into Dombraatu etymology. And when something is placed on its side like that, it seems to be a negation of the concept in question."

Kirk looked up from the tricorder screen. "A not-sickness. A cure."

"Yes. And it comes from the creature itself. If I'm not mistaken, via a second sting."

"A second sting?" the captain repeated incredulously.

"Yes." She showed him some more etchings, smaller ones. "See? The process leading to sick and not-sick is the same. Identical."

He grunted. "A second sting. And that's the blasted cure."

The ensign nodded. She looked into his eyes—and seemed to linger there, as if caught and unable to free herself. Nor did it seem she *wanted* to free herself.

Suddenly, Kirk was more aware then ever of the way her hair caught the sunlight—of the fullness of her lips, and the green depths of her eyes.

He was more aware of the jungle around them, with its subtle but exotic fragrances, and the warm breeze that ran through it, making the leaves flutter as if with excitement.

Something was happening here—something he couldn't allow to go any further. The captain cleared his throat, steeling himself.

"Good work," he told her, sounding as clinical as he possibly could.

Inwardly, he winced. That wasn't what he wanted to say. That wasn't what he wanted to say at all. But this was still a *mission*.

Karras regarded him for a second or two. Then, obviously disappointed and embarrassed, and maybe a little confused as well, she averted her eyes.

"I guess we should get going again," she suggested, her voice steady.

"Absolutely," he responded. Damn. He sounded like some stuffy admiral—not like Jim Kirk. But he didn't know what else to say. *Ah, the things I do for Starfleet.*

And without another word, they resumed their trek through the Octavian jungle.

Dreen looked at McCoy across the desk of the colony administrator. "And why, may I ask, does Spock need a doctor?"

McCoy cleared his throat, all-too-aware of the

armed Merkaans standing behind him. *Sell,* he told himself, *sell.*

The Merkaan's brows came together. "I asked a question."

The doctor frowned. "Spock's sick, Acquisitor. He's *very* sick."

Dreen was interested. "Sick in what way?"

McCoy told him about the serum in the Vulcan's blood and what it was doing to him. "As a result," he finished, "he's not going to last very long out where you've sent him. So, if it's revenge you're after, you may be disappointed. It's not going to be very satisfying. Not with Spock in that kind of shape."

The Merkaan nodded. "And so you followed him down here—risking your own life—in an attempt to provide me with more of a contest. How nice of you to be so concerned. How altruistic."

The doctor shook his head. "Not altruistic at all, Acquisitor. You made a deal. You said as long as Spock complied with your wishes, you wouldn't harm the colonists—and Spock wouldn't have beamed down here if he didn't think you'd keep your word."

Dreen stroked his chin with the tip of his forefinger. "So you're trying to keep the colonists safe. By prolonging Spock's ability to elude me."

"Yes. But I'm also giving you a sweeter, more memorable revenge. There's something in this for both of us."

The acquisitor weighed the information. "And for Spock as well, eh?" His finger traced the line of his jaw. "Then why didn't Spock wait for you? Why didn't you transport together?"

"Because," McCoy explained, "Spock didn't think you'd let me medicate him while we were down here. He said I'd be putting my life on the line for nothing."

Dreen paused, considering the doctor's argument. And why not? There was nothing more convincing than the truth.

Nor had McCoy done a bad job of presenting it, if

he did say so himself. Especially when one considered the situation he'd beamed down into: Spock already gone, scrambling through the hills somewhere, and a bunch of snarling Merkaans looking at him like it was time for target practice.

"Listen," he went on, "don't take my word for it about Spock's condition. See for yourself. Call in one of your physicians."

The acquisitor shook his head. "Not necessary. I believe you when you say the Vulcan is debilitated."

Inwardly, the doctor cheered. He'd done it, damn it! He tried to picture the look on Spock's face when McCoy showed up with his medication.

"On the other hand," Dreen continued, "there may be another reason for your wishing to delay the Vulcan's demise. For instance, the possibility that if I linger here long enough, I may have to face not one Federation vessel, but several." He skewered the human with his eyes. "Perhaps that occurred to you as well, eh, Doctor?"

McCoy licked his lips. "It's possible," he agreed, not knowing what else to say.

"Good of you to grant me that," the acquisitor sneered. "I think you'll stay right here, Doctor McCoy. But by all means, keep on hoping that Spock doesn't falter too soon. Because when he does, I'm going to execute you—for the crime of audacity."

He made a gesture of dismissal and McCoy felt Merkaan hands on his arms. As the meaning of Dreen's words sank in, he was dragged to his feet.

He'd blown his chance. Blown it royally.

Dreen's guards tugged at him; the doctor was in no position to resist. In trying to negotiate a path around his chair, however, he barked his shin on it—hard enough for him to curse out loud.

"Boyce's birthday," the acquisitor jeered.

Before McCoy had a chance to think, he shot a look at Dreen—a look which communicated his surprise.

How had the acquisitor gotten hold of Spock's message?

A moment later, he realized the truth: the acquisitor *hadn't* gotten hold of it. He'd heard it in some other context and knew nothing about its true meaning.

Nor had he suspected. At least, not until now.

"Did I misuse your phrase?" Dreen asked. He wasn't sure if he was on to something or not, McCoy thought; he was probing. "Perhaps you would care to correct me, then."

The doctor searched frantically for an answer. "We say that when—" When *what?* Why had the acquisitor used it when he had? "When someone gets hurt," he finished.

It was the right answer. He could tell by Dreen's expression. But there was still a shade of doubt there.

"And this is an expression you borrowed from the Vulcans, yes?"

McCoy had a fifty-fifty chance. He took his shot. "No. Actually, they borrowed it from us."

Right again. The suspicion faded.

"Why do you ask?" the doctor went on, for good measure.

"Never mind," the acquisitor told him. He turned to one of the guards. "Take him away. Lock him up somewhere."

As McCoy was half-lifted out of the office, he sighed inwardly. And hoped that Dreen would never press him further on the subject.

# Chapter Seventeen

THE *MESIRII* WERE YELPING in the distance. Spock resisted the impulse to look back, concentrating instead on what lay ahead of him—a long slope rife with tiny stones, the largest of which seemed to have piled up at its base.

Careful of his step, he descended the escarpment, then picked his way over the debris at the bottom. And kept going, across a wide, shallow riverbed, where only prickly orange weeds the size of his hand had been able to survive.

His breath coming harder than it should have been. It was getting more and more difficult to keep his metabolism in check while at the same time making increasing demands on it.

How much time had elapsed since he'd been transported to the hills? Four hours? Five? The sun was still high in the sky, but he'd beamed down to the colony shortly after dawn. More than five, then—possibly six or seven.

And already, his thoughts were fuzzy. It was not a promising development. On the other side of the dry riverbed, an unusually long and gentle flank was presented to him. Grateful, he began to ascend.

More yelping. And it was getting louder—slowly, gradually, but getting louder nonetheless. The beasts were closing in on him.

Spock accepted the fact with grim inevitability. After all, there had never been any hope of winning this race; the only question was when he'd lose it.

Nonetheless, he found himself trying to gauge the distance separating him from his pursuers. *Sounds carry farther in the cold air,* he told himself. Dreen and his *mesirii* could still be a mile away.

No, that wasn't necessarily right. Dreen might not be with them. Spock had figured that out some time ago, hadn't he? He'd realized that the Merkaan, unable to keep up with his hunting beasts, would have to rest sometimes. Then, after he'd refreshed himself, he could have his transport tech beam him across long stretches of terrain.

It was the only way Dreen could maintain the pace. Which meant if Spock could elude the *mesirii,* he could elude their master as well.

Suddenly, there was a flash of green fire off to his left. Turning, he saw a piece of the hillside consumed in a disruptor blast.

The first officer didn't dare glance over his shoulder. Obviously, the acquisitor had beamed well ahead of his *mesirii*—and with the help of his transporter technician, materialized close enough to Spock to use his disruptor.

Pushing himself up the slope as hard as he could, the Vulcan zig-zagged to make it difficult for his pursuer to hit him. There were other explosions of matter-rending force on either side of him.

But none, he noted after a while, as close as the first. None that could have been intended to kill.

And then he realized, with a certainty that exceeded the facts at hand, that Dreen was only playing with him, taunting him.

When he heard the Merkaan's laughter, Spock finally looked back over his shoulder—and saw his antagonist standing at the top of the hill he'd left behind, his weapon aimed at the sky.

"Run, Vulcan! Run for your life!" Dreen's voice came to him in hollow, echoing waves, one after the other. "Just don't think you can run far enough to save yourself!"

At this range, the acquisitor could certainly have cut him down if that had been his wish. But he'd chosen not to.

". . . save yourself . . . save yourself . . ."

Resolutely, Spock turned again and resumed his flight. So much for eluding the beasts and thereby eluding Dreen. There was obviously no hope of that.

Better to clear his mind and focus on getting the most out of his dwindling reserves. Doggedly, he drove himself up the incline.

As Spock disappeared over the crest of the next hill, Dreen put away his disruptor and laughed. It had been a long time since he'd enjoyed himself so thoroughly.

He tapped a stud on his communicator. Immediately, he heard Balac respond: "Yes, Acquisitor?"

"How are the transports going?"

"Well, Acquisitor. The level of cooperation has never been higher."

Dreen grunted. "Really? Perhaps they foresee a spate of bloodshed once my agreement with the Vulcan has, shall we say, run its course. Nor would it be an unreasonable expectation." He paused. "However, we must treat any change in behavior as suspect. Increase security in the vicinity of the mines and the processing plants."

"It will be done."

"That is all."

"As you wish, Acquisitor."

Once the link was broken, Dreen thought for a moment. Was he being overly suspicious? Probably.

Just as before, when he'd questioned that simple phrase. What was it again? Oh, yes. *Boyce's birthday.*

It was just that it had seemed so . . . quirky. Out of place, somehow. And then, when the human doctor had given him that strange look upon hearing it . . .

No. It was his imagination, he told himself.

Of course, it would be easy enough to find out one way or the other. He could have the doctor tortured. Force him to disclose the phrase's secret meaning, assuming there was any.

On the other hand, he didn't want to look unsure of himself in front of his expeditors. Or worse, paranoid. Competent acquisitors didn't hunt for things that weren't there. *Gareed Welt* didn't hunt for things that weren't there.

And if it turned out there was no secret meaning, no rebellious message hidden in the phrase, he would look foolish and insecure. No matter how large his haul was, there would be a shadow on his acquisition.

He shook his head. He'd just emerged from the shadows. He didn't need any more of them. Up until now, the expedition had been an exercise in efficiency. He would keep it that way.

Besides, even if there *were* some sort of information couched in those two words . . . what could the colonists possibly do with it? They were watched all the time. The threat of death was their constant companion. Even if he'd allowed them to talk freely with those on the *Enterprise,* there was no way his acquisition could be stalled now.

Having set his mind at rest, Dreen looked to the hills again. And smiled.

The hunt called.

"Damn," Karras exclaimed.

Negotiating his way over a fallen tree trunk, Kirk turned to look at her over his shoulder. "What is it?" he asked.

She stopped. "How could I have been so stupid?"

The captain was honestly puzzled. "About what?"

The ensign regarded him, though her mind was somewhere else. "Those symbols," she told him.

"Yes?" he prompted.

Suddenly, Karras whipped out her tricorder. "I can't believe I missed it," she said, exasperated with herself. "Look."

Once again, Kirk found himself peering at the tricorder's screen. What he saw was a configuration of a half-dozen symbols, none of which were the by-now-familiar creature-glyph. However, he did recognize a couple of them.

He pointed. *"Sick* and *not-sick,"* he told her. "Right?"

"Yes. And remember these? The description of the process leading to *sick* or *not-sick?"*

The captain nodded. "The ones that told you about the sting."

Karras indicated one in particular. "Look closely. You see this mark?"

He saw it. It seemed to accompany the *not-sick* sign.

"At first, I couldn't figure out what it meant. Just now, it came to me. It's this symbol"—she pointed to another of the tiny carvings—"but it's turned on its side. Just as the *sick* glyph was turned on its side to mean *not-sick."*

Kirk frowned. "But what does the original symbol signify? I mean, when it's turned right-side up?"

"It's a command," she explained. "It means *stay."*

The captain looked at her. "Then, if it's on its side . . ."

"It means *go.* Presumably, to another of the creature-locations. That is, if you want to be *not-sick."*

He considered the information. "So, someone can be cured of a creature's sting by getting stung again, but not by the same creature? It has to be a different creature?"

"Unless I'm way off base, yes. That's what the glyphs seem to be saying."

"But why?" Kirk asked. "Why would nature have created that kind of mechanism? Whom would it have benefited?"

The ensign didn't have an answer for that one. She shrugged.

He pondered it some more. Finally, he shook his head. "It doesn't seem to make sense."

Karras nodded. "I know. But there it is, nonetheless."

The captain remembered their purpose. "We can talk more about this later. The beam-down site can't be too much farther."

In response, Karras closed her tricorder and put it away. But Kirk could tell that her mind was still on the glyphs.

At least, for the next couple hundred meters. Because shortly after that, they reached their goal—the point of their arrival on Octavius Four. The beam-down site.

It was a mess, to say the least. The tangle caused by the creature's emergence had been consumed in the much larger confusion of earth and rock and foliage created by the ground collapse.

As Kirk approached the brink of the affected area, it was hard for him to believe that any of them had come out of it alive. Huge slabs of rock had been upended, leaving gaping holes that plunged twenty feet down. Tall trees had been half-buried or turned upside-down or just cracked in half.

What's more, there was no apparent exit from the cavern below—if there still *was* a cavern below. So the decision not to backtrack out of the hollow had probably been a good one.

But they hadn't made the journey here to sightsee. They'd come to learn something about the prospects of their being rescued.

"Captain?"

Kirk looked up and saw Karras kneeling on the

opposite side of the jumble. She seemed to have found something.

Joining her, he knelt too, and got a better look at her discovery: a couple of bootprints in the dark, overturned earth. Nor was their significance lost on him.

"Someone was here after the collapse," he said.

The ensign nodded. "Mister Sulu's party, maybe. Or some other. In any case, they knew something happened to us, and they came to investigate."

Kirk felt a small twinge of gratification. So, his instincts had been right. There *had* been something to be learned here.

It was still possible that something terrible and unforeseen had claimed the *Enterprise,* and that Sulu's party had been stranded here along with the captain's. But the far more likely conclusion was that Sulu's people had been beamed up—and Kirk's crew of four hundred and twenty was still alive.

Which made his emergency theory sound better and better. After all, Scotty wouldn't have given up in the few hours it took them to reach the hollow. Barring an urgent call from Starfleet, he would still have been around to pick up the signal from Owens' communicator.

Kirk shared his thoughts with Karras. Her reaction was a hopeful one—and why not? If the *Enterprise* had only been called away, it would eventually be back. And it would find them waiting for it.

There was still a question left unanswered, however, and it was a rather big one. Namely: *Why* had the ship taken off? What kind of crisis had the *Enterprise* been called on to confront? The captain wondered.

"Sir?"

He emerged from his brief reverie. "Yes, Ensign?"

"It may not be a good idea to linger here. If the creature senses our presence . . ."

Kirk agreed. "Let's take a quick look around, see if we can find out anything else."

As it happened, there was nothing else to find. Minutes later, they left the beam-down site and headed back for the hollow.

Abruptly, Spock became aware. He looked around, saw the winding trail on which he was crouching, felt the bite of the wind.

And heard the cries of beasts—of *mesirii*. Following the sound to its source, he looked down. The beasts were below him, climbing the trail to get to him. And if he didn't move soon, they would accomplish their objective in a matter of minutes.

With an effort, he rose and began to go forward again. Forward and up.

What had happened? How long had he been hunkering here?

He remembered seeing the *mesirii* from far off. But it had been very far off, maybe half a mile. And at the time, Dreen had been with them; now he was nowhere to be seen.

There was only one possible answer—the rigors of his struggle with the alien substance had blacked him out. Pushed to its limit and beyond, his mind had finally obtained a respite the only way it could—by shutting down at the conscious level.

On the other hand, it hadn't let the poison gain the upper hand. At least, he *thought* it hadn't. Not having been cognizant of what was taking place, he couldn't be sure.

In any case, the poison wasn't in control now. If anything, his mind was a little clearer than it had been, his senses a little sharper.

He recalled a Vulcan expression: *shali bahn*. Literally, the calm before the storm. The clarity of vision, both internal and external, that preceded the dark tumult of death.

Was this lucidity he was experiencing a variation of *shali bahn?* The next time his mind shut down, would it be for good?

The *mesirii* yapped below him, as if to remind Spock that they had a claim on him too. And he wondered which of his adversaries would finally overtake him: the beasts, the poison, or his own tortured brain.

As the Vulcan ascended the switchback path, he saw how cluttered it was with boulders, particularly in the area of the bend just ahead. In fact, the rocks were so numerous there, the trail was essentially narrowed to a width of a few inches.

Normally, Spock would have possessed the balance to get past the rocks with ease. But in his present state, he could depend on nothing, least of all so delicate a faculty as balance.

As he considered the problem, an idea came to him. He looked down at the ground-eating *mesirii*, who appeared every bit as fresh as when he'd seen them in the plaza.

What was the phrase of which Doctor McCoy was so enamored? *Killing two birds with one stone?*

Not that his objective was necessarily to kill, nor were the *mesirii* even remotely related to birds. But the jargon seemed apt nonetheless.

Ascending the trail to the point where the rocks began to pile up, he selected one of the larger specimens. It was too big to lift, especially now, but it appeared he could roll it without too much trouble.

He glanced again at the *mesirii*, who were negotiating a sharp turn in the trail seemingly without breaking stride. Perhaps, he thought, they sensed that the end of the hunt was approaching.

And perhaps it was, though not the way they anticipated.

In less than a minute, the beasts would be directly below him. They were too absorbed in their pursuit to be aware of anything else. If he timed it right, he could catch them unawares.

Inserting himself between the hillside and the boulder, he got his weight behind the latter and waited. Then, when the moment seemed right, he pushed.

At first, the rock wouldn't budge. Determined not to squander his opportunity, Spock increased the pressure, straining as hard as he possibly could. After a second or two, his efforts paid off.

The boulder rolled toward the brink of the trail, picked up speed for a moment, then dropped out of sight. Leaning forward to follow its flight, the Vulcan saw it plummet toward the *mesirii* with an accuracy he had not dared to hope for.

As close as the beasts were to one another, the boulder would hit one and perhaps both of them. They would be disabled, though not killed, Spock hoped. He hated the idea of causing the death of another life form, even when that life form was bred for destruction.

As it turned out, he need not have been so concerned. At the last possible moment, the *mesirii* noticed the impending danger and veered off—one into the hillside, the other toward the edge of the trail.

The Vulcan's effort wasn't wasted, however. Not entirely. As the boulder bounded farther down the slope, the animal that had swerved toward the verge of the trail went over it—and slid after the missile in a roiling mass of teeth and claws.

By the time the *mesirii* landed on the switchback below, it had apparently broken one of its hind legs. The beast tried to get up once, twice, but failed. Ultimately, it just lay on its side and snarled.

However, its companion hadn't suffered any damage at all. As Spock looked on, it resumed its ascent up the trail as if nothing had happened.

Nor was there a chance for a second attempt. The uninjured *mesirii* had already scrambled out of range.

In the end, ironically, he'd done it a favor. The beast was closer to him now than if he'd merely skirted the pile of rocks and kept going. And if he didn't start climbing again immediately, it would narrow the gap even more.

Containing his disappointment, Spock began picking his way around the rocks. For now, his mind was still clear, his strength still sufficient to move him.

He had to make use of those advantages while he could.

Dreen bent over Sarif, stroked the *mesirii's* flank. In response, the animal looked up at him with its large, golden eyes and whimpered. Its wounded leg was tucked underneath it.

"Ah, Sarif," he said. "What have you done to yourself? Or should I say, what has been done *to* you?"

There was no doubt in his mind that Spock was responsible for this. *Mesirii* didn't simply slip; they were much too sure-footed for that.

It was yet another score to settle with the Vulcan. And settle it he would.

The acquisitor stood. Reluctantly, he took out his disruptor. And aimed it at the crippled *mesirii.*

As if it sensed what was coming, the animal tried to drag itself farther up the trail. Tried to show him it hadn't let him down.

But of course, it had. A *mesirii* who had failed was no *mesirii* at all, regardless of the reasons for its failure. It could not be allowed to live.

The transport tech had known it when he noted the animal's immobility and reported it. Tezlin had known it when he contacted the acquisitor. And Dreen himself had known it.

It was his duty to put the *mesirii* to death. But it was not a pleasant duty—not pleasant at all.

Gritting his teeth and ignoring the animal's pitiful look back, he activated the weapon. A moment later, Sarif was invaded by the disruption process. He didn't even have time to squeal before being devoured.

The acquisitor shook his head. "Goodbye, my beauty."

Restoring the disruptor to its place in his tunic, Dreen considered his options. He could have his tech transport him to Memsac's side—which would by now, more likely than not, place him in disruptor range of Spock. If he wished, he could end the chase here and now.

There were some—Balac among them—who would have him do exactly that. They would have him return to the *Clodiaan* immediately, so they could flee as soon as the mineral transports were complete.

But he had begun this, and he would finish it. He would take his revenge to the greatest length possible.

Memsac was still on Spock's trail. Why let the Vulcan off more easily than he had to? *No*, he told himself, starting up the path at a leisurely pace. *Let the pointy-eared deceiver run.*

*Then I will kill him.*

# Chapter Eighteen

As SPOCK DESCENDED into a long, barren valley, he finally allowed himself to accept the fact: for some time—it could have been an hour or several, he could no longer judge—the *mesirii* had failed to gain on him.

At first, he'd believed it was just his imagination, or a trick of the terrain. But as he looked back yet again, and saw the beast topping the rise behind him, he was convinced his observations had a basis in reality.

Could the *mesirii* be tiring, even as Spock was tiring? Had Dreen's failure to feed it backfired? Or was it simply that the Merkaan had not expected the race to last so long?

It didn't matter. Sooner or later the acquisitor himself would reappear and end the contest then and there. But for the time being, Spock could take heart in his accomplishment.

Truthfully, he'd lasted longer than even he would have guessed. And he could not deny that it pleased him. No matter how stridently his Vulcan training cried out against pride and self-aggrandizement, he couldn't help it. He was proud of what he had—

Before he could finish the thought, a familiar agony took hold in his gut. He doubled over, clutching at his middle, but somehow managed to stay on his feet.

Behind him, the hunting beast yipped, suddenly animated. No doubt, it sensed his pain. It saw how vulnerable he had become.

Stumbling, he wrenched himself upright. Tried to submerge the alien madness—to keep it in check, if only for a little while longer.

But this time there was no postponing it, no denying it. This time he didn't have the strength to make it go away.

He could feel its influence pumping through him like a bristling, black tide. He could feel the madness ravaging him, consuming him . . .

And still he kept going somehow, kept staggering forward. Then something hit him from behind with stunning force, spinning him around. He landed on his back, felt a weight on his chest.

Flinging up an arm out of instinct, Spock opened his eyes just in time to see the *mesirii's* jaws close on his wrist. The pain was terrible, terrible—even greater than the conflagration in his blood.

With his other hand, he tore at the beast's muzzle, but to no avail. Finally, he scrabbled wildly in the dirt, seeking a stone. Found one. And with all the energy he could bring to bear, he cracked the *mesirii* over the head with it.

Abruptly, the pressure on his wrist ceased. The animal slumped on top of him, still breathing, but unconscious. Spock pushed it off his chest and rolled onto his belly.

One thought still drove him. One urgent need still held steady in the mounting chaos of his mind.

He had to keep going. He had to survive.

Reaching, clawing at the earth, he pulled himself past the injured *mesirii*. Reached, clawed, and pulled. Again. And again.

Then the pain became too much for him. The fire

rampaged, out of control. And he yielded to the seething darkness.

Dreen had just stopped to rest on a large boulder when his communicator beeped. Touching the appropriate stud, he activated it. "Yes?"

"Acquisitor, this is Tezlin. I have bad news. It seems the other *mesirii* has been immobilized as well."

The Merkaan could feel his teeth grinding together. He nodded. "And the Vulcan?"

"The transport tech reports he is still in the vicinity."

Dreen drew his weapon and got to his feet. "Transport me there," he instructed. "*Now,* Tezlin."

"As you wish, Acquisitor."

On the Merkaan ship *Clodiaan,* third-in-command Seemal Tezlin had just finished giving the transport tech his instructions via ship's intercom. That done, he returned his attention to the task at hand.

In general, the loss of the acquisitor's pet notwithstanding, he was satisfied with the way this expedition had gone. More than satisfied, in fact.

Not only had they extracted from the colony an impressive number of containers—an extraordinary amount of mineral wealth—as a bonus, second-in-command Balac had shown himself to be less efficient than his reputation suggested.

Perhaps next expedition, Balac would be replaced. And who would be a more logical choice as the triad's new second-in-command than Seemal Tezlin, who had served his acquisitor so admirably at Beta Cabrini?

As he looked on, yet another group of containers materialized on the cargo deck. By Tezlin's count, that left only one more batch. And then they were home free, their destination the Merkaan homeworld.

In theory, anyway. In fact, they would probably

have to linger here a while, until Acquisitor Dreen had tired of hunting the *Enterprise*'s first officer.

Madness. And madder still was Dreen's intention to destroy the Federation ship once the hunt was over. Nor could Tezlin completely discount the acquisitor's casual reference to "the slaves they'd be taking" with them.

What if Federation reinforcements arrived before the Vulcan was caught? All their efforts here would fall by the wayside. And they might lose a ship or two into the bargain, depending on how angry the reinforcements turned out to be.

No matter. Tezlin wasn't going to be the one to impress a sense of urgency on Acquisitor Dreen. He had worked too hard to advance his career to wreck it all now on the shoals of insubordination.

Forty hells, he'd served under Sorra Buthatchef on the Kantrul for more than a year and never uttered a word of protest, though Buthatchef was so mad he'd delay transports for hours while he preened in his bath. If he could keep his mouth shut at Norith Four and Abin's world, he could do it at Beta Cabrini.

Besides, how much longer could it take to hunt down the Vulcan? He'd been fleeing from Dreen's beasts for upwards of ten hours. The *mesirii* themselves had to have been tiring by—

Abruptly, he noticed a commotion in the area of the most recent transport. As Tezlin watched, a crowd began to gather.

"What is going on there?" he called.

A couple of expeditors turned in response to his query. "It's Mongis," one called back. "He's collapsed."

Collapsed? Tezlin frowned. "Well, don't just stand there. Take him to the infirmary."

The expeditor who'd answered him raised his fist in obedient salute. "As you wish, third-in-command."

But before the order could be carried out, a second

Merkaan fell to the deck. And a third would have joined him, if those around him hadn't caught him first.

"What in the name of the potentate—?" Tezlin cut short his exclamation and strode over to the troubled group. Was it possible that they'd caught some sort of disease down on the planet? Something that was only now beginning to affect them?

No. That didn't make sense. There were others who'd been in the colony just as long or longer. And *they* weren't coming down with anything.

As Tezlin approached, he smelled something. It was subtle at first, then a bit stronger as he got closer to the afflicted ones. He sniffed the air, wrinkled his nose. Yes, there was definitely something there.

Not exactly unpleasant, he noted, but hard to ignore. Did it have something to do with the problem at hand? He snorted. Did a Merkaan love other people's wealth?

"All right," he said, loudly enough to be heard over the hum of trepidation, "get these men out of here." He picked out the nearest expeditor, the one named Collix. "You. Get up to environmental systems and have the tech check the ventilation system. There's something in the air and I want to know *what.*"

"As you wish," the expeditor replied and started off. Tezlin turned to the others, who'd already begun lifting their peers off the deck.

"Move quickly," he advised. "We've no time for this; there's work to be done."

But before he could get any further, the third-in-command heard a thud directly behind him. Turning, he saw that the Merkaan he'd dispatched to environmental systems had gone down on his knees like a pensioner. A moment later, he slumped forward and lay motionless.

Tezlin cursed. Obviously, this was more serious than he'd cared to believe. And if the expeditors could be affected, why not a third-in-command?

Without bothering with further instructions, he hurried back toward the vertical lift. He had to isolate the problem, he told himself. He had to isolate it and deal with it before it slowed down the transport schedule.

What if the acquisitor finished sooner than expected, and wanted to know why the last shipment was still sitting on the ground? Then Tezlin might find himself in the same stew as Balac. And that was not where he wanted to be.

Halfway across the deck, he realized that the odor was as strong here as it had been back there. It was spreading. Filled with the knowledge, he ran faster. As fast as he could, in fact.

The lift wasn't far now. Another half-dozen strides and he'd make it. Just a few more now . . .

But he'd no sooner reassured himself than his legs seemed to turn soft and heavy. And before he knew it, the deck came flying up at him.

Tezlin recovered and eyed the door again. It was almost within reach; he still had a chance. His mind was lucid, and there was feeling in his upper body. If he could drag himself with his hands, get into the lift, he might clear his head of the odor. And meanwhile, the lift would be whisking him to the infirmary . . .

Then even that hope died. He'd barely begun to pull himself along, when his arms became useless as tree stumps. Slowly he settled to the deck, until his cheek was pressed against it.

Tezlin never lost consciousness. Not quite. He stayed awake enough to see the expeditors rushing toward him, and the way they crumpled before they could reach him. He saw them pile up one on top of the other, each as helpless and as numb as he was.

And after a while, he saw the others—the humans —who materialized in the cargo hold with their gas masks and their phaser pistols. And he began to understand what kind of fools they had been.

* * *

In accordance with his instructions, Dreen was surrounded by the scarlet glow of transport. He gripped his disruptor more tightly in anticipation of a confrontation.

When he materialized, however, he was surprised to find his vigilance unnecessary. He'd expected to find Spock still on his feet, still fleeing with what was left of his strength; instead, he was stretched out on the ground, his breath coming in spasms, his body shuddering with chill and exhaustion.

Not more than a couple of meters behind the Vulcan, Memsac lay senseless. There was a thin line of blood trickling from a wound over one eye. And a rock beside him—no doubt, the weapon Spock had used to disable the beast.

The acquisitor shook his head. First Sarif, now his handsome running companion. An awful pity. But he wouldn't dispatch the *mesirii* just yet. He had other business to attend to—happier business.

Approaching Spock, he stood over him and kicked him in the ribs—once, twice—to make sure his apparent helplessness wasn't a trick. Satisfied, he then knelt beside his enemy and smiled at the prospect of killing him.

"Isn't it interesting," he remarked, "how fate sours on its favorites, Spock? How one star rises while another falls?"

The Vulcan didn't answer. Obviously, he was incapable of answering. He was too weak, too wracked with cold.

Dreen laughed softly. He was in no hurry. This was a moment he had dreamed about. A moment he had never thought he'd reach.

He wanted to savor it, to remember every aspect of it. The heft of the disruptor pistol in his hand. The sight of Spock lying there, humbled, defeated.

Nor could he help but relive the details of his own humiliation, still vivid in his mind's eye. That was appropriate as well, was it not? One had to remember the depths to truly appreciate the heights.

The wind blew, cold and sweet. Carrion eaters circled high overhead, drawn by the imminence of death. The acquisitor noted that as well.

Then, his preparations complete, his hunger for retribution honed to a fine and exquisite point, he grabbed the Vulcan by the shoulder. And anticipated the expression of horror on Spock's visage as he contemplated his utter and irreversible destruction.

But as he turned his prey face up, he saw that there was another kind of horror there—a shivering, sweating, feverish horror—something so terrible, so consuming, that he didn't even seem aware of Dreen's presence, much less what the acquisitor had in mind for him.

So, in the end, he was indeed to be cheated, just as the human McCoy had predicted. He would have his revenge, but not on the sharp-witted Vulcan whose name he'd cursed down through the years. This was just a creature—a quivering, unthinking lump of flesh who didn't even merit the favor of a disruptor blast.

Bitter and repulsed, Dreen put his weapon away. With the toe of his boot, he rolled Spock over again, so that his face was pressed into the ground. Then, turning his back on the Vulcan, he went and got the rock that had been used on Memsac. It wasn't as heavy as it looked, but it would do.

Returning to where Spock lay trembling, the acquisitor raised the rock over his head. And taking one last look at the object of his hollow vengeance, he prepared to bring it down on the Vulcan's skull.

"Stop right there!" came a cry from behind him.

Dropping the rock, he drew his disruptor and whirled. But whoever had snuck up on him was too alert. There was a blast of red light and a hammer blow to his chest, knocking the breath out of him, sending his weapon flying out of his grasp.

As he lay there, gasping to fill his lungs again, Dreen looked up to see who had stopped him. What he saw was not one figure, but three.

A trio of Starfleet officers, all of them armed with phasers. One stood in front of the other two, his eyes narrowed in barely contained anger.

"Sorry to interrupt," he said. "But that is my commanding officer you were about to pound into the ground."

The acquisitor shook his head. How was this possible? Tezlin had the *Enterprise* under close watch. And besides, no one on the Federation vessel could have located Spock so quickly, not after he'd transported the Vulcan into the hills. Only his transport tech had the coordinates.

"You seem surprised," the officer noted. He recovered Dreen's disruptor, which lay on the ground. "Vait until you get back to your ship."

The Merkaan reached for his communicator. Nor did his enemies make a move to stop him. On the contrary, they had turned their attention to Spock. Activating it, he rasped: "Tezlin!"

There was no response. He cursed under his breath. He'd just spoken to his third officer a few minutes ago.

"Mister Chekov," one of the humans said. They had turned Spock face up. "Look. There's something wrong with him, and it's not just exhaustion."

The one who'd stunned Dreen knelt beside the Vulcan. His face became a mask of apprehension. He muttered something about "Leslie" being "right."

Then, flipping open his communication device, the human barked a command: "Mister Kyle. Five to beam aboard."

By that time, the Merkaan had recovered enough to sit up. And to remember the daggers in his tunic. Watching to make sure no one noticed, he reached for them with both hands—

Until the one called Chekov froze him with a

glance—and a well-aimed phaser. "I vouldn't try that if I vere you," he said.

An instant later, they vanished in a subtle, golden glow: the officers, Spock, and Acquisitor Hamesaad Dreen.

McCoy paced in the narrow office that had been set aside as his cell. Outside, his guards exchanged guttural comments with a decidedly sadistic tone to them.

*Damn,* he mused. *What in blazes was I thinking of? I'm a doctor, not a poker player. Maybe Jim could have sold these Merkaans a bill of goods, but not yours truly. Hell, I couldn't even make the truth sound convincing.*

At least he hadn't given away Spock's plan. At least he'd managed to—

His ruminations were cut short by a cry from outside. And then, right on its heels, another.

At first, he thought the marauders were killing humans in the plaza outside, which would have meant Dreen's hunt was over and Spock was dead. Then he realized the cries weren't human at all. They were *Merkaan.*

His guards must have noticed the same thing, and at about the same time. After a quick exchange, one of them bolted down the corridor, leaving the other one to guard him. The remaining Merkaan shot him a warning look and McCoy held his hands up, signifying his willingness to cooperate. Sure, he had thoughts of trying to escape, but he wasn't about to give them away.

There were more sounds from outside. More cries —and some of them *were* human now. They seemed to be getting louder, closer.

The doctor's watchman appeared to be caught in a dilemma. McCoy tried to put himself in the Merkaan's place.

If he were to leave his post, he might be of some help

in putting down the disturbance, whatever it was. But then he'd be leaving the prisoner all alone—against the orders of his superior.

Of course, if the colonists had rebelled and gotten hold of weapons somehow, it would be dangerous for him to remain in a naked hallway. But if the acquisitor determined he'd been wrong to leave his post, the penalty would be a severe one—the doctor could only guess *how* severe.

In the final analysis, the more immediate of the guard's fears won out. He took off as had the other guard.

McCoy smiled. He was free. Not bad.

But if there was a war going on outside, he wasn't about to plunge headlong into the middle of it. He'd take it one step at a time.

And the first step was to survey the corridor, to make sure no one was going to take a potshot at him before—

No sooner had he stuck his head out than there was a blast of red light and his guard came lurching backwards, spinning into the wall. A second blast hit the Merkaan squarely and knocked him off his feet altogether.

Nor was he going to get up again. Not for some time, anyway—McCoy could tell that at a glance. He could also tell it was a phaser that had scuttled him—but who had access to a phaser down here?

Then he got his answer, as Lieutenant Leslie and another security officer, the woman who'd stopped him en route to the transporter room, came swinging around a corner at the far end of the hall.

"Leslie!" the doctor shouted, not wanting to be taken for a Merkaan hiding in ambush. "It's me, McCoy."

Recognizing him, the security chief stopped himself short of firing again. "Doctor McCoy—it's about time. I thought we were going to have to search every building in the colony!"

"What's happening?" McCoy asked.

Leslie shot a wary look down the corridor. "What's happening," he said, "is we're taking back the colony. The square, the plants, the mines—all of it."

The doctor smiled approvingly. "Then, Spock's plan worked?"

The security chief nodded. "Couldn't have worked much better. The colonists managed to gas all three of the Merkaans' ships. When we saw the transport activity had stopped, we knew the gas had done its work. Then all we had to do was punch a few holes in their shields, beam over, and take control."

"What about Spock? He's up in the hills somewhere."

"He *was*. Chekov found his coordinates on the Merkaan flagship. He beamed down just in time to stop Dreen from killing him."

"So he's alive," McCoy confirmed.

Leslie nodded. But there was a shadow behind his eyes that told the doctor the news wasn't all good. "Now, come on," he said. "We've got to get you beamed up. It's not safe around here."

For an instant, the doctor felt the urge to stay and fight. Then he thought better of it and kept his mouth shut.

Spock needed him; that had to be his priority. Besides, he was no more a fighter than he was a poker player.

As Leslie made contact with the ship, McCoy braced himself for transport.

# Chapter Nineteen

DREEN HAD BEEN SITTING in the *Enterprise*'s brig for nearly an hour before someone came to see him. It was one of the officers he'd seen on the bridge behind Spock.

Gathering himself, the acquisitor effected a posture of arrogance. He didn't know what had happened on the *Clodiaan* to prevent his reaching Tezlin, or how the humans had managed to effect his capture. However, it was merely a minor setback.

He still had nearly three hundred hostages planetside. Knowing the humans, they would try to use him as leverage to free the colonists. But when Balac would refuse to deal with them, they would relent and release him.

"At last," he spat as the officer came to stand before the energy-barrier. "I assure you, you have not improved your chances for survival by keeping me waiting."

The human smiled grimly. "I think ye need to be a little better informed," he told the acquisitor. "Ye're in no position to be makin' threats."

Dreen was taken aback. He swallowed. "And what does that mean?"

His visitor frowned. "What it means is that we've taken all three of yer vessels, not to mention the force ye had on the ground. Now, if ye're willing to talk surrender—"

"Surrender!" the Merkaan exploded.

The human smiled grimly. "That's what I said. Of course, ye dinnae have to discuss it if ye've got nae stomach for it. It's really just a technicality."

"You're bluffing," Dreen told him, grasping at the shreds of his confidence. "I don't believe a word you're saying."

The man shrugged. "Fine with me. Ye'll have plenty of opportunity to see for yerself. Of course, ye might not recognize yer ships without their armaments, but at least ye've got a ticket home, which is a good deal more than ye deserve." And with that, he started to go.

The acquisitor cursed. "Wait," he commanded.

His visitor stopped, and turned. "Aye?"

Dreen licked his lips. "If you're telling the truth, then tell me all of it. What happened? How did you do it?"

The man shook his head regretfully. "Sorry," he replied. "Ye'll have to figure it out for yerself." Then he disappeared down the corridor.

The acquisitor looked at his guards, but they only turned away. Obviously, they weren't going to tell him anything either.

One thing was certain: they didn't look very worried. No more than had their superior.

It could still have been a bluff. *Still.*

But he had the feeling that his adversaries had somehow outmaneuvered him. *Again.* His jaw tightened.

He had lost his precious haul—all twenty-six tons of it. He had lost his beautiful matched *mesirii.*

And more. Much more.

He'd been disgraced—just as surely as Pike had disgraced him. There would be no triad for him, not even a hope of one. People would laugh at him the rest of his days.

The weight of his realization was too much for him. The acquisitor took an uncertain step backward, felt his knees buckle, and sat down heavily on his bunk.

He'd spent the last ten years forgetting a nightmare. But the nightmare was back. He was living it all over again.

As Montgomery Scott entered sickbay, he saw McCoy standing at the foot of Spock's bed. The man was lost in some private thought.

"Doctor McCoy?" he said, so as not to catch the doctor by surprise.

The chief medical officer looked up. Wordlessly, he acknowledged Scotty's presence. Nor was it difficult to discern the reasons for his mood; McCoy didn't like the prospect of his patients dying on him.

Nonetheless, as the engineer approached, he dredged up a few words: "They gone yet?"

"Aye," Scotty replied. "They're gone, with their tails between their legs. And without so much as a disruptor to their name, they won't be causin' any trouble on their way home."

McCoy grunted. "Good riddance. But who's to say they won't come back?"

"Maybe they will. Next time, though, we'll nae be taken by surprise. The *Excalibur's* on its way now to discharge a security contingent. Y'know, to set up defense systems and such."

The doctor scowled. "All those people, Scotty— dead. And their cold-blooded killer gets off without so much as a slap on the wrist. Doesn't seem right."

"Maybe not," Scott agreed. "But there are some prime directive considerations at work here. According to Starfleet headquarters, we dinnae have the right t' try him in our courts—or for that matter, attempt to rehabilitate him. Dreen was acting according to the demands of his culture imperatives. And ye know we cannae tamper with such things."

McCoy snorted. "Yes. I know."

"On the other hand," Scotty continued, "dinnae think he's going to avoid punishment altogether. From what we know of the Merkaans, they dinnae take failure lightly. And this is the *second* time Dreen's let them down. I'd say he's pretty much washed up as an acquisitor—which, for him, is probably a fate *worse* than death."

The doctor nodded. "How long before we can leave for Octavius Four?"

"A couple of hours, I'd say. Maybe a little more. Depends on the *Excalibur,* of course."

"Of course," McCoy agreed.

Silence. Cutting through it, Scotty spoke again. "Doctor, there's someone who'd like to see Mister Spock. I said I'd have to clear it with you first."

McCoy's eyes narrowed. "Who is it?"

Scotty told him.

After a moment, the doctor shrugged. "Sure, why not?"

They both found themselves looking at Spock. The doctor sighed.

"I dinnae suppose there's any change in his prognosis?" Scotty asked.

McCoy shook his head. "No, though we have had an interesting development. When we got Spock back from the planet's surface, there was something new in his blood samples. Infinitesimal quantities of organic material, of a sort we've never encountered before. Certainly nothing like anything we've ever found in Beta Cabrini."

"Could it be from Octavius Four? Something Spock might have picked up along with the poison?"

"That would be the obvious conclusion, all right. Except we didn't notice it until now. Of course, it could have snuck by in quantities too small for our instruments to pick up. But then, how did it get big enough to be detectable? Did something trigger a growth spurt—something in Spock's system, maybe, or a component of the environment around the mining colony? We just don't know. More importantly, what relationship does it have with the poison?"

Scotty frowned. "So it's another piece of the puzzle. But ye're no closer to solving it."

"That's about the size of it. It'll probably help us figure out what happened to Spock after—" The doctor swallowed. "After he's gone. But as for helping him *now?*" He shook his head. "I don't know, Scotty. I just don't know."

"To tell the truth," the engineer remarked, "despite everything, I've still got a feeling he's going to make it. Maybe it's nae very realistic, but . . ." The sentiment faded, unfinished.

McCoy took hold of his shoulder. "You keep thinking that way, Scotty. Hell, Spock's come through worse, hasn't he?"

Scott smiled at the doctor. "That he has."

McCoy rubbed his hands together. "All right, then. Now why don't you get on up to the bridge and let us doctors go about our business?"

Scotty looked at the physician in a sad and comradely sort of way. And said: "Aye. Why don't I?"

Leaving sickbay, he charted a course for the nearest turbolift. And tried not to let on, to those he passed in the corridor, how heavy a load he carried inside.

As Wayne left the transporter room, alongside Lieutenant Sulu, who'd been assigned as his escort, he looked around appraisingly. "It's been a while since I was on the *Enterprise.*"

"So I understand," the helmsman responded. "Has she changed much?"

Wayne thought about it, and shook his head. "Not

really. Still the same proud lady she used to be." He turned to the other man. "You're the helmsman, right?"

"Most of the time."

"Does she still have that little list to port at top speed?"

Sulu shook his head. "Not that I've noticed."

The administrator grunted. "Good. I used to hate that. And our engineer couldn't seem to do a damn thing about it."

He surveyed the place some more, trying to remember if there had always been a computer terminal in this corridor. In the end, he couldn't.

Sulu searched his face. "It must bring back memories."

Wayne nodded. "Some."

Quite a few, in fact. But he hadn't beamed up just to reminisce. He'd had a purpose in mind. And as they approached sickbay, he was reminded of it.

"Maledoric acid," he said admiringly. "Would you have thought of that?"

Sulu looked at him. "Hmm? Oh, right. Maledoric acid and duranium ore. And no, I wouldn't have. But then, I'm not Spock."

Wayne smiled. "He always was in a class by himself."

The doors to sickbay slid open, revealing a more modern facility than the one the administrator recalled. And a flock of unfamiliar faces as well. Where was Boyce? And Castelano?

"This way," Sulu told him. Taking the older man's arm, he guided him to the area that used to be critical care.

Apparently, it still was. There was only one bed there, and Spock was on it. As Wayne got a look at his former colleague, his heart went out to him. The Vulcan seemed sunken, depleted.

"Administrator?"

He turned and saw a slender man in a chief medical officer's garb. Uniform styles had changed over the years, but medical-section attire seemed to have changed less than that of other specialties.

The doctor held out his hand; Wayne grasped it. "Bradford Wayne—good to meet you."

The doctor nodded—solemnly, Wayne thought. His eyes were a window on his disappointment, his bitterness. "Leonard McCoy. Now remember, you'll have just a few moments with him. We've got to break orbit in a little while." He frowned apologetically. "And he's not in a position to hear you, I'm afraid. He's been heavily sedated."

"It's all right," Wayne said. "I understand."

Leaving McCoy to his duties, the administrator advanced to the side of Spock's bed. There was no chair there, which was just as well. He felt like standing.

Up close, the patient was even paler, weaker-looking. The bones of his face were so prominent, it hurt to look at them. But Wayne forced himself to look. It was the least he could do, after what Spock had done for them.

He cleared his throat. "It's funny," he began, then stopped. His voice sounded so flat, so self-conscious. He'd forgotten about sickbay acoustics.

Anyway, there was no reason to say the words aloud. The Vulcan wouldn't hear him any better that way.

*It's funny, Spock. When we were serving under Chris Pike, I didn't know you very well. At first, I didn't even like you. You were such a go-getter, always eager to do that little bit extra. I figured you were putting a shine on the old apple. Trying to get the captain to notice you.*

*I mean, I was so laid back, so casual—so damn glad just to be a helmsman. And here you were, making me feel like I should have been striving for something more. Making me uncomfortable.*

*Of course, I began to understand you after a while. I realized you weren't just putting on a show. That earnestness, that drive to do well—it was just you, just the way you were. You weren't out for a promotion. You were doing what all of us should have been doing: learning as much as we possibly could as fast as we possibly could.*

*But I wasn't open to the possibilities the way you were—which is why I wound up in charge of a colony, I guess, and you became first officer of the* Enterprise. *Anyway, even after I got to know you, we never really connected. We never really got to be friends.*

*I'm sorry about that now. I really am. I've heard what you risked to help free the colony. I've heard what kind of price you paid. I wish I'd been closer to you, Spock. And I envy those who were.*

Wayne sighed. He hadn't meant to stand here so long. He hadn't realized he had so much to say.

But the *Enterprise* had to take off. She had to go back to Octavius Four and see if her captain might still be alive. It was time for him to get to the point.

*I just wanted to thank you, Lieutenant—I mean, Commander. I just wanted to let you know we won't forget you.*

Having said his piece, the administrator nodded to Sulu. Together, they walked out of sickbay and headed for the transporter room.

"Care for another stalk?" Kirk asked.

Karras shook her head. "No, thank you." She didn't even look up from her tricorder, with which she'd been fiddling for the last few minutes—in fact, almost since they'd decided to give in to the heat of the day and take a load off their feet.

Idly, he wondered if curiosity was the whole reason for her preoccupation, or if it was also a way of avoiding conversation. After all, she might still be uncomfortable about what had happened earlier.

Either way, it was her right to do as she pleased. Nothing in Starfleet regulations said you had to be charming during rest periods.

Finishing the last of his own stalk, the captain wished for a stream. All that sugar had made him thirsty. Too bad they had nothing to carry water in, or they could have brought some back with them from the beam-down site.

Karras grunted, and shook her head. And finally put the device down.

"Anything further?" he asked.

"Nothing." She sighed. "There are still some symbols that escape me. I don't like it when things escape me." The woman regarded him. "Sir, may I speak frankly?"

He nodded. "Go right ahead."

"What I suggested before . . . you know . . . I was in a romantic setting with a handsome man and—"

"Ensign," he said, "there's no need to—"

"But there is," she insisted. "You're uncomfortable around me—don't deny it. And there's no reason for either of us to be uncomfortable. I think we should just forget it ever happened and go about our business."

A mature philosophy, Kirk decided. One befitting a future officer. A philosophy he should have been pleased with.

Then why wasn't he? Was he a trifle offended that any woman smitten with him could so quickly become *un*-smitten?

"I agree wholeheartedly," he told her. He extended his hand as a token of their understanding.

Karras reached out to take it . . .

But before she could complete the gesture, the jungle behind her exploded in a fit of unbridled fury. Trees toppled and boulders were shunted aside as the ground itself rose and then split apart.

And an all-too-familiar form emerged from the

chaos, tentacles writhing, orifice working hungrily. It was every bit as monstrous and as ghostly white as the creature that had attacked Spock. Every bit as deadly. Grabbing Karras' arm, the captain pulled her toward him. But as he did so, she screamed, her eyes opening wide with terror.

A moment later, he saw why. There was a pale, whip-like tentacle wrapped around her ankle. And it was dragging her backwards.

The ensign clutched at him, tried to reinforce his grip with her own, but it was no use. The creature pulled her feet out from under her. And then, as Kirk tried to anchor her with his weight, to dig his heels into the ground against the pull, it tugged harder than he expected.

There was a bone-jarring impact as something came rushing up to meet him—and he found himself sprawled on the jungle floor, his forehead warm and wet with blood. Dully, he realized he'd been yanked face first into a tree.

More importantly, the creature had what it wanted. As the captain looked up, wiping the blood from his eyes, he saw Karras dangling upside down above the treetops—her features contorted as Spock's had been contorted, clutching wildly at the tentacle that was crushing her ankle.

Kirk reached for his phaser—and remembered too late that he didn't have one. He watched as his ensign was drawn toward the monster's orifice, despite her struggles—watched as she opened her mouth to scream, but couldn't, because the pain was too great.

Desperately, the captain looked around for something he could use to help her. Something, anything. His eyes fell on a tree branch splintered by the force of the creature's emergence. A fraction of a second later, his fingers closed on it, hefted it.

There were only a few meters separating him from the creature; they were relatively free of obstacles.

Putting his head down, Kirk charged the thing's underbelly, driving his makeshift spear into the sickly-white flesh with all the force he could muster.

But the creature's hide was tougher than it looked —even here, where it should have been most vulnerable. The spear barely pierced it at all. Nor did the creature seem to feel it.

A second later, though, the organism began to shudder in the vicinity of its wound. And out of the corner of his eye, the captain saw the tentacle that came plummeting in his direction.

Kirk threw himself to one side, barely avoiding the thing as it snatched at him. Then, as it snatched a second time, he used a tree for cover.

This was no good, he told himself. He had to help Karras. And how could he help her if he could barely help himself?

With no better alternative in sight, he picked up a couple of rocks and hurled them at the creature's maw. *Follow through,* he told himself, remembering who'd given him that advice. One rock missed, but the other seemed to hit its target dead on.

This time, the creature didn't just shudder a little. It jerked. Obviously, he'd hit something sensitive.

But a high-intensity phaser blast hadn't been able to separate the other creature from Spock, and no rock was going to separate this one from Karras. As the captain's mind raced, searching frantically for another way to attack it, he saw that anything he did would be too late.

The creature had already lifted the ensign near its mouth, where a smaller tentacle unfolded and touched her on the thigh. Lightly, almost as if it were a caress. Then, apparently having accomplished its purpose, it let Karras go.

She dropped like a stone through the interwoven branches overhead and landed with a disheartening thud on the jungle floor. As Kirk made his way to her side, forgetting about his own vulnerability, he remembered what it had been like with Spock—the shivering, the feverish flush in his face, the wide and staring eyes, the bellows-like pumping of his lungs.

He barely noticed as the grub-thing retreated, slipping back into the snarl of debris it had created. He barely noticed as its tentacles slithered after it through the undergrowth.

The captain had only one thing on his mind: saving his ensign's life.

Leaves torn loose by Karras' descent were still floating down around her when he reached her. Kneeling, he saw that the symptoms were only beginning to set in. She was an unhealthy pink, but not burning up—not yet. Her breathing was labored, but not with the terrible convulsing force that was sure to follow.

Kirk's teeth clenched. What could he do for her? He didn't have any medical devices with which to arrest her accelerating metabolism. He didn't—

Wait. What was it Karras had said about a *cure?*

He forced himself to think, to remember . . .

*"So someone can be cured of a creature's sting by getting stung again—but not by the same creature? It has to be a different creature?"*

They were his words, though he hadn't quite believed them at the time.

And they made no more sense now than they had then. But it was all he had to go on. All that stood between Karras and the alien poison that was already turning her body against her.

*Find another creature,* the captain told himself. But where?

The hieroglyph map was useless; without a deeper knowledge of the region, there was no way of establishing its scale. Besides, he didn't know where the ensign's tricorder had fallen when the creature grabbed her.

Meanwhile, Karras was deteriorating before his eyes. Her complexion was turning darker by the second, her eyes getting more and more protuberant.

And she was starting to shake as Spock had been shaking.

Abruptly, he knew where to find another creature. Damned if he hadn't known all along!

He didn't know if he could reach the place in time, but he was sure as hell going to try.

# Chapter Twenty

KIRK HAD NO IDEA how long it took him to return to the beam-down site—maybe just minutes, the way he was plunging through the jungle—but it seemed much too long.

Nonetheless, Karras had survived—so far. She was shaking and twitching like a rag doll, her uniform drenched with perspiration. But she was still alive.

As they broke out into the clearing, pelting across the shallow stream, the captain focused on the jumble from which the first creature had emerged. It was as still as when they'd seen it last. Not a sign of the behemoth that had stung his first officer.

But now he *needed* that behemoth. He needed it to come crashing out of the earth as it had before, rearing and stretching and sending out its tentacles in search of Karras.

Not that there was any guarantee it would save her—none at all. It might just add a second sting to the first and make her death that much quicker.

Still, he had to try. His legs aching from his exertions, his parched throat claiming the warm, humid air in great gulps, Kirk fell to his knees before the tangle of soil and rocks and foliage. A moment later, he eased Karras down from his shoulder and set her on the ground before him.

"Come on," he gasped, staring into the hole. *"Come on."*

Nothing happened. The place was still—still as death and decay.

Only Karras was moving. Trembling. Convulsing. But not much longer, the captain knew. No one could go on like that much longer.

For a moment, he had a feeling they weren't alone. He sensed the presence of spirits all about them—the souls of the ancient Dombraatu, kneeling as he was kneeling, praying to their great and terrible grub-god.

But praying wasn't in his nature. Kirk had never been one to ask meekly, and he wasn't about to start now.

"Come on," he cried, "damn you!" Anger surged within him, hot and irrational. "I didn't come all this way to let this woman die!" He shook his fists at the churned-up stretch of jungle. "I'm *not* going to let her die, not when there's a chance that you can save her! Now, get out of that pit or—or so help me, I'll drag you out!"

The spirits were staring, he thought, wondering at this madman who dared to shout at their god. It was all right. *Let them stare,* he told himself, *as long as that big, white worm comes up and does something about it.*

But there was no response. No sundering of the earth, no monster, no nothing. And after a while, he sensed that even the spirits had fled.

The captain hung his head. Karras' convulsions were slowing. Her body's resources were depleted; she simply had nothing left.

It was over, wasn't it?

Suddenly, he felt a rumbling in the earth. The ruined area in front of him shrugged, surged, grew mountainous, and finally spewed out its monstrous inhabitant. The creature uncoiled, horrific as it towered over Kirk, a ghostly-white tower of living flesh. His heart beating against his ribs, his skin crawling, the captain withdrew from Karras, leaving her all alone.

Nor did the creature fail to notice her. Dropping a tentacle over the ensign's tortured form, it lifted her up. Brought her right toward its mouth, still black and oozing from Kirk's phaser blast.

*An offering,* he thought. *That's what she is. An offering to a primitive deity who hasn't had one in thousands of years.* He swore at himself for having brought her here.

No. The captain wouldn't curse himself yet. Not until he'd had a chance to see if the woman's theory was right.

As he watched, the creature brought Karras level with its maw. Then, just as it had with Spock, it extended a small tentacle and ran it gently over her shoulder.

The ensign cried out once: a shrill, pitiful wail that made Kirk's blood turn cold. Then she went limp. Lifeless.

Finished with her, the creature lowered her body—the spent form that had been Selena Karras—almost to the ground. When it let her go perhaps from ten feet up, the captain was there to catch her.

It made no move to snare him. Apparently, it was sated.

As he set Karras down, he had the opportunity to wonder at his foolishness. To sweep a lock of yellow hair from her dark, staring face.

And to ask himself: *What have I done?*

The bridge of the *Enterprise,* Scotty noted, was normally a cheerful place. The kind of place one looked forward to visiting now and then.

Right now, it was like a tomb.

Everybody was moving as if in slow motion. And why not? Despite the speed with which they'd returned to Octavius Four, who was in a hurry to discover what they already knew in their hearts?

Bad enough that Mister Spock was *this* close to death. Now they had to face the loss of four others, including Captain Kirk.

It was a black day on the *Enterprise,* the engineer told himself. He shifted in the captain's chair. A black day, indeed.

"Approaching the planet," Chekov announced from his seat at navigation.

"Slow to orbital speed," Scotty instructed.

"Slowing to orbital speed," Sulu confirmed.

Octavius Four loomed on the forward viewscreen. "Mister Chekov," the engineer said, "check the area around the beam-down site for signs of life. Lieutenant Uhura, scan for communicator signals on all frequencies."

They all did what they had to do. But none of them held out much hope. They were seasoned; they knew the odds of finding the captain and the others were—

"Scotty!"

He turned to face Uhura at the mention of his name, surprised by the informality. It was one thing to call him that down in the rec, but on the bridge . . .

Then he saw the look on her face, and the way she held her communications headphone to her ear, and he forgot the lecture he'd been formulating in his mind. Uhura was grinning. Grinning!

Could it be? "What is it, lass?" he snapped, trying to not hope too hard.

For once, the communications officer was speechless. All she could do was shake her head—and patch whatever she was listening to into the bridge intercom.

"—Kirk. Repeat: is that you, *Enterprise?*"

Finding her voice, Uhura answered. "Aye, sir. It's . . . it's good to hear your voice."

"That goes double for us down here, Lieutenant. I need to speak with Mister Scott."

Scotty spoke up. "Right here, sir. And still a little stunned, I might add. How the divil did ye—"

"Plenty of time for that later," the captain interrupted. "How's Spock?"

The engineer sighed. "Not well, sir. Doctor McCoy doesn't give him much time."

Strangely, Kirk seemed undaunted by the news. "Scotty, I want Spock beamed down immediately. Have you got our coordinates?"

Chekov turned and nodded in answer to the captain's question. The engineer acknowledged him with a glance.

"We've got them, all right," he said. "But are ye sure ye want him beamed *down,* sir?"

"Positive. And have Doctor McCoy accompany him."

Scotty exchanged puzzled looks with Uhura. "Whatever ye say," he responded. "I'll see to it immediately."

"Good man. Kirk out."

Shaking his head, the engineer pressed the required stud on his armrest. "Doctor McCoy, this is Mister Scott up on the bridge . . ."

Busy as he was in the lab, McCoy had been listening to Scotty's message with only one ear. At least, until the word "captain" worked its way into his consciousness.

He raised his head. "Could you repeat that, Mister Scott?"

A pause. "I said I just heard from the captain, Doctor. His party appears to be all right."

McCoy got to his feet. "Jim's alive?" he repeated numbly.

"That he is. I just spoke to him myself."

"That's *great,* Scotty. And the others who were with him?"

"It seems they're alive as well."

The doctor smiled incredulously. "Well, then, what are we waiting for? Let's get them up here so I can take a look at them!"

A longer pause. "I'm afraid that's nae what the captain had in mind."

McCoy's smile faded. "What do you mean? Spit it out, man."

"Captain Kirk does nae want to beam up. He wants you to beam *down*. And he wants ye to bring Mister Spock with ye."

The doctor was tired. Maybe he hadn't heard right. "He wants me to do *what?*"

A sigh. "To beam down. With Mister Spock."

The doctor just stood there for a while, open-mouthed. Finally, he got out: "That's what I thought you said."

"I know it does nae make sense," Scotty added. "But the captain seemed to know what he was doing."

McCoy grunted. "I need to talk with the captain. Maybe he doesn't realize what kind of condition Spock is in."

A suffering silence. "Aye," the engineer agreed at last. "I'll ask Lieutenant Uhura to put you through t' him."

The doctor sat down again and waited. Beam Spock down? In his present state? He'd have his head examined first.

At first, McCoy thought that Kyle had made a mistake. As he materialized with Spock in his arms, he saw the evidence of a huge upheaval not a hundred feet in front of them—the kind left by the creature that had attacked the Vulcan in the first place.

"Of all the—" he began.

"Problem, Doctor?"

McCoy turned and saw Kirk standing behind him, along with the rest of his party. Owens was sitting down; his leg was held rigid with wooden splints.

"Here," the captain said, "let me give you a hand." Coming over, he eased Spock into a vertical position, pulled an arm over his shoulder and relieved McCoy of the Vulcan's weight.

"Jim," the doctor rasped, taking hold of the other arm, "are you out of your mind? One of the creatures has been here. What if it decides to come back?"

But Kirk didn't seem to be paying him much attention. He was gazing at his friend and frowning. "I've seen him look better," he commented.

"Damn it, Jim, did you hear what I said? One of those monstrosities could come ripping out of that hole at any moment!"

The captain turned to him. "I know, Bones. In fact, I'm counting on it." His eyes became hard and flinty. "I know it sounds crazy, but one of those monstrosities is what's going to cure Spock."

McCoy looked at him. "It's the heat. It's gotten to your brain."

"Take a look at Karras, Doctor. Does she look the least bit unhealthy?"

Reluctantly, McCoy did as he was told. "She seems fine," he concluded. "But what's that got to do with—"

Kirk stopped him. "Bones, she got stung the same way Spock did. Exhibited the same symptoms." He indicated the creature's egress with a tilt of his head. "But one of these monsters got her well again. Don't ask me why or how, but it worked. And it'll work for Spock too."

Then the captain told him about the hieroglyphs. And the way they had enabled him to save Karras' life.

The doctor thought for a moment. "It's insane." He shook his head. "But Spock *is* running out of time, and nothing I do seems to have any effect."

Kirk looked him in the eye. He was dead serious. "It's not a theory, Bones. It's proven. I've seen it."

McCoy scowled. "You'd better be right."

The captain nodded. "Do you think I'd try this if I

had any doubts? Now, come on, help me get Spock over there. In these parts, the mountain doesn't come to Mohammed."

Wondering what his med school professors would have said if they could see him now, McCoy shouldered his half of the burden all the way to the perimeter of the ruined area. And at a cue from Kirk, he helped set Spock down.

"Now step back," the captain told him. "And watch."

Nothing happened right away. There was just the sigh of the wind in the trees. Then the ground started to tremble.

A moment later, it erupted with a tearing of roots and a scraping of rocks, and a creature—just like the one they'd seen before—came shooting up out of the chaos. McCoy's mouth went dry; fear tightened the muscles in his belly. It was all he could do to keep still, to keep his hand from reaching for his phaser, to keep his feet planted firmly on the ground.

How could he have agreed to be a party to this? How could he have assigned Spock to such a fate?

The monster stretched out to its full height, dwarfing the nearby trees. Sweeping about with its tentacles, it found the Vulcan with one of them. Then, as if with an unholy hunger, it raised Spock to the level of its puckering mouth.

Lord, the doctor thought. It's going to *eat* him.

At the last moment, however, Spock was diverted from the thing's maw. Out came a heretofore-hidden tentacle—like the one with which the other creature had injected its poison. It descended toward the Vulcan's shoulder.

McCoy shivered, absolutely horrified. And then he felt a hand grip his shoulder.

Turning, he saw it was the captain's. "It's all right," Kirk said.

But even *he* was shaken, unnerved by what he was

witnessing. Despite his words of assurance, he looked anything but assured.

Scotty drummed his fingertips on Mister Kyle's transporter console. "What's taking them so long?" he asked.

The transporter chief shook his head. "I don't know, sir."

Scott frowned. "If only the captain had nae been so mysterious."

Kyle nodded. "It's a puzzle, all right. I just hope poor—"

Abruptly, Kirk's voice invaded the transporter room. "Mister Kyle?"

The transporter chief straightened, as if the captain himself had been in the room. "Aye, sir?"

"Six to beam up."

"Six to beam up," Kyle acknowledged. With a quick glance at Scotty, he turned his attention to his controls. A moment later, he'd activated the transporter.

The engineer watched the platform as the energy shadows of six forms began to take shape. It was impossible to tell which one was Spock, much less what kind of shape he was in.

Then the shapes took on definition and substance. In the back row, there were the three younger crewpeople who'd been part of the original survey team. Two men and a woman, though Scott didn't know their names.

In the front row, there was Kirk on one end and McCoy on the other. And between them, the first officer, standing upright and alert.

"For the love of . . ." Scotty began. He shook his head in wonder.

As Kirk and McCoy stepped down from the platform, Spock followed. There was no sign of the condition that had been plaguing him. Noticing the engineer's interest, he acknowledged him with a subtle nod.

Breaking out into a grin, Scotty nodded back.

"Just where do you think you're going?" McCoy asked, scurrying after his patient.

Spock turned to him, fully in charge of himself again. "If you check the duty roster," he said, "I believe you will find I am supposed to be on the bridge."

"Like hell you are," the doctor replied. "You're coming with me back to sickbay." He turned to the three younger people. "In fact, you're *all* coming with me back to sickbay." He shot the captain a feisty look. "No exceptions."

Kirk and Spock exchanged glances. The captain shrugged. "Not much I can do. He is the doctor."

"You're damn right," McCoy told them. "Now let's go. Everybody."

As the captain passed Scott, he clapped him on the shoulder. "Hang on to the conn," he said. "This is liable to take a while."

As Scotty watched them all exit, he sighed happily. It was amazing how quickly things could return to normal around here.

# Chapter Twenty-one

By THE TIME Kirk and Spock reached the conference room, McCoy had already finished setting up and was tapping his fingers on the table. He looked up as they entered and shot them a sour look.

"Nice of you to show up," he remarked.

Spock arched an eyebrow. "We were detained," he replied.

"No kidding," McCoy commented.

"We would have been here sooner," the captain chimed in, spotting an argument in the making, "but I had to field a call from Admiral Kowalski."

McCoy's eyes narrowed warily. "Now what?"

"Nothing important," Kirk told him, pulling out a chair. "Just congratulations on a job well done. Clearing up some details. That sort of thing."

The doctor harumphed. "In that case, I forgive you. Now sit tight and be amazed." Leaning forward, he flipped a toggle on the desktop monitor, activating it.

What Kirk saw was a split screen with two microscopic images. They were identical, as far as he could tell.

"The sample on the left," McCoy explained, "is a tissue fragment we found on Ensign Karras' clothing. It's from the beast that cured her of her hyperthyroid symptoms. The one on the right is part of the stuff we found floating in Spock's blood after we beamed him up from Beta Cabrini—the stuff which vanished without a trace when he was cured."

The captain nodded. "So the material you found in Spock's blood was deposited along with the poison."

"That's right," the doctor confirmed. "In very small quantities. It was only afterward that it grew, eventually becoming big enough for us to notice it."

Spock considered the evidence. "Fascinating."

"To say the least." McCoy leaned forward again and called up a second picture. It was a computer-generated representation of a humanoid life-form Kirk didn't recognize.

Apparently, however, Spock was better informed. "A male member of the Dombraatu race," he said. "The now-*extinct* Dombraatu race."

"Very good," the doctor told him. "Now, what do we know about the Dombraatu?"

As the Vulcan began to answer, McCoy stopped him with a gesture. "I'll tell you what we know. They were some of the most dedicated explorers the galaxy has ever seen. They colonized like crazy. And if their ship specs are any indication, they were one of the doggone toughest peoples we've ever encountered, living or dead. In fact," he went on, "they made the Vulcans look like pantywaists."

Spock looked to Kirk.

"Weaklings," the captain translated.

"I see," the first officer responded. If he took umbrage with the metaphor, his tone didn't give it away. It was as neutral as ever.

"Now," McCoy said, "let's take a look at Ensign Karras' hieroglyphs." He brought up a third image—the creature-symbol, magnified a few times, but otherwise just as Kirk remembered it from the carvings.

"It may look like a weeping willow," he told Spock, "but it's meant to be one of the creatures."

"Thank you, Captain. However, I have had occasion to peruse the ensign's report."

Kirk grunted. "I should have known. Please proceed, Doctor."

"As I was saying," McCoy continued emphatically, "the glyphs show us quite a bit. First, that the Dombraatu co-existed with the creatures at some point in the recent or not-so-recent past. Second, that the creatures were doing the same kind of stinging then that they're doing now. Third, that the creatures were basically stationary, or why have a map in the first place? And fourth, that the Dombraatu—even after being stung—were strong enough to get from one creature-site to the next."

"Couldn't those who were stung have had help?" the captain asked. "Couldn't their friends have carried them?"

The doctor shook his head. "Not according to Karras' interpretation of the glyphs. It seems the wounded made the journey alone."

Spock nodded. "I read the glyphs the same way."

Kirk made a gesture of surrender. "I withdraw the suggestion."

McCoy scowled. "Now that *that's* settled, I ask you: what did the creatures have to gain by breaking up the scenery, grabbing a Dombraatu, and injecting him— or her—with a combination of poison and rapid-growing organic material?" His eyes gleamed. "Better yet, let me ask you a simpler and—you'll appreciate this, Spock—infinitely more poetic question: Why do blossoms smell so sweet in the springtime?"

The captain felt a smile coming on. "Damn your hide, Doctor. I believe you're on to something."

The Vulcan tilted his head judiciously. "Are you postulating that the organic matter injected by the creatures was a collection of gametes? The equivalent of sperm in humans or Vulcans?"

McCoy bobbed his head. "That's *precisely* what I'm postulating, Mister Spock. These creatures are hermaphrodites. They play the role of the male by making the stuff, and the role of the female by accepting it. But of course, they can't impregnate themselves, or all they'd have would be a race of clones. That's why once you're infected, you can't go back to the same creature to get *not-sick*—to use Karras' terminology. You've got to go to a second creature and thereby complete the procreative process."

"So the Dombraatu, and more recently Spock and Karras, were like the bees that carry gametes from flower to flower," Kirk said. "But what about the serum? And its effect on the carrier's metabolism?"

The doctor restored the image of the humanoid to the monitor. "Remember how strong we said these people were? Well, what almost proved fatal to Spock and Karras might have only been a matter of discomfort to your average Dombraatu—little more than an annoyance." He leaned back. "In fact, they may have needed the injection. Maybe their thyroids, or whatever served them in place of thyroids, required a boost periodically, and the creatures gave it to them."

Spock nodded. "Unfortunately, there hadn't been any Dombraatu on the planet for some time. So, when the creatures perceived a reasonable facsimile—"

"They settled for sloppy seconds," McCoy said, completing the thought in his own words.

"That is not exactly the way I would have put it," the Vulcan remarked. "But it expresses the sentiment." He thought for a moment. "An interesting theory, Doctor. It would also explain why the creatures treated us so roughly. They were not used to dealing with such fragile carriers."

"And don't forget," McCoy added, "you struggled. The Dombraatu wouldn't have done that. What's more, it might have been hundreds of years since the last time they'd done this sort of thing. The creatures might have been a tad out of practice."

The captain absorbed it all. It *was* a good theory; Bones had outdone himself. "Good work," he said. "Good work, indeed."

"There is only one mystery that has yet to be cleared up," Spock commented.

The doctor looked at him. "And what mystery is that?"

"The set of conditions which allowed the Dombraatu homeworld to remain wild and primitive while at the same time spawning a race of star travelers. Of course, one answer seems more likely than any other."

"And that is?" Kirk prodded.

"It is possible," the Vulcan said, "that Octavius Four was not always a primitive place. Imagine a society torn between its earliest traditions and the lure of space travel, not unlike Vulcan in its recent past. As most of the society's population moves out to the stars, colonizing, exploring, those who remain purposely revert to their race's ancient ways. And part of the reversion process is the obliteration of all traces of modern society."

McCoy sat back and stroked his chin. "Could be, all right. Then the carvings on those stones may be even newer than some of the Dombraatu colonies we've discovered."

"That may be true," Spock confirmed. "In any case, we will know that soon enough. The computer has almost completed its cross-analysis of Ensign Karras' tricorder readings."

The captain thought of something. "Doctor, if the gamete that our first officer here delivered has the desired biological effect . . ." He kept a mischievous smile under wraps. "Wouldn't that make Mister Spock a father, in a manner of speaking?"

McCoy grinned. "I guess it would, at that." He

turned to the Vulcan. "I'm going to have to find a food processor and whip up a batch of cigars for you, Spock. Just in case, you old hound dog."

The Vulcan regarded him. "Cigars?"

"An old Earth custom," Kirk explained, "abandoned long ago for its negative effects on one's health."

Spock looked from one of them to the other. "I see," he replied. "In that case, I think I will avoid that particular tradition." A pause. "However, I must say: if I had a hand in proliferating the creatures' species, I am not displeased. In the course of my second encounter with them, while the creature was withdrawing the serum from my blood, I had a chance to brush against its consciousness. What I found was crude, to say the least; hardly what one would call intelligence. Nonetheless, it was characterized by a certain . . ." He searched for the right word. At last he found it: "Nobility."

"Nobility?" McCoy wondered. "Spock, it's not much more than a giant insect."

Kirk turned to the doctor. "Let's not forget where *we* came from, Bones—slimy things that crawled out of a primordial ocean. When did the seeds of *our* nobility first start to take root?"

McCoy thought about it and nodded. "Interesting question," he decided.

The captain pushed his chair out and got up. "Interesting questions all around, I'd say. And interesting answers as well." He looked from one of his officers to the other. "However, it's getting late, and I've a personnel matter to attend to."

The doctor's features screwed up in suspicion. "Personnel matter? What personnel matter?"

Kirk smiled affably as he negotiated a path around McCoy's chair. "I'm afraid," he said, "that's going to have to remain a private affair—between me and the personnel in question."

\* \* \*

As the strains of Bartlett's *Symphony for Celestials in D Major* filled his quarters, Kirk gazed across the dinner table at Ensign Selena Karras of the *Horizon*, formerly Ensign Selena Karras of the *Enterprise*.

"Mm," she said, listening appraisingly. She smiled. "Nice. Very nice."

"Tell me more about your assignment," he said, reaching for the wine decanter.

Karras watched as the captain replenished her nearly empty glass. "It's a pure research mission. The Soolahn system. You know, just beyond Antares."

He paused, on the verge of refilling his own glass. "Beyond Antares. Like the song."

Her eyes sparkling in the subdued light. "That's right. Like the song."

As he tipped the decanter, and the ruby liquid flowed, he asked: "When did you make the application?"

Karras looked at him. "A year ago. About the same time I applied for a berth on the *Enterprise*." She paused. "You see, I wasn't sure exactly what I wanted."

"But now you are?"

She sighed, gazed into the depths of her wine. "To be honest, I'm less sure than ever." A trace of a frown. "I could explore the Soolahn system for years and never find what I found on Octavius Four. Ironic, isn't it? I'm transferring to a pure research vessel, when I had the pure research opportunity of a lifetime on the *Enterprise*."

Kirk eyed her. "But you're still making the switch."

Karras confirmed it. "Still. I know what this is like, but I've never worked with Doctor Erdel of the *Horizon*." She shrugged. "I may love it. I may hate it. But I've got to give it a try."

He nodded. "I can't say I blame you. I've heard it's almost impossible to sneak onto one of Erdel's voyages. But what about your work on the Dombraatu hieroglyphs?"

Karras wrinkled her nose. "I've taken that about as far as I can," she said. "Now it's up to the *real* experts." She regarded him. "You think I'm making a mistake?"

The captain smiled. "It's not for me to say. It's your life. That makes it your call. But I can tell you this: if you ever decide you want to serve on a Constitution class vessel again, there'll be room for you on the *Enterprise.*"

She seemed pleased, almost—relieved? "That's good to hear, sir. For a while, I was afraid you might take it personally. You know, with all that happened down on Octavius Four . . ."

Kirk feigned a memory lapse. "You must be thinking of someone else. A captain, maybe, who had a mission to worry about—and a certain ambivalence about personal relationships with members of his crew."

Karras looked at him askance. "Those are no longer considerations?"

He shook his head. "Not as far as I can tell. Twenty-four hours from now, you'll be on someone else's ship. Part of someone else's crew." He leaned forward. "And stop calling me sir. The name's Jim."

"Jim," she agreed. She raised her glass. "To my captain. A pity he couldn't be with us tonight." The corners of her mouth quirked as she thought about it. "Or maybe not such a pity."

He grinned, raised his glass, and clinked it gently against hers. It promised to be a most enjoyable evening.

# Epilogue

PIKE SET DOWN his morning cup full of steaming, black, shiny coffee and touched the stud that activated the kitchen faucet. A fraction of a second later, it shot out a steady stream of water at room temperature, dousing the breakfast plates and assorted silverware.

Of course, he and Vina could have avoided dishwashing if they'd had a mind to. They could have just *wished* the dishes clean. But they'd decided long ago to maintain as much normalcy in their lives as possible.

That didn't preclude someone else in the illusion, someone like Derret, from taking care of the more mundane chores. After all, real people on real primitive-area vacations often hired someone to help with the housework.

But once they'd decided to make their stay at the beach house an extended one, Vina had voluntarily banished Derret from the illusion. He would have been extraneous, to say the least. And also, she had sensed how much the houseboy's appearance bothered Pike, despite his protests to the contrary.

Procuring a sponge from the dish full of biodegradable detergent to his right, Pike selected a plate and got to work. A moment later, Vina emerged from the back of the house.

He glanced at her. "Find it?"

She nodded. As she joined him at the sink, she held it out so he could see it—an old-fashioned children's book. *Alice in Wonderland.*

"It was in the storage room, just where I remembered putting it," she said, her flawless brow creasing a little. "Though I guess I shouldn't be so surprised. I mean, if I *remembered* putting it there . . ."

"Then it would have to be there," he finished for her. "Annoying, isn't it?"

She shrugged. "I don't know. I kind of like it—knowing that things are where I expect them to be."

Suddenly, she looked past him, her attention drawn to something else. Following her gaze, he turned and peered out the kitchen window to the beach beyond.

At first, he thought she might have glimpsed the whales that had been approaching the beach the last couple of days. Then he saw it wasn't the whales at all.

The Keeper was standing out there on the sand, not ten meters from the house. He nodded as his eyes met Pike's.

"He's back," Vina said. She looked at him. "He must have some news."

Pike grunted his assent. Swiping a dishtowel from the rack that extended from one of the cabinets, he wiped his hands halfway dry and tossed the towel on the counter. Then, taking Vina's hand, he led her out the door and down the steps. The sand was cool beneath his bare feet, not warmed yet by the sun.

The blood vessels at the Keeper's temples twitched and squirmed. "Greetings, Christopher. Vina."

"Good morning," Vina returned. "How long have you been standing out here?"

A faint smile. "Time is an illusion as well."

She nodded. "I should have known you'd say that."

The Keeper eyed Pike. "We have done as you asked."

"You've gotten word about my friends?" the human asked.

"We have," the Talosian confirmed. His smile deepened. "Nor do we believe you will be displeased with what has been discovered."

Pike felt a wave of relief wash over him. It was unexpected; he must have been worried more than he wanted to admit, even to himself.

"Would you like to come in?" he asked the Keeper. A pause. "Yes."

The next Pike knew, they were all standing in the kitchen. He looked at Vina. She laughed.

Turning to the Keeper, she said: "I think Chris intended for us to walk in."

The Talosian absorbed the information. "Would you prefer that?" he asked telepathically. "If so, I can place us outside again."

Pike shook his head. "That won't be necessary. We're here already." He was full to bursting with curiosity. "My friends?" he prodded gently.

The Keeper accepted the hint with equanimity. "Shall I begin with the one called Spock?"

The human nodded. "That's as good a place as any."

"Very well." His dark eyes narrowed. "Spock encountered some difficulties recently. However, he surmounted them. He is as we saw him last—whole, healthy, and engrossed in his labors."

Pike sighed. "I don't suppose you've got any of the details?"

The Keeper's features took on a rueful cast. "I regret. I do not."

The human waved away the suggestion. "The important thing is that he's all right. And the others?"

The tiny being told him—describing each former comrade's condition, one by one. By the time he finished, Pike had a funny feeling in his gut.

"I appreciate it," he said in earnest.

The Keeper nodded beneficently. And was gone.

Vina slipped into Pike's arms and looked up at him. "Happy?" she asked.

"I guess," he replied. "I mean, I couldn't have asked for more. Everybody's doing fine, it seems."

"Then what's the problem? Feeling a bit nostalgic, are we?"

He thought about it and nodded. Vina knew him better than he knew himself.

"Maybe I am," he conceded. "Somehow, I feel like I should be out there with them. Exploring. Testing my limits."

She shook her head in amazement. "Wasn't it you who told me you used to lie awake at night, feeling the weight of command pressing down on you, wishing you could just find a beach somewhere and someone nice to share it with?"

He laughed. "You know, it's a good thing your memory is better than mine. I did say that, didn't I? And I meant it too."

"Mm. Then prove it. Let's take a walk in the surf."

Pike frowned. "Don't you think that's a little daring?"

"You're a starship captain," she told him. "You can handle it."